AUTUMN'S BANE

A Wild Hunt Novel, Book 13

YASMINE GALENORN

A Nightqueen Enterprises LLC Publication

Published by Yasmine Galenorn

PO Box 2037, Kirkland WA 98083-2037

AUTUMN'S BANE

A Wild Hunt Novel

First Electronic Printing: 2020 Nightqueen Enterprises LLC

First Print Edition: 2020 Nightqueen Enterprises

Cover Art & Design: Ravven

Art Copyright: Yasmine Galenorn

Editor: Elizabeth Flynn

A Nightqueen Enterprises LLC Publication

Published in the United States of America

ACKNOWLEDGMENTS

Welcome back into the world of the Wild Hunt. We're at book thirteen, and into the second story arc. Typhon is bearing down on the world and, as the gods try to figure out how to stop him, it's up to Ember and the Wild Hunt to do their best to keep the collateral damage from hurting too many people.

Thanks to my usual crew: Samwise, my husband, Andria and Jennifer—without their help, I'd be swamped. To the women who have helped me find my way in indie, you're all great, and thank you to everyone. To my wonderful cover artist, Ravven, for the beautiful work she's done.

Also, my love to my furbles, who keep me happy. My most reverent devotion to Mielikki, Tapio, Ukko, Rauni, and Brighid, my spiritual guardians and guides. My love and reverence to Herne, and Cernunnos, and to the Fae, who still rule the wild places of this world. And a nod to the Wild Hunt, which runs deep in my magick, as well as in my fiction.

You can find me through my Website at Galenorn.com and be sure to sign up for my newsletter to keep updated on all my latest releases! You can find my advice on writing, discussions about the books, and general ramblings on my YouTube channel. If you liked this book, I'd be grateful if you'd leave a review—it helps more than you can think.

July, 2020

Brightest Blessings,

~The Painted Panther~

~Yasmine Galenorn~

WELCOME TO AUTUMN'S BANE

Life isn't easy when you bear the mark of the Silver Stag.

The Father of Dragons has returned to the world and all hell is breaking loose. A shadow dragon has let loose a group of vrykos—undead creatures who are cunning, hungry, and looking to feed on the living. In the midst of the chaos, Ember finds herself facing a major decision brought on by a twist in her status with the Queen of Dark Fae.

But when the shadow dragon drags her friend Viktor, the half-ogre, into the world of the dead, Ember must journey to the Underworld to rescue him. Will she be able to save Viktor before it's too late? Or will she lose her own soul to the armies of the dead?

Reading Order for the Wild Hunt Series:

- Book 1: The Silver Stag
- Book 2: Oak & Thorns
- Book 3: Iron Bones
- Book 4: A Shadow of Crows

- Book 5: The Hallowed Hunt
- Book 6: The Silver Mist
- Book 7: Witching Hour
- Book 8: Witching Bones
- Book 9: A Sacred Magic
- Book 10: The Eternal Return
- Book 11: Sun Broken
- Book 12: Witching Moon
- Book 13: Autumn's Bane
- Book 14: Witching Time (forthcoming)

CHAPTER ONE

THE AFTERNOON SUN SPLASHED THROUGH THE WINDOWS overlooking the alleyway, the blinding glare so bright that I squinted, tilting the blinds to block out the light. I was in the break room, foraging through the refrigerator, looking for lunch. I had forgotten to bring anything, and Angel was away from her desk so she hadn't remembered to order in. I finally chose a frozen fried chicken dinner and popped it in the microwave, turning as Viktor entered the room.

"She said yes!" He bounced into the break room, rattling the floorboards like a troupe of dancers on a rickety stage. "She said yes, she said yes, she said—"

"Let me guess," I interrupted, grinning. "She said yes!"

The half-ogre nodded, beaming. "I can't believe I'm getting married!" He looked around. "Where is everybody?"

The break room was empty except for me, surprising given it was one P.M. on Friday afternoon. We normally all ate lunch together, but today was different.

"Herne's in his office, talking to the mayor. Angel's downstairs at urgent care."

"Urgent care? Is she all right?" Viktor's smile slid off his face.

I hurried to reassure him. "She's fine, or she will be. She got into a fight with a splinter. She rammed it right under her nail this morning."

"Ouch. How'd she do that?"

"She was out in the garden, trying to prune one of the bushes. One thing led to another. She tried to coax the splinter out, but half an hour ago she gave up and Herne told her to go down and get it looked at. As for the others, Talia took the afternoon off. She's got a headache. Kipa's not coming in today, and Yutani is in his office, talking to ComputaGeek. We need an upgrade to the computer system, apparently, and he's giving them the specs. Rafé won't be in till later, of course. Charlie, either."

Rafé was our new company clerk, and he came to work in the evenings, so that he could do all the filing and organizing needed after we were all gone. It also prevented him and Angel from getting tired of working together, although it did cut down on how many dates they went on. But Angel said it had been good for their relationship, and they both seemed happy. Rafé working evenings served another purpose. He was able to work with Charlie Darren, our resident vampire, on the evenings Charlie came in, and they got more done together than apart.

"Oh. All right." Viktor sounded a little dejected.

I took one look at him and realized he was disappointed. He was bursting to tell his good news, and I could tell that he wanted everybody in the office to know. I settled back in my chair, fork and TV dinner in hand.

"So tell me, was she surprised?" I had planned on eating at my desk, but Viktor needed to celebrate and I was determined to make him smile.

He thrust his hands in the pockets of his jacket, sitting down beside me.

"Yes and no, actually. Sheila told me that she thought I might be about to propose, but she hadn't wanted to get her hopes up, just in case she was wrong. However, she *didn't* expect a diamond. My mother gave me my grandma's ring to give to her," he added, suddenly somber and staring at the ground.

"Oh, that sounds lovely. Your grandmother, is she still alive?"

"No, I'm talking about my mother's mother, who was human. My maternal grandmother. Besides my mother, Nanna was the only one who fully accepted me for who I was. I still remember her telling me, 'I love you because of *who* you are, and everything you are goes into making up your nature, Viktor. Both your human side and your ogre blood.' Nanna never once tried to deny my ogre heritage, nor did she praise my human side more."

Viktor had told us many times that he was estranged from his father and his father's people, but I hadn't realized that his mother's side hadn't accepted him either.

"I'm sure she's watching over you," I said. "When did she die?"

Viktor shrugged. "Long ago. My father had traveled to Russia and that's where he met my mother, back in 1767. He married her and brought her home on a sailing ship, back in 1768. Her parents and her two little sisters came along with her. They settled up on Mount Rainier in the ogre compound. The ogres accepted Tatiana—my mother. She and her family were among the first settlers in this territory, but they lived in the village Keyren, the ogres' village. It was hidden deep in the mountain, though now it's moved to the area surrounding the national park."

"I knew your father's people had first lived up there, but once Mount Rainier was turned into a national park, I wasn't sure what had happened."

"After my parents split, we moved down into what's now the Puyallup area. My grandpa Viktor was strong and with me to help him, we made our homestead thrive. I'm named after him. He wasn't all that fond of me, but he didn't mistreat me."

"I wondered about your name."

"Right. At first my name was Yalt. In Ogrísh—the language of the ogres—it means *Blessed Between Worlds*. My father named me. But when the clan leader instructed him to disown me, my father formally reclaimed my name and gave me to my mother. Among my father's people, if you're turned out from the community, they steal your name and you're no longer allowed to use it, under pain of death. So Mother renamed me after my grandpa."

That seemed harsh, but then, ogres weren't a gentle people. They could be brutish and crude, although you'd never know it by how Viktor acted. "How did the local natives feel about you and your family?"

"They were friendly enough. They didn't care for the ogres, which was understandable given my father's people are given to thievery and loutish ways, but they didn't hold my blood against me. We farmed and my mother kept the cows and chickens. We traded with the local tribes for what we needed. I think my grandparents longed for their days in Russia, but they never blamed my mother or me."

"They never went back, then?"

He shook his head. "How could they? If they took me along with them, there would be so many questions and no one would accept me back home. If they left me and my mother, we would have died in the wilderness. No, my grandmother swore up and down we'd make a comfortable home, and we did."

"She sounds like a strong woman." I wondered if Viktor had any living relatives besides his ogre family. I had heard him speak of his mother, but she was human. "Your mother..."

"Tatiana is still alive. She remarried when I was eighteen. I don't often talk about it, because my stepfather died twenty years after they married and he's long gone. He fell into a river and drowned before anyone could save him."

"But she's *alive*?"

"Yes, Pierre was one of the magic-born. On their wedding day, he offered her a potion that would extend her life by some three hundred years and she decided to accept it. He offered it to the rest of her family as well, but no one else wanted it. The only problem is, longevity potions and spells don't guard against accidents and murder. So my mother lost him in 1817, and decided that she'd live out the rest of her life, but she wouldn't seek to extend it further. She told me she's seen and done more than most people ever get the chance to." He suddenly blushed. "I'm sorry, I don't mean to be so chatty today. I'm sure this is all very boring."

"On the contrary. I'm fascinated." I finished my meal and crossed to the counter, where I poured myself a cup of coffee. Viktor was usually reticent about his family, so him opening up made me feel like he trusted me a little more. "Coffee?"

"Thanks, with cream."

I handed him the mug and set the dish of creamers in front of him. "What about your grandmother? You said you miss her?"

"Oh, I do. Grandmother Anna used to call me her 'big boy' and she'd hold me on her lap. By the time I was four, I was the size of a ten-year-old human, but she never said anything bad about my size. My grandmother's hair smelled like apples and hay, and she always had a cookie in her pocket for me."

"How old were you when your parents split?"

"I was…oh…ten? Eleven? Somewhere around there. As it became apparent I wasn't going to reach the expected size of an ogre male, my father started acting out against my mother. He blamed her and wanted nothing to do with me. The leader of the ogres ordered him to either cast me out into the wilderness, or for her and me to leave. My father told my mother she had to choose.

"I overheard that fight. It isn't a pleasant memory," he said, closing his eyes. "In the end, Mother chose me. She told my father to go to hell. The next day, we gathered our things, and my father relented enough to give us the supplies to last through the summer while my grandpa and I built a little cabin. We left the mountain and moved down into the Puyallup valley. Grandpa died of a heart attack five years later, but my grandmother and my mother kept the homestead going. Pierre came along a year or so later and he did wonders adding on to it."

I pressed my lips together, thinking that all of us at the Wild Hunt had been through one form of hell or another. Well, maybe not Herne, and probably not Kipa, but we had all faced our demons as we grew up.

"I'm sorry it was so hard. Your mother has always supported you, hasn't she?"

He nodded, his voice softening. "She's never stopped being my cheerleader. She loves Sheila, and while we'll never have children of our own—Sheila really doesn't want to go through pregnancy—we thought we'd adopt. My mother likes the idea. You'll meet her at the wedding, which will be on Imbolc. Sheila honors the goddess Brighid, though she's not a priestess. So we thought it would be nice to get married then."

"I'll be there with bells on, Viktor. Congratulations again." I reached up on tiptoe and threw my arms around his neck, giving him a long hug. "You deserve happiness, and so does Sheila."

At that moment, Herne entered the room. I spun around, poking Viktor on the arm as I did so. "Tell him before I do."

Herne glanced from me to Viktor and a slow smile spread across his face. "You did it! You asked her?" He tossed his file folders on the table and hurried over to Viktor's side, grabbing the half-ogre's hand and shaking it as Viktor nodded, grinning.

"Yes, I did—we're engaged! The wedding will be on Imbolc. We were wondering if you would mind hosting the wedding at your house, Ember? We want a garden wedding—we're hoping for snow, but that's something we can't control."

"Of course you can! We'd be thrilled to host it. I know Angel will agree."

"Thank you. And…Herne, I have a special request. If the answer's no, that's fine, but I don't want Sheila to know until our wedding day."

"What is it? You know you can ask me for anything, man." Herne pumped Viktor's hand again, his voice cracking just a little.

One look at Herne's cornflower blue eyes and I knew that he was putting on a good show, but behind the smile was a trace of worry.

I hadn't answered *his* proposal yet. I was close to an answer, but the ramifications of what it meant to be the wife of a god had set in, and I wanted to be fully aware of what I was promising before I gave my word. But Herne was struggling with my hesitation and I knew I had to give him an answer soon.

"I was wondering if you might ask the Lady Brighid if… You see, Sheila reveres her, and I know—I just know if Brighid were to oversee the service or even send her blessing…" Viktor faltered, wincing. "I just realized what I'm asking."

"No, good gods, man, it's not a problem for me to ask her. She might say yes. The Lady Brighid can be extremely generous about things like this." Herne turned to me. "I have to go visit my father in Annwn tomorrow.

I'll drop by Brighid's palace then and see what she says. Do you want to go with me?"

I shook my head. "Actually, your mother's coming to dinner at my house tomorrow around six."

Morgana had been to my home once or twice, but always with Herne, and sometimes with Cernunnos. It felt awkward asking her to come solo, but I wanted to have a heart-to-heart chat with her, and I didn't want Herne listening in.

Herne cocked his head, squinting at me. "All right, then. Well, you *are* pledged to her."

That was another thing. How would that work once Herne and I were married? If I became a goddess—a thought that freaked me out—what the heck did that mean for my interactions with Morgana? It was too much to think about right now.

"So, are we on for Lughnasadh tomorrow night? Marilee's leading the ritual, if we're still all good for it." I leaned back in my chair, thinking about marriage and holidays and all the celebrations that made up our lives.

Milestones were important. They were reminders of crossroads in our lives, and the touchstones that kept us connected to the cycles of the earth. We called it the Wheel of the Year, and the Fae and other Cryptos weren't the only ones who celebrated the Sabbats—the name for the eight great festivals that marked the quarters and cross-quarters of the year. Human pagans also celebrated the holy days, and together, we bridged gaps in age and race and even species, coming together to mark the tides of life in joy and in sorrow.

"We'll be there with bells on. Or, corn tassels. Marilee has done wonders for you, and for Angel." Herne gave me a quick peck on the forehead. "I've got to run. Will I see you tonight?"

I shook my head. "No, Angel and I decided we need a girls' night. It's been too long since we've just climbed into our PJs and binge-watched some of our favorite shows with a big bowl of popcorn and a tub of ice cream."

Snickering, he merely nodded. "I get it. No boys allowed."

"Right." And because I wanted to set him somewhat at ease, I added, "You know before too long I won't have that option. Not if you and I are..." I paused, biting my lip. Was I *really* ready to say yes? But then I caught a glimpse of Viktor over at the refrigerator. This was his night and I didn't want to spoil it for him.

Herne leaned in and gazed into my eyes. "Are you saying..."

"Not yet." I gave a covert nod toward Viktor. "But soon. I promise you, before the week is up, I'll have an answer for you. I just have a couple more things to decide." I kept my voice low, not wanting Viktor to overhear. "Meanwhile, why don't you take Viktor out tonight, to celebrate his engagement? Get Yutani to go as well, although he doesn't drink much."

Yutani, our IT guy and a coyote shifter whose father was the Great Coyote himself, was a borderline alcoholic. He kept himself sober and when he did drink, he never had more than one or two drinks. He was tightly wound, and a Dom, and altogether, a good man who walked on the freaky side of life. But then again, weren't we all a little freaky?

"Good idea. We don't have to go to a bar. I think I could persuade Yutani to go bowling." He glanced over at

Viktor. "Hey, want to go bowling to celebrate your engagement? We can take Yutani and Rafé with us as well."

At that moment, my phone rang. I glanced at the caller ID. It was Angel. Frowning, I answered. "Hey, what's up? How are you? When are you getting your butt back up here?"

She didn't bother to answer. "Ember, turn on the TV. Channel 8 KPOZ. Hurry."

I grabbed the remote from the counter and pointed it toward the break room television and switched it on to channel 8.

"This just in," the newscaster said from behind the desk. "The town of Klarkson, on Highway 2, has been overrun by creatures that no one has yet been able to identify. They're attacking the townsfolk. Several people have been seriously injured, including five children. Right now, police are swarming the graveyard from where the creatures are believed to have originated, but officers have been forced to fall back twice. Bullets are proving useless, and the creatures are inhumanly strong and appear entirely uncommunicative. Mayor Willis of Klarkson has appealed to the National Guard for help, and there's so much chaos that no one seems to know what course of action to follow."

The news anchor held her hand to her ear, pausing, then looked bleakly at the camera. "I have a report from the Klarkson Hospital. They are reporting the admittance of four adults in critical condition, along with three children who are also critical. If you are in Klarkson, police ask that you please stay in your houses and lock your doors and windows."

I turned down the volume, looking at Herne. "What the hell?"

He was staring at the screen, a solemn look on his face. "This started in the *graveyard*? You know what I'm thinking."

"Yeah, me too. Typhon." I returned to my phone call with Angel. "How did you find out about this?"

"Urgent care has a TV in the waiting room and I'm waiting to pay my bill. You think it's Typhon?" She paused, then added, "I have a feeling in my stomach, Ember—it's not good."

When Angel had a gut reaction to something, we paid attention. She was human, mostly—and I say mostly because we suspected that she had some degree of magic-born blood in her system—and she was an empath. She was also my best friend and had been since we were eight years old and got in a mud-wrestling battle that netted us both a trip to the principal's office. After that less-than-auspicious start to our friendship, we bonded instantly.

"Not good, how? Not good as in, gee this sounds nasty, or not good as in, we'd better get ready or get our asses kicked?" I wasn't sure where Klarkson was, but I knew that I didn't want to go there.

"Not good as in, we'd better get prepared because there's something much bigger on the horizon." Her voice drifted off and after a moment she said, "I'll be up shortly."

I shoved my phone back in my pocket and turned to Herne. Both Viktor and he were watching the footage out of Klarkson. There wasn't much yet, and they were running the same clips over and over, along with video taken by the townsfolk using their cell phones. A lot of it was fuzzy and indistinct, but after a few moments, a clip came on that was clear as a bell.

The creature looked a lot like a zombie in many ways, but there was a brightness to the eyes that whispered "cunning" to me. But zombies *weren't* cunning. They had some form of sentience, but they weren't the brightest bulbs in the socket. These creatures were corpses in varying stages of decay, but they crouched low, skulking along, and there was a malevolence to them that felt like more than the feeding frenzy of zombies. Nor were they ghouls. Given I'd spent most of my adult life cleaning up messes with sub-Fae and the undead, I could spot the differences.

"What do you think they are?" I asked Herne.

He shook his head, his gaze fixed on the screen. "I don't know, but we'd better find out."

"Angel thinks we're in for something big."

As we watched the report spinning out, I could feel the hair standing up on my arms. Angel was right. Typhon was sending something new at us and, whatever it was, we weren't going up against a mere batch of skeletal warriors.

I took a deep breath, letting it out slowly. All the joy that I had felt over Viktor's announcement had drained away. We were truly entering the war against the Father of Dragons, and life wasn't going to let us forget what we were facing. After a moment, I turned and headed down the hall, poking my head into Yutani and Talia's office. Yutani glanced up and I saw that he was watching the news on his tablet.

"You saw?"

He nodded. "Yeah. But it's worse than that. The local

channel just came out with a report. Something similar is happening in the Worchester District. We'd better get ready to rumble."

As he stood, I cursed under my breath. Just what we needed right now. Angry that we couldn't have one day to celebrate—just *one* day to breathe—I gave him an abrupt nod and headed for my office. It was time to get suited up and ready to go.

CHAPTER TWO

So I guess here's a good place to introduce myself. My name in Ember Kearney, and I'm what's known as a tralaeth. I'm half Dark Fae, half Light Fae, and according to my respective heritages, I shouldn't exist. I live in Seattle, where I spent most of my adult life working by myself as a private investigator and troubleshooter. Goblin problem? I put an end to them. Someone rifling your chicken coop? Call me and you'd be back in eggs in no time.

But then a little over a year ago, my best friend—Angel Jackson—and I ran into a situation and we almost lost her little brother. With that, Herne appeared in our lives. The Lord of the Hunt, Herne is the son of Cernunnos—the Lord of the Forest—and Morgana, a goddess of Fae and of the Sea.

Herne swept us up in his net, recruiting us to work for the Wild Hunt Agency. The Wild Hunt's primary focus is to prevent the collateral damage that happens due to the frequent and petty wars between the Courts of Light and Dark Fae. But unfortunately, we've had to evolve over the past few months. Now, we're facing a far greater danger, one that threatens the entire world. Typhon, the Father of Dragons, has returned. And with his rise out of stasis, the monstrous son of Tartarus and Gaia is bringing with him hordes of the undead, thanks to his paternal lineage. He's also managed to open the portal for his children to return to this world. The dragons are coming home, so to speak.

Meanwhile, Herne and I clicked, and now he's proposed. I love him, more than I could ever imagine loving anybody. But there's one problem. If I accept, I must become a goddess like his mother did. And that means my entire life will change.

I put the proposal on hold for a while in order to think things through. But I can't wait much longer, and meanwhile, our enemies keep lining up at the door. Sometimes, it feels like there's no place left to hide.

"HELL AND HIGH WATER," Herne said, coming out of his office as I was sitting by Angel's desk. He looked downright dour. "Everybody back in the break room."

Angel and I immediately followed him. He poked his head around the corner and shouted for Viktor and Yutani before opening the break room door. Angel and I seated ourselves at the table. When Yutani and Viktor came in, Herne motioned for them to sit down.

After they were settled, he said, "I just talked to the mayor. There's trouble at several cemeteries in the Worchester District. Whatever those creatures are we saw on TV, they're here, too. The cops tried to stop them, but bullets are useless. Three officers have been hurt, along with several people who were visiting their loved ones' graves. They're in the hospital right now."

"Are these creatures trying to exit the graveyards?" I asked.

Herne nodded. "Yes, they're definitely trying to break though the barricades. The cops are doing their best to pen them in, but at least a few of the creatures have made it past them. The police are trying to keep them at arm's length while doing their best to avoid getting attacked. The mayor wants to know what we're dealing with. She texted me several pictures of them. Yutani, I'm forwarding the pics to you. Find out what they are and what we can do to them."

He pulled out his phone and tapped away. Yutani received his texts and opened his laptop, transferring the photos to the computer. He immediately buried his nose in the screen, searching for something that would tell us what we were dealing with.

Angel walked over to the TV and flipped it on. The local stations were all breaking news reports. She paused, then grabbed the remote and flipped to a cable news show.

"Um, guys?" she said.

I glanced up to see that a channel outside of New York was running a similar story, but they weren't replaying our footage. "Oh shit. Is this taking place on the East Coast, too?"

Angel raised the volume.

"According to local police, in Gardenia, New York, dozens of bodies have risen in the graveyards and are on the loose. These are not the same as vampires. We repeat: these creatures are *not* vampires. Governor Kamar has been in touch with Regent Chambers of the Vampire Nation, East Coast Region. Regent Chambers had this to say."

The film cut to what looked like an office with a pale man behind the desk, whose eyes were almost glowing. "We want to reassure the citizens of New York that these creatures, while they are undead, are not vampires. The Vampire Nation has no knowledge as to who brought them back to life or what danger they may pose."

Herne paled. "Try another channel—nationwide."

Angel flipped through till we came to another news story, this time out of Tampa, Florida. "Florida, too. And it looks like Denver as well." She turned off the sound then, letting the horrific images become silent.

"Angel, call Talia and tell her we need her, headache or not. Also, call Rafé in." Herne stared at the muted television. "If they absolutely cannot make it in, get them on Zone and we'll conference them in. Also, conference Charlie in, if he's not in class. I'll be back in a moment." He abruptly withdrew from the room.

Angel handed me the remote and headed back to her desk to make the calls.

Viktor and I stared at each other. It was bad enough when a problem this deadly was local, but nationwide? The Wild Hunt's reach only extended so far, given our focus was on the Fae Courts, which were located in western Washington.

"What the hell are we going to do about this?" I asked, watching the live images on the television.

Officers were shooting at the walking dead, but to no avail. The keen, twisted smiles on the corpses' faces were enough to unnerve anybody. And then, one of the officers tripped. Before his comrades could reach him, the nearest creature grabbed hold of him, dragged him to his feet and bit deep into his throat. The officer was screaming—that much I could tell from the picture. His buddies rushed in, trying to beat the thing off. They managed to separate the cop from his attacker and quickly carried him off.

"They remind me of ghouls," I said. "Unlike zombies, ghouls have a sentience that's twisted, but cunning. And there's intelligence behind the eyes of those creatures. Hey, I bet Raven would know. She's a bone witch and deals with the undead. Why don't you call her?"

"Good idea," Yutani murmured. "I'm not getting anywhere on my own. Not yet." He pulled out his phone and moved away from the table.

I leaned forward, watching Viktor. The ogre looked somber. "I'm sorry." I reached out and took his hand. "This was supposed to be your day to celebrate."

He shrugged, smiling gently. "One thing I've learned over the years: No matter what your heart feels, reality will do as it will. There are very few days that are either completely wonderful or completely horrendous. Life's always teetering on the balance beam, and we have to take joy when and where we can."

"You're right about that." I squeezed his hand, then leaned back in my chair. "If we can find out what these creatures are, then we have a better chance of putting a stop to them. So I hope Raven has the answer."

"As it so happens, Raven did give me an answer," Yutani said, returning to the table. "She looked them up in her copy of *Beltan's Bestiary*. Apparently, the undead are called *vrykos* and they're a Greek form of ghoul." His brow furrowed, he quickly returned to his computer. "Now that I've got a name, I have something to go off of."

I carried our mugs and plates to the sink and poured soap on them, leaving them to soak. At that moment, Angel returned.

"Talia's on her way, and so is Rafé. Charlie's waiting on Zone. I'll just set up the connection on the break room laptop." She crossed to the rolling cart that had a laptop on it, booting it up before setting up the video meeting with Charlie.

College agreed with the young vampire. Charlie had been turned a couple years ago, when he was barely nineteen. We met him when we needed to interview him on a case, but he had quickly become friends with first Viktor, then Herne. Now, he worked for the Wild Hunt and Herne was putting him through college to finish his degree. When he graduated, Charlie would take over as the accountant for the business. Currently, he did data entry for us and sometimes came into the office in the evening hours to polish and service the weaponry.

He appeared on the screen. A far cry from the scruffy, self-conscious vampire we had first known, he was neat and tidy, and had his hair pulled back in a sleek ponytail. There was something appealing about him, in a boyish way. His vampire glamour was beginning to shine through.

"I've been watching the news," he said, as soon as the feed was clear. "Do we know what they are? I saw that the Vampire Nation, the East Coast rep at least, says they're not vamps."

"We just found out—" Yutani started to say, stopping as

Herne entered the room. Behind him was Rafé. He silently took a seat next to Angel, first holding her chair for her. They were dating, and while he was Dark Fae, Rafé wasn't particularly welcome in TirNaNog, the Court of the Dark Fae. He had always been a black sheep in his family.

"Talia will be here in a few moments," Angel said. "She was getting ready to come in, anyway. Apparently, her apartment is right next to a new construction zone and it's only making her headache worse."

"We'll wait till she gets here so we don't have to repeat anything." Herne looked at me. "You guys have any luck figuring out what we're dealing with?"

Yutani nodded. "Yep, we called Raven and she tracked it down. Like you, though, I'd rather wait till we're all together before discussing it."

Angel turned the volume back up and we continued watching the news reports that were coming in from all areas of the country now. The vrykos seemed to be everywhere, or at least, all of the major cities. Via the laptop, Herne waved to Charlie, who waved back. Five minutes later, Talia entered the room.

"All right, I'm here. Somebody get me a cup of Head-Eze." She slid into the chair opposite me, grimacing. She glanced over at the laptop. "Hey, Charles. Good to see you."

He waved at her. The old myth about vampires not being able to be seen in the mirror or on camera was just that—a myth.

Angel jumped up to fix the tea—she was a tea snob and didn't like it when anybody else thought they knew the proper way to brew tea. Even herbal tea.

"Hangover?" Yutani asked, giving Talia a sideways grin.

Talia bared her teeth at him. "Be nice. I may look human but I'm still a harpy, even if I don't have most of my powers. I could gnash that pretty face of yours before you had time to shriek, pretty boy."

Yutani snorted. "Good luck on that. But I take it booze is not at the bottom of your condition?"

"No. I'm not sure what caused it. Maybe change in air pressure, maybe a strained neck or something. But I woke up in a fog and with a headache the size of Mount Rainier." She rubbed her temples.

I glanced out the window. The weather was bright—too bright for my liking. We had had a bit of a heat wave in May, then pleasant weather in June. Now, at the end of July, we were experiencing another heat wave and the weather was gearing up to be hot and muggy. But I could feel some moisture in the air and I knew that a thunderstorm was likely within the next week.

"Thunderstorm weather. Don't be surprised if we have a doozy of a storm over the next couple days." I shifted in my seat. Thank gods we had air conditioning in the office.

"Okay, we're all here," Herne said, ignoring the weather chat. "First, Yutani, you said we have a name to put to these creatures?"

Yutani nodded. "I called Raven. She combed through *Beltan's Bestiary*. She thinks we're facing a Greek form of ghoul called vrykos."

"Lovely. Can they reason?" Viktor asked.

"Yes, to a degree, and they're forced to obey the necromancer who summoned them back to the corpse. They aren't necessarily the same soul who inhabited the corpse during life, though. Basically, they're pissed off, and they have a hunger that cannot be satisfied. They feed off the living." Yutani was reading off of an entry he found online.

"Great. Just what we need. So... how do they attack? Do they eat their kills? Drink blood? Just what are we talking about here?" I was jotting down notes, though Yutani would be sending everyone the info. But sometimes I found I remembered things better when I wrote down what I heard.

Yutani paused, skimming the article. After a moment, he pushed the laptop back. "All right, this is what we know about them. They will eat those they attack; however, they don't siphon off life force. But there's a different concern. Their saliva carries a virulent form of bacteria, a lot like a Komodo dragon. And that bacterial infection is not only deadly, but it can spread. It's highly contagious, through touch, airborne droplets, and bodily fluids exchange."

My heart skipped a beat. "Are you talking a potential plague here? How many of these creatures are considered carriers?"

"Almost one hundred percent. If you get bit, you'll almost certainly end up infected. Add to that their bite also has a necrotic toxin in it and you've got one hell of a potent weapon." Yutani leaned his elbows on the table. "If this is happening on a nationwide scale..."

"It means we could end up with a plague sweeping through the country." Talia let out a slow breath, accepting the tea that Angel handed to her. "What about the rest of the world? Is this happening in other countries as well?"

Yutani pulled his laptop closer and began tapping away. "Let me check." A few minutes later, he looked up. "Yes. This is going on worldwide. Only it's not just the vrykos. There are reports of skeletal walkers, ghouls, and zombies cropping up all over. The dead are pouring out of their graves."

Herne reached for his phone. "I'm texting my father. He and some of the other gods have to meet with the United Coalition and other world leaders. This could blow up into a nightmare if the governments take the wrong actions."

"What stops the vrykos?" I asked. We had already been dealing with an upswing in skeletal walkers, though we hadn't seen zombies or ghouls so far.

"Same thing that stops skeletal warriors, ghouls, and zombies. Cutting them to pieces. Bombs—maybe. Fire will destroy them." Yutani was glued to the screen. "I was right. In France, they're noticing the beginnings of a new disease. Bacterial, and linked to the victims of the vrykos. There have been ten cases, and they all died. Two of them weren't victims of the creatures—they were family members who sat with their loved ones at the hospital."

"Are there any known antidotes?" I asked.

Herne once again took to his phone. "I'll get Ferosyn on it." He stepped away from the table and moved over near the window.

Yutani paused, then shook his head. "Some antibiotics seem to be slowing the progression of the disease. The bacteria shuts down the internal organs, even as the necrosis begins to eat away at the flesh. And...we have one report of one of the victims who died and reanimated as a zombie. The doctors had to *torch* the corpse in order to stop it. So zombie-like aftereffects."

"What about luring them into anti-magic zones? Will that deactivate them until the spell runs out or the vrykos are removed from the area?" Angel frowned. "I don't even know if there is such a thing."

"Oh, there is," Yutani said, "but I can't find anything that answers whether it would work on them." The coyote shifter was still reading.

Herne returned. "I talked to Ferosyn, who's looking into antibiotics that will work on the Fae and Cryptos, given most human antibiotics have massive side effects for them." He paused. "No groans—I know tomorrow is Lughnasadh and it's also a Saturday, but I need you guys to be on board with this. Everybody be here bright and early and ready to work tomorrow morning."

I restrained myself from sighing. I had been looking forward to having the day off before ritual, but I sucked it up.

"We'll be here," Viktor said, motioning to the rest of us, and we nodded.

"Good, because I also called Mayor Neskan. She asked us to meet with Jana Wildmere, the president of the Shifter Alliance, to discuss forming a militia formed of shifters. And tomorrow afternoon at one o'clock, Ember and I are going to parley with Saílle and Névé to ask them if we can commandeer the Fae militia they drummed up during the Iron Plague. Humans simply aren't strong enough to cope with these creatures, so the Cryptos have to take the helm on this one. I also convinced the mayor to call for a statewide curfew until the situation is under control. She's going to discuss it with the governor."

The last thing I wanted to do was parley with Saílle and Névé, but this wasn't the time to complain. "We should talk to the Vampire Nation, too." I glanced over at the screen. "Charlie, who runs the show for this state?"

"The regent for the Pacific Northwest is Dormant Reins. He's a thousand years old and was here long before any white settlers ever came to the area." Charlie leaned back, crossing his arms. "Getting an audience with him isn't going to be easy."

I worried my lip. "What about calling Eldris? He seems to have a lot of power in the Vampire Nation." Eldris was the manager of a nightclub called Fire & Fang, and he was too slimy for my tastes, but he had connections and he might actually be willing to talk to us.

Yutani caught my gaze. "You might be on to something there."

"Should I call, or should you?" I asked.

Yutani thought it over for a moment. "Probably you. He was intrigued by you. And now that he knows you're not my sub, I doubt if he has much interest in talking to me."

Herne cleared his throat—hard—and leaned forward. "Don't you think *I* should have a talk with him instead of Ember?"

There it was again, that flicker of jealousy. Herne didn't want to share me. I was fine with that, even though a number of the gods and the Fae were far from monogamous. But I wasn't a piece of property. I had conflicted feelings every time Herne's possessive side reared its jealous little head.

"Yutani's right. I caught Eldris's eye, and as uncomfortable as that made me, I'm not above using it for all it's worth." I pulled out my phone. "Should I ask him to come in tomorrow night, or are we going to go down to Fire & Fang?"

Herne's smoldering look told me exactly what he thought of that idea. "I'd prefer here, but I doubt we have the upper hand on this. Find out where he's willing to meet."

I brought up my contacts and found Eldris's number. He answered on the first ring. "Hey, it's Ember Kearney. Remember me?"

"Most definitely. I never forget a beautiful woman." His words were smooth and flowed over me like sweet honey.

I shook my head, trying to chase away the strands of glamour that flickered through the phone. Eldris was old, and he was a powerful vampire. Try as I might, his ability to charm overwhelmed my ability to ignore it.

"We need your help on a matter that's going to affect everyone, including the vampires. We need to talk to the regent of the Pacific Northwest." I paused, waiting for his answer.

Silence…then, "You really think you can just walk into his office like you would a city official?" Eldris laughed. "Pardon me, but that's the funniest thing I've heard. You won't get in by namedropping your boyfriend's name at the door. Let me work on it. I can't promise you I'll have you an invitation by tomorrow, but I'll do what I can."

"It's *really* important," I said. "Please, don't take too long. A lot of lives hang in the balance."

Eldris paused, then when he spoke again, his voice was somber. "I've seen the news. I know why you're asking. I'll do what I can. I'll call you when I have anything to report." And with that, the line went dead.

I sat back, closing my eyes for a moment. I glanced over at Herne. "He'll do his best and I believe him. Should we head out to the Worchester District now?"

Herne pressed his lips together and shook his head. "Just killing a few of them won't solve the problem. The mayor said she'll assign the strongest Fae officers she's got to the outbreaks. Meanwhile, we need a systematic plan of action. Until then, everybody be on your guard. I think the war has come to us."

CHAPTER THREE

It felt wrong, not charging in to do something, but Herne pointed out the police could barricade the vrykos into an area for the night and keep watch over them. We had to be at our best for our meetings with the Fae Queens and the president of the Shifter Alliance. Reluctantly, I agreed that we needed to focus our efforts where they would do the most good instead of just going in swinging.

"Just relax, love. I know that's a tall order, but we have to take advantage of every chance we get. We're headed into the trenches, so we sleep when we can, smile when something good happens, and deal with death when it's in front of us. We may not have much downtime for the foreseeable future. I'll tell you what, I'll go over to the Worchester District and find out how things are. If needed, we'll go in to help."

Herne pulled me to him as we stood in his office. He wrapped his arms around me and leaned down for a long kiss. His eyes were the purest blue I had ever seen, untouched by all the horror and pain he had been through, gentle as a young buck in the field, and yet, as deep as the early morning sky.

ANGEL and I had ridden in to work together, and as we headed home, we stopped at Ben's Big Burgers to grab dinner. They made the best shakes in town—especially in March, with their biggy-piggy lime milkshakes. But the restaurant was good any day of the year. We ordered double-stack bacon cheeseburgers, orange cream shakes, and double-crisp curly fries.

As we pulled into the driveway, I felt a warmth run through me. Our home, a safe haven. It was *my* house, technically—Angel rented from me—but it really was *our* home. I stopped as the thought crossed my mind that if—when—I married Herne, either he would have to move in, or I would have to give up the house to move into his home. The thought of living without Angel as a roommate gnawed at me. I wasn't ready to let go of seeing her face every morning. We had developed a rhythm to our lives, and I wasn't sure I was willing to give that up.

"What are you thinking about? You have that mopey look on your face," Angel said as we headed toward the door. She was carrying the takeout bags so I paused at the mailbox to get our mail. "You might as well tell me, because I'll pry it out of you one way or another."

I snorted. "All right, I was just thinking that if I accept Herne's proposal, what will that mean for this house? For you and me being roommates? I love living with you.

You're my best friend and I can't imagine...not being in the same place."

Practical as always, Angel said, "We'll deal with that when the time comes. You can't let a house be a deal-breaker to accepting Herne's proposal. I sure wouldn't," she added, giving me a long, hard look. "I refuse to be your excuse for you not giving him an answer. And I won't be the reason you say no to him. If you don't want to marry him, then don't. But you have to give him a good answer, either way, soon."

I stared at her, surprised by her tone. She usually wasn't so abrupt. But as her words sank in, I realized she was right. I was coming up with obstacles to either accepting or refusing him. I needed to figure out why. I loved Herne more than I had ever loved anyone. He was the man of my dreams. But then...he wasn't really a man. And that was where my confusion lay. Herne was a god, not a man. And I'd have to become a goddess. And *that* meant so many changes.

As I unlocked the door, letting Angel enter first, I took a deep breath. "Okay, you're right. Confession time. I'm scared."

"Scared of what? Living happily ever after?" Angel carried the food into the kitchen.

I followed her, setting the mail on the table before washing my hands. I brought out plates and forks as we settled at the table. Mr. Rumblebutt jumped up on the chair next to me and let out a loud purp, reminding me that I had been gone all day and he desperately needed acknowledgment. I kissed him on the nose and scratched behind his ears while Angel opened the takeout bags and began to spread out our meal.

"What am I afraid of? It's the whole *becoming-a-goddess* thing. The thought of it scares the hell out of me. I *just* went through the Cruharach. That was such a huge change. I don't know what becoming a goddess means. I suppose I'll ask Morgana tomorrow, during dinner." I sipped my milkshake, staring at my plate. "Once you marry a god, it's forever, Angel. I mean, even if we split sometime down the road, there's no going back. I'd be a goddess, adrift in a world that I wasn't sure of. There's no way to reverse the process."

Angel thought for a moment, then said, "All right, let's look at that. So, Herne lives here for the most part, on Earth. He doesn't spend most of his time in Annwn. He goes grocery shopping at the Q-Mart. He eats fast food and watches television and likes to grill steaks. That's about as human as you can get, god or not. He's not going to suddenly sweep you off to Annwn, is he?" Angel licked ketchup off her fingers, then picked up her shake.

I blinked, suddenly realizing that was exactly what I had imagined happening. That we'd get married, go back to Annwn, and I'd be lost in a world I didn't know.

"Um...yeah, I guess not."

"That's what you really thought, wasn't it? That he'd take you back to Annwn and you'd lose your life here." Angel laughed. "Ember, use your brain. Herne's been in charge of the Wild Hunt for over two hundred years. He spends most of his time here on Earth. We're fighting a war against Typhon and that means he's needed here more than ever. So I don't think I'd worry myself if I were you. You won't be going anywhere soon."

I rubbed my head. "You're right. But..."

"But what? The house? I do understand. You love this

house—you bought it. But nothing says you have to sell it, even if you end up moving in with Herne. Hell, I'll rent it from you if that happens. I'm sure Rafé would move in, if we're still together by your wedding. He hates that crappy little apartment of his and I think he'd welcome the chance to move."

I felt like an idiot. Angel was looking ahead at a positive future. She was seeing possibilities I hadn't even really thought about. Which reminded me...

"So, how are you and Rafé doing? I know you're doing better, because...therapy. He's come a long way in the past few months."

"We're good. The Elves are really good with their therapeutic techniques and he's coping with the PTSD so much better. He's the Rafé I remember, only more thoughtful. And he's glad to have a steady job that doesn't require him to wait on tables. When I asked him if he misses his acting career, he said no. He's looking into online classes so that he doesn't have to disrupt his schedule at the office."

"What's he want to do again?" Rafé had been a waiter/actor trying to make it to the big time and having a hard time advancing.

"Counseling. The idea of being a mental health therapist for the Fae appeals to him. He's been talking to his counselor over in Annwn a lot about that. By the way, speaking of counselors, how's Raven doing with Sejun?"

Our friend Raven had been through a traumatic kidnapping a few months back. While she was Ante-Fae—the race that preceded the Fae—even with her potential and powers, she had sunk into a deep depression. She had been talking to a therapist from Cernunnos's palace for a couple months now.

"It's helped a lot. She told me that she's getting the nightmares and flashbacks under control. She and Kipa are on an even keel again. Her mother has helped a lot, too, although quite frankly, just having the Queen of the Bean Sidhe as my mother would be enough to freak me out. But Phasmoria has been checking on Raven a lot lately."

We moved on to other topics as we finished our dinner, and then I fed Mr. Rumblebutt as Angel rinsed the dishes and put them in the dishwasher. She pulled out some cookie dough she had frozen earlier in the week, and set a couple batches to baking. I popped the popcorn and made myself a triple decaf caramel latte. By the time the kitchen was clean and the cookies were done, we were ready for our binge-fest. We had recorded four episodes of *English Gardens Explored*—one of our favorite shows—and we curled up on the sofa with our goodies and dove into watching.

As the light outside faded into dusk, we tried not to think about the vrykos. Tomorrow was Lughnasadh—the first of August—and Marilee was set to lead the ritual. We would celebrate the season of sacrifice, and hopefully wouldn't be interrupted by dragons and undead and all the things that were currently going bump in the night.

Mr. Rumblebutt joined us on the sofa, and I pulled him on my lap, burying my face in his fur. He purred up a storm as I petted him, and once again—even though I tried not to dwell—my thoughts turned toward the future. Could Mr. Rumblebutt become a god, too? Could cats become immortal? And what about best friends who were human?

With a score of unanswered questions on my mind, I brought my attention back to the show and lost myself in a garden filled with wildflowers and ferns, enjoying the sedate pace of the narrator's voice as a village filled with flowers soothed my frayed nerves.

WHEN I WOKE the next morning, the day was partially overcast, with a loose layer of clouds patchworking the skies. I rolled out of bed and, grabbing my robe, headed for the shower. I could smell cooking coming from downstairs. Angel usually woke earlier than I did and she almost always made breakfast because she loved to cook.

I lathered up, then stood beneath the shower of water, closing my eyes. The energy coiled around me like an old friend. My mother's blood made me half Leannan Sidhe—the Light Fae side—and so I was intimately connected with the water and Mother Ocean.

The waves called to me, the sirens on their mist-shrouded rocks, the naiads in their grottoes by the lakes, and the undines, guarding the rivers—all of these were deeply rooted in my nature. The Leannan Sidhe were among the most predatory of the Water Fae. I could charm men and women, bringing them into my control. If I wanted to, I could suck the life out of a man, draining his chi—his breath—even as he swore to love me forever.

For a long time I had never known the specifics on my heritage, but when I joined the Wild Hunt, Morgana—Herne's mother—had claimed me as one of her own, as my mother had been. She was goddess of the Fae, and goddess of the Sea, and she helped me understand why I had to embrace my blood, even though both sides were predatory and dangerous. So I was learning to accept who I was, and to use the powers I had been born with.

Now, I soaked up the energy of the shower, of the water streaming over my body as it ran down my skin, pooling in droplets on my breasts, trickling over the gentle curve of my stomach. I had a lot of scars that interrupted the smooth stretches, but they were visible reminders of the battles that had helped make me who I was.

Finally, I stepped out of the shower and toweled off. I sat at my vanity, staring in the mirror as I pulled out my blow dryer. My hair was getting long—it was nearly to the middle of my back now—and it was as dark as a moonless night. My eyes were brilliant green, and as I flexed, my muscles were definitely apparent. I had big boobs and curving hips, all with a soft layer of padding. I would never be called "slender," but I didn't care. I was fit, happy, and healthy, and that's what mattered.

Finally, shaking myself out of my thoughts, I dried my hair, pulled it back in a ponytail, and put on my makeup. Finally, I dressed in a nice pair of black jeans, a pale green tank top over a sturdy but sexy bra, and a pair of ankle boots. Low heeled—about two inches—they were easy to run in, if need be.

Fastening my crow necklace around my throat that marked me as belonging to Morgana, I glanced down at my newest tattoo. A few weeks back, I'd had the same crow inked on my right upper arm to honor Morgana.

Before I headed downstairs, I paused at my nightstand.

I opened the drawer and pulled out a small ring box. As I cracked it open, I caught my breath again. Herne had given me the most stunning sapphire set in platinum. Diamond and amethyst baguettes adorned the sides of the square-cut solitaire. As I stared at it, I heard a voice inside asking, *What are you waiting for?*

"What *am* I waiting for?" I whispered. And just like that, I made up my mind. I slid the ring onto my left ring finger and held it out. My decision was made. I held out my hand and admired the ring.

"Get your ass down to breakfast," Angel called up the stairs.

And so I turned and walked into my future.

"When's Morgana due?" Angel asked as I entered the kitchen.

"Around six. Hopefully, we'll be back from Ginty's by then." I glanced at the clock, wondering how long it would take us to get through the business with the Fae Queens.

Angel paused. "Girl, what's that on your finger?" She gasped, then squeed as she ran around the kitchen island to grab my hand. "You never showed me the ring before!" Whistling as she looked at it, she took my hand. "Wow, that's gorgeous."

"I didn't want you to fall in love with the jewelry and pressure me to just accept so you could look at it. I think it's a family heirloom. Maybe from his grandmother? I don't know. I suppose I should ask him when I get the chance." I felt odd wearing the ring. But it also felt right, and it fit snuggly on my finger. Something about it felt magical.

"Here's your food," Angel said, still mesmerized by my ring. "I've never seen a ring so beautiful. It feels like it was made for you. And it packs a punch of energy."

"Doesn't it? I can't seem to get Herne on phone. He's not texting me back. I was going to tell him that I accept his proposal, but I don't want to do it via text message. I'll try calling."

Angel stared at me. "Are you joking? You don't just accept a proposal over the phone."

I blinked. "Betty White did! She accepted Allen Ludden's proposal over the phone. I saw it on a documentary."

"*She's Betty fucking White.* The woman could go on a rampage and people would cheer her on. She's as close to a goddess as we humans have. You *aren't* a goddess. Not yet." But her eyes were twinkling and I realized she wasn't actually scolding me.

"You're probably right. Herne deserves more than a phone call. I just know how anxious he's been about my not answering him yet. He even talked to Raven about it, I found out." I paused, then shrugged. "Hey, I know." I held out my phone and took a picture of my left hand. The ring sat prominently on my finger. "I think I *will* text him. Just not in words." I glanced at Angel, waiting for her to frown but she just shook her head, laughing.

"Oh, go on. Of course, if you just walk into the office with it on, the impact might be—"

"Yeah, but I want him to know before the rest of the office." I hit send and watched as the picture made its way through cyberspace to Herne's phone. Holding my breath,

I waited. After sixty seconds, I let it out in a long stream, staring at my phone. "Why isn't he answering?"

"Maybe he hasn't seen it yet? He could be on the phone, or he could be in a meeting, or he could be driving. Remember, you guys have to parley at Ginty's today, so he could be setting things up." Angel slid a plate of bacon and eggs in front of me, along with four pieces of cinnamon toast.

I fretted as I ate. Had he changed his mind? Was he regretting having asked me? I was driving myself crazy with possibilities. After a moment, Angel brought me a large travel mug filled to the brim with ice, milk, and espresso.

"I don't think you need the caffeine, but you might as well. Come on, finish your breakfast and we'll head to the office. I really wish we didn't have to work today. It's Lughnasadh."

I grinned at her. "Until last year, you didn't celebrate Lughnasadh."

"Old dog, new tricks. It just doesn't seem right to work on holidays."

"A lot of people have to, regardless of what holidays they recognize. I'd rather stay home and focus on the celebration, too, but the reality is we don't have that luxury. We'll meet at Marilee's tonight, and that will be fun. Meanwhile, let's head out for the office."

I finished the last bite of my breakfast and, after slipping my dish into the dishwasher and grabbing my latte, I slung my purse over my shoulder and followed Angel out to the driveway. We decided to go in separate cars in case Herne and I ran long at the parley. As I pulled out of the driveway, I glanced back at my house. I still didn't know what we'd do about our living situation, but I'd deal with that later. For now, I felt far more settled, having made a decision. I was going to marry Herne. And that put a smile on my lips and a song in my heart.

WHEN ANGEL and I stepped out of the elevator, the office seemed terribly quiet. Talia wasn't at the front desk, like she usually was until Angel got there. I walked over to Herne's office, knocked, and peeked in, but he was nowhere to be seen.

I looked back at Angel, shaking my head. "I don't know where they are. Herne's not in his office."

"That's odd," Angel said. "Let's check the break room. Maybe they started the meeting without us?"

We started every workday with a staff meeting. But usually, the elevator was locked from stopping at our floor during meetings, so to find no one in the reception area and the elevator unlocked seemed strange.

Angel hung back, looking in her purse for something, so I headed down the hall. I had a feeling something was amiss and I wished that I had armed myself. I usually wore my dagger in a thigh sheath, but it was in my tote with the rest of my gear.

I paused at the door to the break room, hesitating. Glancing over my shoulder, I met Angel's gaze and she gave me a nod.

"You might as well open it."

I glanced down the side hall, but there was no sound from Yutani and Talia's office, either. The supply room door was closed, as was the door to my office. Taking a deep breath, I put my hand on the knob and slowly cracked open the door to the break room, prepared for anything.

There was a blur of movement and before I could move or speak, shouts of "*Surprise!*" echoed around me. I was so surprised that I nearly fell back into Angel's arms.

She laughed and pushed me forward, as I realized that everybody had been hiding in the break room. And there in front of me stood Herne, a bouquet of red roses in his arms. He held out his hand to me, smiling.

"You've made me the happiest man in the world. The happiest *god* in the world. Ember, my love, I will cherish you for all the days to come."

And with those words, Angel gave me a little shove, pushing me into his arms, as everyone clapped and cheered.

CHAPTER FOUR

In the short time that it took Angel and me to drive to work, somehow Herne had pulled off the impromptu party complete with a cake and a bottle of champagne. Talia had the company camera and was snapping pictures right and left. I was surprised and gratified to see that Sheila was there, too. Both she and Viktor were dressed up. The cake not only read "Congratulations, Herne and Ember," but had Viktor's and Sheila's names on it as well.

"How did you get this done so fast?" I asked.

Talia laughed. "You'll find out anyway, so I'm going to tell you whether Herne wants me to or not. We already had the cake here, but it just had Viktor's and Sheila's names on it. This was going to be a surprise party for them. But when you texted Herne the picture of the ring, I hustled to add your names to the cake. If you'll notice, the icing's a different color and the letters aren't nearly as steady."

Grinning like an idiot, I gave Herne a long kiss and then, carrying the roses, slid into a chair. Sheila also had a bouquet of roses, and I had the feeling that mine had been an afterthought, probably from one of the boutique shops across the street. But I didn't care.

"The only thing I feel bad about is I feel like we're upstaging Viktor and Sheila," I said.

Sheila shook her head, and when she spoke her voice was throaty. It had changed since her neck had been slashed, but she considered herself lucky to even be able to speak. She was actually lucky to be alive. "I don't mind. I'm just grateful I'm here. And I appreciate all of your congratulations. I know I'm not a member of the Wild Hunt."

"That will change the day you get married," Herne said. "When anyone gets married into the Wild Hunt, their partner is automatically brought into the agency for protection." He paused, his smile slipping away. "I just wish we could've protected you against what happened with Falcon Smith. I know he hasn't been found yet. Trust me, we're keeping an eye out for him. But meanwhile, I hope you don't have any objection to a tattoo. Everybody belonging to the Hunt gets the same mark."

Sheila shook her head. "I'm fine with it. I plan on being married to Viktor for a long time. I'll accept life as the wife of a member of the Wild Hunt without complaint." She paused, then asked, "Have you set your date yet?"

Herne started to shake his head, but I broke in.

"I want to get married in the autumn, so I'd say probably a year from either this Mabon or Samhain." I paused, realizing I hadn't even consulted Herne. I looked at him. "Is that all right with you?"

He nodded, a big goofy grin on his face. "That's fine with me. It will take some time for all the details to be worked out. So even though we're photobombing Viktor and Sheila's engagement party, we won't be upstaging their wedding."

Angel poured champagne around while Talia cut the cake.

I stepped forward, holding my glass up. "I'd like to propose a toast. To Viktor, one of the most gentle giants I know—or ogres, rather. And to Sheila, the love of his life. May the two of you have many years together spent in love and laughter, and may you be blessed with peace and health and joy."

Everybody clapped, and cheered as they clinked their glasses together.

Then Angel stood up. "And I would like to make a toast as well. To the best friend I could ever have, to my sister in arms. We may not share blood, but we share the bonds of sisterhood. From the very first day when I pushed you into the mud, and you dragged me down with you, I realized that you would always fight for what was right. I've never been disappointed in you. To you, and to Herne, may you live in joy and magic together. I'm not going to wish you peace because I don't think that comes with the territory, but certainly joy does."

My eyes fogged over as tears flecked my lashes. I tried not to cry, but Angel's words hit deep, and I jumped up and hugged her tightly.

"You know that everything that you said, I want for you, too. You are always and forever my sister."

She ducked her head, smiling. "I know, but today's not about me. It's about Viktor and Sheila, and you and Herne, and that's as it should be."

"All right, waterworks off! Let's eat cake and drink

champagne and then, I'm afraid we have to get to work." Herne cleared his throat, looking suspiciously like he had tears in his eyes as well. But he downed the champagne, and then gave Angel a long hug.

After the cake was two-thirds gone, we moved it off the counter so we could have our morning meeting. Sheila excused herself, heading out to do some shopping.

"Rafé, since you're here as well, you might as well stay for the briefing. Charlie, can you hear me?" Herne glanced over the laptop where Charlie was watching through the screen. He had Zoned in for the party.

"Loud and clear. Again, congratulations to both you and Ember, and Viktor and Sheila. I only ask that you hold your weddings in the evening so that I can attend?" He gave us a pleading look.

I laughed. "Of course. It wouldn't be right without you there."

As we settled down to work, I paused to get myself another piece of cake and to whip up a second iced latte. I edged into the seat next to Herne, and he covered my hand with his, fingering the ring and smiling softly. As everybody shuffled papers and got ready, I lowered my voice and whispered to him.

"Thank you for being patient. It wasn't that I didn't want to marry you—"

He slowly pressed one finger against mine. "Hush. I know *exactly* what it was. And that's all right. I'd rather have you accept with your whole heart than go into it with doubt."

I ducked my head, smiling softly. "I had no doubts about loving you, but I have to admit I'm a little afraid. Turning into a goddess, and what that might entail...it's daunting, to say the least. But if your mother was able to do it, I can too."

"Of course you will. There's no doubt in my mind, and no doubts cloud my heart."

AS WE RAN through the minutes, I tried to focus on the task at hand. But my heart was pounding. Now that I had actually accepted, an excitement swept over me that I hadn't expected.

"Talia, have you been able to get a hold of the Shifter Alliance?"

She nodded. "I talked to Jana Wildmere this morning. She's agreed to meet with you on Sunday at four. And I contacted the mayor after that. She'll set up a meeting with the United Coalition as soon as we have verification from both the shifters and the Fae that their militias will be on hand."

Herne turned to me. "Have you heard from Eldris yet?"

I shook my head. "No, but that doesn't surprise me. He won't call until he has an answer, and you know the vampires have to be looking at what they can get out of this." Suddenly, I realized that Charlie was listening. I blushed and glanced over at the laptop. "I'm sorry, Charlie. I didn't think before I spoke."

"Not *all* vampires are out to get everything they can from the living. But enough are that I understand your hesitation. The truth is, I wouldn't have chosen this life if it were offered to me as an option. But it's what I am now, and I aim to prove that I don't have to live down to the stereotype. I don't own a black cape, and I'm not running around seducing women and sinking my fangs into unsuspecting tourists."

"Point taken," I said. "All right then, this afternoon." I turned to Herne. "What do you think Névé and Saílle will say? Do you think they'll agree to help us?"

He thought for a moment, then shrugged. "Honestly? I have no idea. I don't know whether they'll help us out or walk away from the parley. Especially since we forced them to hand over Callan. I doubt they've forgiven us for that yet. There's not much I can do to change their minds if they decide to ignore our request. I can't force the issue."

"I guess we just wait and see." I frowned. Saílle and Névé were unpredictable, but they seldom forgave slights and injuries to their images and rules.

"Right." He stared at his notes, then cleared his throat. "All right. Let's get moving. Ember, Viktor, and I will head out to Ginty's at noon. Talia and Yutani, will you gather all the information you can on any vrykos attacks that you come across? Search all the news outlets, even the tabloids. Sometimes there are shreds of truth behind some of the wild stories. Charlie, I suggest you get back to your studies for the moment. Rafé—why don't you help Talia and Yutani? Angel, you can have the rest of the day off. Did you and Ember come in separate cars?"

Angel nodded. "Thanks." She glanced at me. "I'll go home and do some chores. We want the place to look nice when Morgana comes to dinner. What did you want me to cook?"

I bit my lip. "I'm not sure." I glanced at Herne. "What does your mother like? What's her favorite food?"

Herne laughed. "You can't go wrong if you serve her a platter of fish and chips, especially if it's halibut. And don't stint on the portions. My mother can eat four or five pieces of fish and a double side of fries in a single go. She's not a fan of coleslaw, however. In fact, sometimes I wonder if my mother would touch a vegetable without Cernunnos pushing her."

Angel thought for a moment, then asked, "Does she like clam chowder? That's a good pairing with fish and chips."

He nodded. "New England. If you offer her Manhattan-style clam chowder, she's going to laugh you out of the kitchen. I suggest peach pie for dessert. That's her favorite."

My stomach aflutter, I realized that I was going to be telling Morgana tonight that I had accepted her son's proposal. She'd not only be my patron goddess, but my mother-in-law. And *that* was a daunting thought. My consternation must have shown on my face, because Herne reached over and gave me a little rub on the shoulder.

"My mother loves you. You already know that. It's not going to change just because I'm bringing you into the family."

That really set me to sweating. I was going to be part of Herne's *family*. And when you married somebody, you married the family along with them. Which meant Cernunnos would be my father-in-law. But I said nothing, simply forcing a smile as I stood and gathered my things.

"I'll go get ready for the parley." I escaped out of the break room before he could catch me. We had long enough to talk in the car, although I was grateful Viktor was going with us. I was suddenly feeling extremely awkward, and I wasn't sure how to deal with the unexpected shift into insecurity. I headed into my office, closing the door behind me. And there, I sank down on the sofa, trying to calm my stomach.

WE WERE on the road on the way toward the 520 floating bridge before Herne derailed the conversation away from shop talk. I had begun to relax, thinking I was off the hook, when he suddenly decided to become chatty. Viktor was in the back seat, thumbing through an e-book.

"We should start planning the wedding. I know you want to wait for a year before getting married, and that's fine, but weddings among the gods are far from simple affairs. Our wedding will be a major event, so we need to start discussing the matter now." He paused. "You do realize it will have to take place in Annwn?"

I nodded. "Actually, yes. I expected that would be the case. But I'd like to bring a few friends over. Marilee, for one. Everybody in the agency, and Raven. How will we manage that?"

"We have a year to figure it out. But anybody you want there, we'll make it happen. I promise you that."

"I suppose you already know who will be officiating?" I was quickly beginning to realize that Herne's customs would take precedence over mine, even though he was doing his best to make it as much my wedding as his.

"Most likely Danu. However, you choose your own bridesmaids and maid of honor. I assume you're picking Angel for the latter?"

"Of course. As far as bridesmaids, I suppose Raven and Talia. I have some other women friends, but not a great many." I bit my lip, then asked, "Who are you asking to be your best man?"

Herne raised his eyebrows. "Kipa, even though I'd rather have Viktor." He glanced in the rearview mirror as Viktor looked up, hearing his name. "Sorry, old man, but custom requires I choose someone in the family. But you and Yutani can be my groomsmen."

Viktor snorted. "That's all right. You know, hearing the two of you talk makes me extremely glad that I am not a god. Or marrying a goddess. Sheila and I want a simple affair, although it would be incredible if the Lady Brighid could preside. Other than that, we just want a quiet garden wedding in the snow, if there is any."

"I can't promise the snow," I said. "But I thought we could weave some red rose garlands to go over the trellises and decorate with sprigs of holly."

"That sounds lovely."

"What about wedding dresses?" I turned to Herne. "Can I choose my own?"

"I think my mother will probably want to have one made for you. However, I know you'll be consulted. Her tailors will make it. But...please try to pick something ornate? I know that you like simple, but I can't stress enough that this will be a huge affair."

By the tone of his voice, I could tell he was worried that he was imposing too many restrictions. And truth be told, I chafed at being told that I couldn't even pick out my own wedding dress. But then a thought struck me. What if we had two ceremonies? One the grand one for Herne and all of his relatives. And then we could have a private one, with just a few friends, perhaps out in the woods near our home. I relaxed. Surely he couldn't object.

"I have an idea," I said.

"What?"

"What do you think about having two ceremonies? One the grand ball, and the other out in the woods, with just a few friends, private and meaningful to us?" I looked at him, expectant.

After a moment, he nodded. "Of course. That's the perfect solution. I fully understand why you want that. And whatever it costs—whether you want two wedding dresses or a dozen, you have only to ask. I'll pay for everything."

Feeling better but still overwhelmed, I decided I'd had enough wedding talk for the moment. I turned my thoughts toward the parley. Ginty's Waystation Bar and Grill was the one place where we could safely have both the Queens of Light and Dark Fae in the same room and be sure nobody was going to get killed.

The Fae had a history of warring with one another as far back as time could remember. The Light and Dark courts weren't that different, but they were mortal enemies, locked in an eternal battle for supremacy. Yet neither one could exist without the other. The balance was necessary between light and dark, between shadow and sunlight. But they still fought, driven by an internal instinct to destroy one another.

The fact that I was a product of both courts proved to be a problem for most of the Fae, who saw me as tainted because of my mixed blood. TirNaNog and Navane—the two great cities—were mere shadows of their mother-states back in Annwn. There, the wars between the two great Courts of Fae were horrendous, the carnage unending. Throughout the eons they had battled, and untold lives had been lost in the wars. It all seemed like such a waste, such a callous disregard for life. But the Fae weren't known for wisdom, and as intelligent as some of them could be, they were also petty, jealous, and arrogant —a deadly combination.

Here on Earth, Saílle was Queen of the Dark Court, and Névé, Queen of the Light Court. They mirrored each other, opposites and yet so much alike. Neither queen appreciated the fact that I sat in on the parleys with Herne. Long ago, when the two cities had been established over here on Earth, both courts had agreed with Cernunnos and Morgana to abide by the Covenant of the Wild Hunt. Through that agreement, the two queens had agreed to give a certain governance to Cernunnos, Morgana, and the Wild Hunt in order to minimize collateral damage. They weren't allowed outright warfare, so all their machinations were covert. They had no choice, given Morgana was goddess of the Fae, but that didn't mean that they wouldn't push the boundaries as far as they could.

As we passed over the bridge heading toward Ginty's, which was located halfway between TirNaNog and Navane, I stared out at the water. The elementals were out in force today. I could feel them even from within the car. They were playing in the Puget Sound, leaping and diving with the waves. To others they would appear just as an upsweep of water, a wave rolling across the surface, but I could see them from here, their glistening translucent bodies merging with the Sound. Part of me wanted to jump out of the car and dive over the edge, to swim out and play with them. It seemed far more appealing than going to Ginty's for parley. But I managed to hold myself in check.

Twenty minutes later, as we approached the outskirts of Woodinville, I shook off the sleepiness that had crept over me. When I wasn't the one driving, the swaying motion of the car made me want to curl up and take a nap. The rocking motion reminded me of a ship.

As we approached the end of Way Station Lane, a side road off Paradise Lake Road near Bear Creek, I flipped down the visor, checking my makeup in the mirror. Everything looked good, and my hair curled out from the ponytail to dangle down my back.

The parking lot was nearly full, which wasn't surprising. Ginty's was a popular attraction, especially for Cryptos seeking a drink among their own kind. While humans were accepted and allowed inside, the bar focused mainly on its not-so-human patrons.

Rustic on the outside, the wood stained a deep pecan, with bronze hardware, to outside eyes, Ginty's was only one story high. Inside was a different matter. The Waystation had a stairway leading into another dimension where it housed people seeking sanctuary. No one could set foot beyond those limits without permission—not even the gods, with a few exceptions. Waystations and Sanctuary asylum seekers were sacred, sacrosanct, and off-limits to anybody except the proprietors who kept watch over them.

As I approached the door, a rush of warmth hit me. I could feel a storm on the horizon. The faint smell of ozone hung heavy in the air and it was hot and muggy. My clothes felt like they were sticking to my skin. I looked around as a dragonfly landed on my nose. Taken aback, I held very still, crossing my eyes to stare at it as it stared back at me.

"That's an omen if I ever saw one," Viktor said softly. "Dragonflies mean transformation. Something's going to happen," the half-ogre added.

Just then the dragonfly skittered off my nose and hovered for a moment before circling around me three times. Then it took off so fast that it vanished as if it'd never been.

I glanced at Herne. "Viktor's right. I feel like something is going to happen."

"Well, we can't prepare for it until we know what we're dealing with. So let's get this over with. Here's hoping that Saílle and Névé aren't in the mood for a fight today. I really don't feel like kicking some Fae queen ass."

I slid my arm through Herne's elbow and we headed inside, Viktor behind us. But my mind was on the dragonfly, and on the unsettled feeling it had left behind. Viktor was absolutely right. Something was going to happen. I just didn't know what.

CHAPTER FIVE

I was surprised to see Wendy manning the door instead of Waylin, the usual bouncer. The tall, black bartender with the platinum Mohawk gave us a scintillating grin.

"Herne, Ember—I take it you're here for a parley?"

I knew better than to ask if the Fae Queens were here yet. The bouncers couldn't tell us who was upstairs. Nobody could, because it went against sanctuary rules.

"I wish we were just here for a drink," Herne muttered and I seconded the feeling.

"Show me your peace-bindings," she said.

I pointed to my dagger, which was attached to my thigh sheath. I had peace-bound it well, because not doing so would get us kicked out of the bar. Herne and Viktor showed her their weapons as well.

As she glanced at my dagger, her eyes lit up. "I spy an incredibly beautiful ring," she said, glancing at Herne.

It suddenly occurred to me that, while we hadn't

talked about it, I wasn't sure if Herne wanted the news to spread yet. I turned to him with a question in my eyes.

But he was all smiles. "She said yes!"

"Well, congratulations. I foresee a long and happy life for you," she said. "You seem well suited. All right, there's a line forming behind you. Let's get this over with. You are now entering Ginty's Waystation Bar and Grill. One show of a magical weapon will get you booted and banned. Do you agree to abide by the Rules of Parley, by blood and bone?"

As always, Herne answered for all three of us. "We do, by blood and bone."

Viktor and I murmured "By blood and bone" behind him. Wendy motioned for us to go on through, and then stopped the next customers from entering. For casual customers who were there for just a drink, Wendy would just check their peace-bindings. Anybody there for parley? Went through the whole oath-taking ritual.

As always, the inside of Ginty's seemed much larger than the outside, because it was an interdimensional space, grounded in this world.

Most of the booths were filled so we made our way through the crowd to the bar and finally found three seats together. A new bartender was on duty. He was tall and gaunt, reminding me of an extremely lean swimmer. His head was smooth, except for a thin braid from a small round of hair on the top of his head. The man was pale and his hair was the color of sunrise, pale yellow against an even paler skull.

"What can I get for you?" he asked, barely glancing across the bar at us.

Since we were on duty, Viktor and Herne ordered

light ale, while I settled for a large cola. At that moment, a familiar voice echoed from behind the curtain that separated the back of the bar from the stockroom.

"Is that who I think it is?" Ginty shouted, barely audible over the clamor of customers.

"If you think it's Herne and company, you're spot-on." Herne wiped the foam off his lips after taking a sip of ale.

Ginty, a handsome dwarf, emerged from behind the curtain. He stood four-five and was the picture of health, with rippling muscles and blond hair that fell to his waist. He kept it French braided, and today he was sporting a five-o'clock shadow. He wore jeans and a tank top, showing off his massive biceps, and his belt was black leather studded with silver. He jumped up on the stepstool that he used to raise himself up high enough to talk to his customers, and leaned his elbows on the counter.

"Good, I'm glad you made it." He glanced over at the television set on the wall, which was tuned to the news with the volume turned down. Once again, the station was showing attacks by the vrykos around the nation. "What the hell's going on?" He nodded at the screen.

"That's what we're here to talk about. Leave it until parley, old man," Herne said. "There are things that are better off spoken of in private." He glanced around the bar. "Have you heard of any trouble over here on the Eastside?"

"No, but we don't always get wind of problems when they first start. Unless they're political, that is. Then, we're usually first on the list for information. Let's go. The parley awaits." Without further ado, Ginty led us over to the right side of the bar, where a staircase was cordoned off with velvet ropes.

The crimson ropes were actually creatures, guardians who protected the way into the portal leading to safe haven. If someone attempted to barge through, the ropes would turn into massive snakes with extremely sharp fangs. Their venom was lethal, and all it took was one bite to stop an intruder in their tracks.

Ginty said something over the ropes and passed his hand over them, and then unhooked the velvet and moved it aside, allowing us to pass through. He swung in behind us, once again hooking the rope across the staircase.

As we headed up the stairs, we arrived at the first landing. The staircase turned to the left as mist shrouded our passage. It was a magical fog, marking the entrance into another dimension. We went by feel, touching the walls as we took one step at a time until we came out into a long hall. There, the staircase turned to the right, leading to yet another floor.

But Ginty led us down the hall to the first door on the left. It seemed to be the conference room where we always met the Fae Queens, and I wondered if it was specifically kept for them and their various parleys. In fact, I wondered how many parleys they had and how many people met with them here.

As he opened the door, we entered the conference room. There was a U-shaped table front and center, with chairs around the outside. As always, Saílle sat to the left, and Névé to the right. They usually brought an entourage of bodyguards and advisors with them, and today was no exception. Ginty, Herne, Viktor, and I took our seats at the cross table that divided the two factions.

Saílle and Névé were—as usual—decked out in full regal attire. Saílle was dressed in yards of slate blue satin and her hair flowed down to her ass, waving rivulets of shining black strands against the muted material. She wore a crown of sapphires and diamonds, and a necklace of amethyst. Her eyes were the color of ice, and she sat unmoving, like a pale statue carved out of alabaster.

Névé was her opposite, and in this—the season of summer—Névé sparkled. But we were past the summer solstice and so her luster had faded a little bit. Her hair was platinum, and her eyes were a rich coffee color. She wore a gown of green and gold that flowed over her like a gossamer dream. Her tiara sparkled with emeralds and diamonds, and her matching choker was the largest emerald solitaire I had ever seen.

I nodded at both, but said nothing. Decorum dictated that Ginty begin the parley before anyone spoke. He stood, holding aloft a golden wand. The smoky quartz on the end glittered as he wove the magic around us. An oath taken under parley was an oath that bound us before the gods, even the Fae Queens.

"I hereby declare the Lughnasadh parley of the Courts of Light and Darkness, in the year 10260 CFE, open. Under this mantle, all members are bound to forswear bearing arms against any other member of this parley until the meeting is officially closed and all members are safely home. I also remind the Courts of Light and Darkness that they are forsworn by the Covenant of the Wild Hunt from inflicting injury on any and all members of the Wild Hunt team, under the sigil of Cernunnos, Lord of the Forest, and Morgana, goddess of the Sea and the Fae. Let no one break honor, let discussions progress civilly, and remember that I—Ginty McClintlock, of the McClintlock clan of the Cascade Dwarves—am your moderator and mediator, and my rule as such supersedes all other authority while we are in this Waystation."

After he finished reciting the Oath of Parley, he pulled out a long scroll covered in small print. "If you stay, you agree to the rules. If you disagree, leave now, or be bound to the parley. I have spoken and so it is done."

He waited, but no one said a word. Now was the time for objections if anybody decided they didn't want to proceed. After a moment, he set down the scepter and the scroll. "Then, if you are all agreed, I shall open the parley. Herne, son of Cernunnos, you have the rights of first speech."

With a long sigh, Ginty sat down next to me. He looked harried, but he always took the parleys seriously. If something went wrong, it was up to him to put a stop to it. He was the keeper of the Waystation, with absolute authority.

Herne cleared his throat as he leaned forward, propping his elbows on the table. "Queen Saílle, Queen Névé, we come to ask a boon from you. A serious situation has arisen. It seems as though Typhon is making his first move."

"Continue," Saílle said, her voice catching on the wind and vanishing almost before we could hear it.

Herne explained the situation, and when he came to the part about the reports we had seen on the news, Ginty pushed a television set over to where we could all see it. I wasn't clear on how he managed to get the signal in here, but he did. He turned the TV on just in time to see the same footage we had seen before. Saílle and Névé watched silently, and it was impossible to read their expressions.

"This is only going to get worse. You know it. We know it. There's no denying the fact that Typhon is here to stay until the gods can figure out what to do with him. And I will tell you this quite honestly, we are nowhere near to having an answer. We haven't even figured out how he was sent into stasis in the first place. Until we know that, we can't figure out how to send him back, or even if it's possible to do so again."

"This is troubling news indeed," Saílle said. She glanced across the room at Névé. "Have you noticed any uprisings among the dead?"

Névé shook her head. "But then again, that's not something we keep watch for. What do you wish from us, Herne, son of Cernunnos?"

"We would ask that you give us control over the Fae militia. Give us the ability to call them out on situations like this. Humans cannot stand against these creatures, and who knows what else the dragons have up their sleeves? We need patrols who can fight supernatural creatures. The Fae have an edge with their strength and speed."

"Are we the only ones you're asking to risk life and limb?" Névé asked.

Herne shook his head. "No, we're also approaching the Shifter Alliance and the Vampire Nation. We hope to form a united front. I know that you aren't especially fond of shifters or vampires, but this is a worldwide threat. Every single one of us faces the danger, and my father wants us to work together. I ask that you put aside your arguments once again to form a truce. I can't tell you how much it will strain the Wild Hunt's resources if we have to settle squabbles between the two of you, *and* go after those summoned by Typhon's emissaries."

I had the feeling neither Saílle nor Névé cared for his tone, but they weren't stupid. I hoped they would make the right decision.

"How much control over the Fae militia do you seek?" Saílle gave me a long look. I couldn't figure out why, but she was staring intently at me.

"I echo that question," Névé added.

"We would like the ability to call out the militia when needed, and the authority to give them orders." Herne paused, then added, "We don't seek to co-opt them for good. But if we are to make a united front against Typhon and his children, then we *must* work together. I cannot stress enough that we don't dare approach this haphazardly. Someone has to be in charge of the master plan against Typhon, and in this quarter of the world, I'm the one in charge."

Saílle paused. "I must speak to my advisor for a moment. I request a recess."

Ginty stood, holding up the scepter. He turned to Névé. "Do you have any objections?"

Névé shook her head.

"Herne, do you mind if the Dark Queen takes a recess?"

Herne shook his head. "That's fine."

"Then I call a fifteen-minute recess. We will convene again when the chime sounds. Bear in mind, that in this room or out of it, until we dismiss the meeting, we are all still bound under the Rules of Parley." Ginty raised the scepter and a low chime emitted from it. He lowered it, then sat down, stretching out with his hands in his pockets.

Saílle and her advisors wasted no time in heading toward the door. They slipped out quietly.

"I wonder what that's all about," I said, watching their departure.

"I have no clue," Herne said. "But I'm sure we'll find out, in one way or another."

For lack of anything better to do, I turned to stare at Névé. She was sitting impassively, looking like a china statue. She was lovely, her radiance so stunning it made her difficult to look at. Where Saílle was magnetic and mesmerizing, Névé was radiant. Opposites again, and yet they achieved the same effects.

I glanced over at Viktor, who had pulled out his phone to read. I thought about trying to engage the Light Queen in some chitchat, but I knew that wouldn't go over well. I finally turned to Herne, who was speaking in low tones with Ginty.

"How much longer?"

Herne grinned at me. "Getting bored?"

"*Is it soup yet?* Kind of… I'd really like to get out of here so I can get ready for Morgana tonight. I'm nervous." I smiled, but I knew that my nerves were showing.

"Well, Saílle has fifteen minutes and it's only been five since she stepped out. I'm not sure what that's all about, but I have a feeling we're going to find out." He paused, then nodded to the door as the knob turned. "Apparently, she didn't need fifteen minutes."

I followed his gaze. Saílle entered the room again, her face once more impassive and impossible to read. She caught me looking at her and just smiled, coolly, before returning to her seat. Ginty called the parley back into session and we began again.

"Herne, you had the floor." The dwarf motioned for Herne to stand.

Herne had barely made it to his feet before Saílle spoke.

"You were requesting the assistance of the Fae militia. I'm willing to give you access to my personal militia." She smiled, saccharine-sweet, at Névé. "I'm sure the Queen of Light will agree, as well."

Of course, Névé felt obligated to follow suit in order to keep face. Saílle had played her hand well, and the Queen of Light fell right into it.

"Navane offers you our faction of the militia as well. When we were facing the Iron Plague and the Tuathan Brotherhood, our courts worked under a truce. I suppose," Névé said, gritting her teeth, "that we should consider another truce, given Typhon's approach."

It was Saílle's turn to glare. I had the feeling the Queen of the Dark Fae hadn't considered that idea to come into play.

Saílle sighed. "Master McClintlock, would you host a parley for our courts to agree upon conditions for such a truce? And Herne, given you have so much at stake, I assume you'll grace us with your experience as mediator?" She had a nasty grin on her face and I realized that she had just stuck it to Herne. But it didn't matter. If we could get the Fae to form a truce for the time being, it would make our job a lot easier.

Herne seemed to be thinking along the same lines. "Of course. Shall we meet tomorrow? No time like the present."

The two queens agreed to another meeting. Ginty looked disgruntled, but decreed that there would be a second Lughnasadh parley the next morning, early.

Saílle spoke again. "The Court of Dark Fae also wishes to extend its congratulations to Lord Herne and...*Lady* Ember on your coming nuptials. In fact, I find it quite a coincidence." Saílle cast her gaze to meet mine.

I froze, staring at her. She had called me *lady*? And how did she know about our engagement? What the hell was she up to? I never underestimated the Fae Queens in how far they would go to one-up not only each other, but everyone else.

"*What's* a coincidence?" I asked.

"Your uncle Sharne is to be married to one of the nobility from the Orhanakai band of the Autumn's Bane peoples. Your father's people. She will come from Annwn, along with Unkai. I believe you *know* the chieftain?" She kept her gaze fastened on me.

I tried not to react but the news boggled my mind. My great-uncle Sharne was the only member of my family who hadn't turned his back on me. He had actually expressed regret over what my grandfather had tried to do to me. We had talked off and on over the past few months, and were trying to build a relationship. But he was a black sheep in the Dark Court, and a confirmed bachelor. Now, the queen was announcing his marriage?

"I had no clue. He didn't mention it to me."

She smiled graciously. "Perhaps he had his reasons. Since your uncle will be marrying nobility, even though she is from Annwn I have decided to move him into the Court. He will become one of the minor lords in the

Outer Court. This means your father's family will take its place under the umbrella of nobility, and *that includes you*."

I froze. Herne froze. The entire *room* seemed to freeze. This was an exceptional move for Saílle, and I wondered what the hell had prompted it.

"Aren't you excited? You'll be a lady in my court!" With a triumphant smile of bared teeth, Saílle quickly turned to her advisor. "You must add Lady Ember to the rolls. As soon as parley is done, send a messenger to make the necessary arrangements and to deliver her the documents that are involved."

What the ever-loving fuck?

I had been anathema all these years and now, suddenly, Saílle was claiming me as part of her court? I glanced over at Névé, who was staring at Saílle like she wanted to kill her. Which she probably did, but thanks to the parley, she couldn't even try.

Herne slid his hand to mine, below the table, and squeezed a warning when I started to speak. I shut my mouth and glanced at him.

"Master McClintlock, may we have a brief recess? I need to confer with *my* team." Herne turned to Ginty and the dwarf sighed, but he motioned that we were into another recess.

Herne practically dragged me out of the room, but Viktor stayed behind. I had a feeling he wanted to see if fireworks were going to erupt between the two queens.

"What the hell?" I turned to Herne as soon as we were out the door and it was shut behind us. "For years they've insisted I shouldn't exist, that I was a pariah—a *tralaeth*. And now, Saílle suddenly announces that I'm part of her court? Can she even *do* that without my permission? And why now? I know Fae governance enough to know that just because one member of your family belongs to the nobility, it doesn't mean they *all* do. Even if Sharne's marriage turns out to be legitimate, that doesn't automatically mean I become one of Saílle's subjects."

He braced my shoulders. "Calm down. I think I know what's going on. Saílle either just noticed that rock on your finger, or she heard about our engagement through one of her informants. Either way, seeing your ring today verified it. She's decided to worm her way into your good graces before Névé has a chance. Because, my dear, you'll become a Fae *goddess* when you marry me. That means that she and Névé will answer to *you*."

I stared at him, both panicking and paralyzed. It hadn't occurred to me what becoming a goddess would mean. But if he was right, then I'd be ruling over the people who both gave me my blood, but had turned their backs on me. All of a sudden, I understood where Saílle was coming from, but that didn't make the news settle on my stomach any better.

"Let me get this straight, because my mind is whirling. When we get married and I go through the ritual to elevate me to deityhood, that means I'm a goddess over the *Fae*? And that the courts of Fae will have to answer to *me*?"

"That's right, love. You'll not only be a goddess over the Fae, but a goddess *of* Fae. You'll rule with Morgana over the Fae who stayed on Earth, as opposed to those in Annwn. And because you're of mixed blood, this will usher in a whole new era for those born into your circumstances."

As his words rang in my ears, my mind was reeling.

The implications were huge—and not just for me. Every tralaeth in the world would be able to claim legitimacy if I became a part of the court. And Saílle was obviously jumping on the bandwagon so she could upstage Névé. If I joined *her* Court, then she could claim that I favored my father's bloodline.

Too stunned to say anything, I stood there, shaking my head. I had no idea what to do next. But I knew that, more than ever, I had to talk to Morgana. She would know what I should do. Or, at least, I hoped so.

CHAPTER SIX

As we headed back into the conference room, I thought about what Herne had said right before we finished our recess. I had asked him to field Saílle's offer for me, but he told me in no uncertain terms to do it myself.

"When you're my wife and a goddess, you aren't going to be able to ask others to handle squeamish tasks," he said. And I knew he was right.

As we settled back into our seats, Ginty called the parley back to order. He was looking frustrated and irritable, and I didn't blame him. I couldn't imagine having his job. I wondered if Ireland—his wife—ended up on the receiving end of a lot of rants. But I also couldn't imagine Ginty taking out his frustrations on her, either.

I paused while he opened parley again, then before anybody could say anything, I motioned to him. "I would like the floor, please."

He cleared his throat. "Ember has the floor."

Nervous—almost shaking—I stood. My knees felt like

they were going to collapse under my weight, but I reached down and steadied myself on the table. I could barely meet Saílle's gaze, but I knew that I had to stand firm on this.

"Queen Saílle, you do me honor by suggesting that I become a part of your court, given my uncle's upcoming marriage and advancement within the halls of TirNaNog. However, I must either refuse, or I must also become a part of Navane's court as well. Given my mixed blood, and given that I am engaged to Herne and will become his wife and join the..." I paused, the words sticking in my throat. "Seeing that I'll be joining the ranks of Cernunnos and Morgana's family and become part of the forces that make up Annwn, I cannot choose sides. I can't give either the Dark or Light court favor over the other."

The last few words squeaked out of my mouth. I felt queasy and I wanted to sink under the floor. Essentially, I was asserting a power that I didn't have yet over two women who would have probably preferred to see me dead rather than set foot in their precious throne rooms.

The room was so quiet that a whisper would have shattered the silence. Ginty slowly turned to stare at me, then glanced at the two Fae Queens.

Saílle's gaze was cool and accusatory, but she said nothing. For once, though, I had caught Névé with her pants down, so to speak. Her jaw dropped as she swiveled in my direction, the look in her eyes validating every fear that flickered through my body.

"You *what?*" Névé said, her words precise and slow.

I cleared my throat and tried to steady my voice. "I must regretfully decline Her Majesty Saílle's offer to sit on the court of TirNaNog, unless I also sit on the court of

Navane. I cannot offer favor to either side." It occurred to me that sometimes the best thing to do was to keep my mouth shut, but that hadn't been an option.

Saílle cleared her throat. "Then the decision is up to Navane. Such a thing has never been done before—"

Herne cut her off. "Yes, *it has*. You haven't forgotten that my mother, Morgana, sits on both of your courts, nobility to both Light and Dark Fae. Every goddess of Fae has had their balancing post with the twin courts and you know that as surely as you know your own name."

I caught my breath, thankful that he had intervened.

Névé glared at Saílle, as if to say, *See what you've gotten us into?* She let out a long breath. "Very well. Navane concedes the necessity of such an unusual request, and given the engagement has already been proposed and accepted, Navane shall follow suit. Ember, you shall be seated on both courts, as nobility. *Honorarily*, of course, as your...future mother-in-law does." She finished, looking like the words had left a sour taste in her mouth.

"Yes, *honorarily*," Saílle said.

I was walking a tightrope. "I...um...thank you."

"Oh, for heaven's sake. Don't act like we're offering you a wasps' nest, girl," Saílle snapped, frowning. "Though such a thing hasn't happened for a long time, and in today's world, this will mean...that others will take their lead from you. Gods only know what the grand city-states in Annwn will think."

Névé snorted. "Oh, *I* can tell you what they'll think. They'll have exactly the same opinion they did when Morgana was elevated to goddess. I was a young girl in Older Navane then."

"Older Navane?" I asked, deciding that interrupting

couldn't be any more gauche than telling them they were going to have to place a statue of me onto their altar tables.

"When we speak about the great city-states in Annwn, we use the word 'older' to differentiate between the ancient Fae homelands and the ones here." Névé glanced across the divide. Saílle had a grim smile on her face. "What say you, Queen of the Dark? Times seem to be changing."

Saílle laughed, shaking her head. "Times may change, some things will stand forever. We shall discuss a temporary truce tomorrow. Be here bright and early, Herne. Six A.M., and Master Ginty, not a word of complaint out of you. We'll bring the documents giving you authority over the Fae militia, Master of the Hunt, so all will be as you wish. And Ember," she added, turning to me, "since you will be the first liaison to belong to both Fae Courts since Morgana, we must discuss a marketing campaign to make your presence palatable to all Fae. I won't be coy. Had Herne not asked you to marry him, I wouldn't have invited you into my court. But as I said, times are changing and we must, I suppose, change with them."

With that, she stood. Before anyone could speak, she motioned to Ginty. "Conclude the parley, old man. I am weary of this discussion."

Ginty frowned, but she stared at him impassively. Finally, he said, "Is there any other business to be discussed? Herne? Névé?"

Herne apparently had decided enough was enough, because he shook his head.

Névé gave Ginty a firm "No," so he concluded the

parley and both Fae Queens swept out of the room, first Saílle and then Névé. They didn't look back.

"Well," I said after they left. "That was...unexpected."

"Most decidedly. You must tell my mother about this when she comes to visit tonight. She can better advise you how to act with them. I don't trust either one, but there's nothing to do for now except hope they show up tomorrow. At least a truce will help. I'm surprised they agreed to it, though," Herne mused.

Ginty sat on the table, propping his feet on a chair. "I know why they agreed."

"Why?" Herne asked.

"They fear Typhon more than they hate each other. Neither will admit it, but they're terrified of the Father of all Dragons. He and his children have no love for the Fae and won't hesitate to decimate their cities along with the humans. All Fae folk, shifters, and humans, we're all in danger. And now that the dragons are beginning to make their move, it's clear this isn't a false alarm." Ginty leaned back on his hands, a dour look on his face.

"Haven't the Fae dealt with dragons before?" I asked. "Aren't there dragons in Annwn?"

Herne gave me a brief shake of the head as he stood up and stretched. "A few, but they're aged and slumbering in their mountains. When Typhon was shut out of the world and driven into stasis, his children retreated to a realm they claimed for their own. But they've always preferred the mortal realms. Life is far different now than it was when they once wandered the Earth, but that makes no matter to them. They can, if they choose, destroy this world and send it into an apocalyptic nightmare."

"Herne is right, and you can bet the Fae know this. The

oldest among them—and the ancient Ante-Fae—have seen the damage dragons can do. Saílle and Névé are looking to close ranks to protect the Fae cities and races. They'll go back to trying to destroy each other if we can stop the threat, but when something from the outside threatens the Fae as a whole, they *will* work together. But that just means that they consider Typhon a deadly foe." Ginty glanced over his shoulder, but we were still alone. "Tell me, Herne. How bad is it?"

"We haven't even seen the first tides of war yet. But it's coming. I have no idea what to expect, but the world is facing dark days, and soon, everyone will know there's an outside enemy looking to destroy society. Panic will set in, and who knows what chaos will follow?" Herne winced, dropping into a chair. "I'm afraid that in a few years, this world will be unrecognizable, unless we can find a way to destroy Typhon."

"Meanwhile, we prepare for war, and we do what we can, and we enjoy every blessing because there might not be another coming," Ginty said.

That silenced all four of us.

ANGEL WAS COOKING up a storm by the time I got home. As I headed to the house from my car, a distant flash of light split the sky as a faint breeze stirred the leaves on the trees. I paused, counting. I reached four when a low rumble of thunder rolled through the air. Another flash, and this time it was only three seconds. I watched the clouds for a moment, uncertain, and then a third flash overhead stirred me and I headed for the house as thunder immediately echoed around me. I dashed inside as a deluge of hail began to rain down, pea-sized pebbles of ice bouncing on the ground as they pelted the earth.

I ducked into the house, turning to watch the hail cover the lawn like some delinquent snowstorm. Finally, after another blinding flash, I shut the door, hoping to shut the storm out. Some storms felt like they had a sentience to them. As though they watched from the heavens, targeting victims at random.

The smell of chowder enveloped me, and I held it tight in my lungs, then slowly let out my breath, grateful to be home. The entire day had felt like one massive cluster-fuck. My mouth began to water as I headed into the kitchen.

Angel was stirring the soup, and I saw a pan of French bread, buttered and covered with grated parmesan, ready to go into the oven. The table was set and a bouquet of fresh roses sat in the middle, along with two rose-colored pillar candles. A peach pie was cooling on the counter, and Mr. Rumblebutt was chowing down on his dinner. Feeling safe again, comfy in the nest Angel and I had built for ourselves, I dropped into a chair at the table.

"You'll never guess what happened," I said, picking a cherry out of the fruit bowl in the middle of the table.

Angel looked up from the stove. "By your tone of voice, I'm not sure I want to know." She turned the heat down, then wiped her hands on a dishtowel and wandered over to sit beside me. "By the look on your face, it wasn't good."

"I'm not sure what the hell it is, to be honest. Good... bad...*weird*? Weird, definitely." I launched into telling her about the meeting. The parleys were private, generally, but anybody in the agency—or the Fae Queens' administrations—could know.

"So, my uncle's getting married to one of Unkai's band, and Saílle tried to co-opt me into her court to one-up Névé. That didn't fly, so now, apparently, I'm to become a member of both courts. *Honorarily*, of course. They couldn't ever give me a real membership or that might legitimize me." I felt spiteful. "It was the oddest, most uncomfortable interchange I've had in a long time. I need to talk to Morgana." I glanced at the clock. It was five-ten. She'd be here within the hour. "I feel like I'm walking on eggshells and everything is going to blow sky-high if I do something wrong."

"Of course this is a huge deal. Not only are you marrying a god, but you're becoming one. This is major, Ember. You're going to be a *goddess*." She blinked, shaking her head. "Did you ever think, in your wildest dreams, that things would come to this?"

I shook my head. "No, and I'm scared out of my mind. I have no clue what to expect." I slowly stood. "I guess I should take a shower. I'm sticky and rain-soaked. And the storm looks like it's just going to get worse."

She nodded. "The weatherman said to expect thunder off and on all night. So don't turn on any computer unless it's a laptop. I'll finish setting the table. Do you want to be alone with her? I can eat in my room if you want."

"No, of course not. I want you there. For one thing, you'll probably remember things I'll forget. I'm sure, with all that's going on, I'll overlook something vital." I headed up to my bedroom, leaving Angel to finish making dinner. Mr. Rumblebutt followed me and I scooped him up in my arms, snuggling his belly with my nose. "Mr.

Rumblebutt, *you'll* still love me, even if things get weird, won't you?"

Being a cat, Mr. Rumblebutt said nothing.

I DRESSED in a blue sundress and pulled my hair into a high ponytail to keep it out of the way. As I finished the last touches of my makeup, I paused, glancing around the room. In a year, would I still be here? Would Herne even *consider* moving into my house? Or would I be living at his place, leaving the house to Angel? It hurt to think of losing her as a roommate. We were best friends, and I loved living with her.

Things have to change, a voice whispered inside me. *You can't expect them to stay the same forever. Life doesn't work like that. If life doesn't evolve, it stagnates, and the last thing you need is stagnation.*

"I know," I whispered to myself in the mirror. "But change can be frightening."

*It can also be exhilarati*ng, the voice answered before falling silent.

By the time I headed downstairs back to the kitchen, Angel had set the table, including a beautiful bouquet of peach-colored roses with rust tips. The roses came from our garden and their fragrance filled the room. I inhaled deeply, holding their scent in my lungs.

The doorbell rang ten minutes later and I answered it. Morgana could easily have just appeared inside the house, but she was always polite, never breaking etiquette. I welcomed her, then led her into the kitchen.

"Angel has dinner ready. I hope you like clam chowder

and peach pie," I said, motioning to one of the place settings at the table. "If you would sit there..."

Morgana took her seat. When she crossed over from Annwn, she took on a more human form—although I had never seen her *not* look human. But she kept herself size proportionate. The gods could—and did—at times, change size, particularly in height and weight. Some had the ability to alter the rest of their looks too.

She stood about five-nine today, with willowy limbs and hair that flowed down to her ass. She had bound it up into an intricate chignon, with a ponytail coming out of the topknot. The hair style reminded me of the main character on an old TV series—*I Dream Of Jeannie*. Morgana was wearing a pale blue linen pantsuit, with a gray shirt that was buttoned to just above her bra. Her eyes were frosty, and she had a perpetual air of glamour and etherealness about her that made it seem like she could just slip away like a wisp of smoke at any time.

"Angel, this looks marvelous," she said as she sat down in the chair I offered her. "Tell me you haven't been cooking all day just for me." Morgana gave Angel a winning smile. She wasn't being polite—she truly meant it. Morgana might have discerning tastes, but she was willing to eat a hot dog with the rest of the gang if that was what was on the grill.

"Only part of the afternoon, and you know I love to cook, so don't sweat it." Angel ladled out the soup and took her seat. I passed Morgana the parmesan bread after taking a piece and placing it on the saucer next to my soup bowl.

"Well, I certainly appreciate it, and the invitation." Morgana paused while Angel filled her bowl, then glanced over at me. "Why do I have the feeling that you have something to tell me?" she added, pointing to my left ring finger. "Out with it, my girl."

I cursed lightly under my breath. I'd meant to take off my ring until I told her, but I had totally forgotten. It felt natural, as though it had always been on my finger.

Angel laughed. "She caught you," she said, breaking the ice.

"I decided to accept Herne's proposal. He proposed some weeks back, but I needed to think things through first. I was going to ask for your advice tonight, but yesterday I jumped the gun and just decided to say yes." I paused, staring at Morgana. "There's more, though. A lot more."

"I see," Morgana said. She didn't look angry. In fact, I suspected she was trying to suppress a smile. "Are you sure you want this? Because I will tell you this: once you make the transition over to our world, there's no going back. Even if something were to happen between you and Herne, you will forever belong to the world of the gods."

I licked my lips. "I know. That's why I wanted to ask you what to expect. What challenges will I be facing? What's the ritual like? And another matter has risen its double-necked wily head." I told her what happened during the parley. "So, both Névé and Saílle intend to claim me as part of their courts. This will give a legitimacy to all tralaeths, but there's bound to be backlash. I'm not sure what to think."

Morgana laughed then, her concerned expression fading away. "Oh, they are wily, indeed. Do you know how old those two are?"

I frowned, shaking my head. "No, not really. Actually, I have no clue."

"They were born a little over two thousand years ago. They are ancient queens indeed, but not anywhere near so ancient nor powerful as the Fae Queens in Annwn are. But Saílle and Névé are cunning and even though they constantly seek victory over the other, they are like yin and yang. One could not exist without the other. If one side were to emerge victorious, it would weaken the balance and both sides would fall."

I shook my head. "And they're worse in Annwn?"

"Lianrial—the mother of the Light Fae, and Pharial—the mother of the Dark Fae—wage horrific wars that never end. The streets of their cities are paved with gold and silver, but the forests and rivers surrounding the twin city-states run red with blood. So many spirits walk the back paths that the forests of the Fae Nation are known as the Haunted Woodlands." Morgana sighed, then added, "I guarantee, they are not offering this because of any change of heart over your mixed bloodline."

"In other words, don't trust them, and they still think I should be dead?" Where Morgana was diplomatic, I wasn't. I didn't kid myself that Saílle and Névé had suddenly become my fans.

"Precisely. They're doing this to incur *my* favor and Herne's favor. They know that we know this, but the Fae governments work on a mutually accepted façade." She leaned back in her chair. "The chowder is excellent. May I have more?"

Angel quickly refilled her bowl. "May I ask a question?"

"Of course."

"What happens if they refuse to acknowledge Ember as a goddess?" Angel quickly glanced at me. "I'm not saying they will, but the fact is, they've been assholes to you since the day I first met you."

"I wondered that myself," I said.

But Morgana just laughed. "If they refuse to accept you as a goddess, then they'll quickly find themselves beset by not only my wrath, but Cernunnos's anger. And the other goddesses of Fae will side with me. We tend to stick together. The Fae—both in Annwn and over here—have strayed too far from the fold. We've been discussing what to do about it through the past few centuries, but now Typhon has drawn attention away from almost everything that isn't an immediate problem."

I hesitated to ask the next question, but I had to know. "How do *you* feel about me marrying Herne? If you object, you know that I'll obey you. I *am* pledged to you."

Morgana held my gaze for a moment, then reached out and took my hand. "Ember, I have been hoping Herne would ask you. I went to Corra, the oracle, not long ago and asked her about you and Herne. She said the best-laid path of fortune lies with the two of you binding your lives together. So I've been hoping that he would propose."

We ate in silence for a while longer, Angel offering us the fish and chips after we finished our chowder. Then Morgana set down her spoon.

"You asked about the ritual to become a goddess. It's not easy. There's no just drinking a potion and *poof,* you're now one of the Immortals. The ritual involves facing your personal fears. If you thought the Cruharach was difficult, then you'll be in for a surprise. The Gadawnoin—the ritual to elevate a mortal to deityhood—is far more complex and dangerous." She pronounced it *Gad-woi-en*. "The actual chance for death is small, but madness...it's an ever-present danger throughout the ritual. I will be in charge of preparing you when the time comes. And that is all I can tell you."

I nibbled on my fish and chips in silence. My stomach was churning. While I was grateful that Morgana was pleased to have me as her daughter-in-law, the Gadawnoin sounded terrifying. Once again, I forced myself to think of Herne, and of what I would be gaining. Because if it wasn't for him, there was no way in hell I would subject myself to what loomed ahead.

CHAPTER SEVEN

Morgana glanced at the clock. "We need to be at Marilee's by eight. I'll meet you there. I have an errand to run first." She gathered her purse—a Louis Vuitton clutch—and paused to give me an awkward hug. She had never really hugged me before and it felt odd.

"My dear, don't worry too much. Cernunnos and I have both been hoping for this. You're a stabilizing influence on Herne, and we think you can keep him grounded. You make him more empathetic. Plus, we like you—a great deal. You'll make a fine addition to our family." She swept out the door after blowing Angel a kiss and another thank-you for the dinner.

I helped Angel carry the dishes to the counter. "Well, I knew the crap Saílle and Névé were feeding me was just that. I'll be on my guard, that's for certain."

"How do we dress tonight?" Angel asked. "Lughnasadh is the festival of sacrifice, and the first harvest, right? So I assume formal robes?"

Marilee had been pushing us to buy magickal regalia.

She insisted that as our training progressed, we'd need it. We finally had broken down and I bought a gown as black as the night sky with silver stars embroidered on it. Angel had bought a black gown with gold embroidery. Both were easy to move in, flowing but not so much that we would chance getting the sleeves caught in a bonfire. I had a silver belt and Angel had a gold one. We felt a little matchy-matchy, but that was all right.

"Yeah, I think she'll be pissed if we don't give the holiday that honor—" I paused as my phone rang. "That's probably Marilee now, wondering when we're going to get over there. We did agree to help her set up." I pulled out my phone, but saw that it was Herne.

"Hello?" I held the phone to my ear as I finished putting the leftover parmesan bread in a zip-bag.

"Ember, you and Angel need to meet us at the Faraday Cemetery over in the Worchester District. The Lughnasadh ritual will have to wait. We've got vrykos coming out of our ears. Or rather, swarming out of the graves. The chief of police called me, begging for help. The cops can't contain them, and they're not sure where to turn." Herne's voice was rough.

"Crap. What do we need to bring?"

"Dress for battle, bring weapons. Tell Angel to bring a bag of first-aid supplies. I know Marilee has been teaching her some healing magic and chances are we're going to need every hand on deck." He paused, talking to someone in the background.

I motioned to Angel. "Everything's on hold. Get the leftovers in the fridge and forget the dishes."

"Ember? I was just talking to Talia, who's on the phone with the mayor. Three cops have been killed. The rest are falling back. They tried using a flamethrower on one of the creatures but the flames weren't strong enough and it just kept coming at them, burning so brightly that it started a small fire when it passed through a patch of dried brush. The rain managed to put out the flames, but the vrykos just kept coming. They've ordered people in the surrounding neighborhoods to stay in their homes, but they're afraid that the creatures will break through the windows."

My stomach clenched. It sounded gruesome. "What kind of weapons should I bring? My bow? Sword?"

"Whatever you have at hand. We're bringing an arsenal. Can you call Marilee and make our apologies? I'm afraid this is one Sabbat that we're going to have to miss." He ended the call, texting me the address of the cemetery.

I turned to Angel who was leaning on the counter, waiting. "We have an emergency. Everybody on board. You'll need whatever magical energy you have and gather up first-aid supplies. We're heading into a nasty fight and Herne wants all hands on deck." As we dashed upstairs to change into battle gear, I told her what had happened.

FIFTEEN MINUTES LATER, we arrived at the cordoned-off side street leading to the Faraday Cemetery. It was on the outskirts of the Worchester District.

Angel and I had driven over together, the back seat filled with first-aid supplies and whatever weapons we could scrounge up. I had brought my bow, Serafina, and my sword, Brighid's Flame. I was proficient with both, but right now I wished that we could just raze the creatures down with a spray of bullets. I didn't like guns, but they had their uses, and facing off against a mass of undead who were out to eat our flesh was unsettling at best. Even more nerve-wracking was the thought that this wasn't an isolated incident. This was happening all over the country.

Angel had brought her training bow and some arrows. She wasn't that good of a shot yet, but she and Rafé were practicing every week with Herne, and both were coming along nicely. She had also brought the crystal shard that Marilee had given her a few weeks back, which allowed her to regroup faster, and to strengthen the energy she was utilizing.

"Are you scared?" she asked. The Worchester District was slammed with ghosts already. This just made it more frightening.

"Am I scared? Yes. I'd be a fool not to be, but I'm more scared of the vulnerable people who are going to be caught unprepared. If these things get into the general population, well—we can pick them off one by one, but that doesn't ensure we can do so fast enough to keep anybody else from dying." I glanced sideways at her. "You scared?"

I didn't have to ask. I knew she was terrified. Angel had been in very few actual fights. But she was doing her best, learning to fight, learning to strengthen her basic abilities. And to me, that was an important step. But not everyone could—or would—take that step. Single mothers didn't have the luxury of time required to learn self-defense, and the elderly didn't have the strength. And then there were the kids who simply couldn't mount their own defense.

"What are you thinking about?" Angel asked.

"All the potential victims out there who can't fight off the monsters under the bed. If this situation gets out of control, cops won't be the only ones dying."

"I know," Angel said. "Truth is, I'm terrified. I think about DJ. He's down in the Centralia–Chehalis area, but this is happening everywhere and it's bound to hit there, too. And DJ's not going to sit around while people are in danger. I just wish he was in the academy now, instead of at home. They'd make sure he stayed there."

DJ was Angel's half-brother. He was twelve and a genius. Scheduled to enter the Rainier Forest Academy for the Gifted come the fall semester, DJ was getting close to puberty, when his full Wulfine nature would blossom. Which was one reason he was fostering with a family of wolf shifters.

DJ's father had been a lowlife wolf shifter who abandoned Mama J.—Angel and DJ's mother—when he found out she was pregnant. DeWayne had come sniffing around recently, trying to find out everything he could about the child he had abandoned. Angel surmised that he was looking to see if there had been any inheritance when Mama J. was killed. She had managed to put him off, but I had the feeling we hadn't seen the last of him yet.

"You think he'd do something stupid? DJ's a smart boy. He's got to realize he wouldn't be able to fight them."

"Maybe, but he's reaching the stage in a wolf shifter's life—especially a male—that they really go all into the protect-the-pack mindset. Cooper was telling me about it." Cooper was DJ's foster father. "We've started having monthly meetings over Zone to discuss DJ and his life and future." As we jogged along, she pointed to the right, up ahead. "Is that the graveyard?"

I squinted. Sure enough, there was a turnoff into what I had thought was a wide, grassy meadow, but as we neared the entrance, I could see the headstones and the line of cops at the fence. They were shouting and pointing. I tried to get a glimpse of what they were pointing at, but we were still out of the sight line. At that moment, I saw Herne ahead of me, talking to one of the officers. We switched directions and headed over to where they were standing. Yutani and Viktor were beside him.

I went up to Viktor. "Where's Talia?"

He nodded at a parked car on the street. "There. We told her to stay in the car and keep tabs of everything via her laptop. She's also our main dispatcher. In other words, if you don't know where one of us is, call her and she'll figure it out by the Find Friends app on our phones. That way we won't risk interrupting a fight or something like that. Charlie will be here after sunset, if we're still fighting, and Rafé is still on the way."

"What do we know—" I stopped, staring at the fence.

There, heading our way with only the fence to separate us, were a handful of what I assumed were the vrykos. They stumbled a bit, reminding me of zombies, but the fire in their eyes was far more intelligent and there was a malevolence about them that was palpable. They were faster than zombies, but not as quick as ghouls —which meant they could outrun someone who couldn't run, or someone who only walked at a fast pace. Which meant a number of people would be vulnerable.

"Crap. Okay, we know they don't feed on energy, but they do eat flesh, drink blood, and can cause contagious infections with their bites, which are necrotic. So what destroys them? I'd say 'kills,' but they're already dead."

"Fire, but it has to be directed and hot enough, or they'll just keep on stumbling through it and end up catching their victims on fire as well. Like skeletal walkers, it should stop them if you make mincemeat out of them. I tried to find magical spells that work against them, but there are only a few necromancers who can work spells of the caliber that will disrupt their energy. And while Raven's on the way, even she's not strong enough to use that spell. But her fire magic should help." He eyed the nearest vrykos.

It was about twenty feet from the fence, and I wondered if the waist-high barrier would keep them from breaking through.

"Can they climb the fence?" I asked, pulling out my bow. "I wonder if an arrow will do any good?"

"If bullets don't, chances are an arrow won't either." Yutani turned to Herne, who was headed our way. "What's the word?"

"The word is, the cops don't have the physical strength to fight these creatures—not most of them. And they came armed with guns, not swords. I called a few friends who should be showing up any minute now." He glanced at me. "Ember, put away your bow. It won't do any good. But Brighid's Flame should cleave through nicely. Angel," he added, turning to her, "there are three ambulances over there. Go join them and offer what help you can."

She nodded.

"Tell them that they need to be ready to bug out in case they break through the lines. We don't have the manpower to cover the medics and fight the vrykos."

"Will do," she said, dashing over to them.

Herne motioned to Viktor. "Go find out how the victims are doing—the ones who've been hurt so far." He turned to me. "I'm glad you wore a leather jacket and sturdy jeans. You do *not* want to get bitten by one of these creatures. Fae aren't immune to the bites, apparently, and neither are shifters. So we're all vulnerable, but at least most Cryptos are strong enough to actually put up a fight." He motioned for Viktor, Yutani, and me to follow him. "Time to go in. Reinforcements will be here soon and Officer Trent over there knows to look out for them."

We headed toward the graveyard. I tried to breathe normally. I had to calm my nerves because fear was the real killer when it came to fights. Fear subverted the best of instincts.

The graveyard was surrounded by a low stone fence about three feet high that encircled the perimeter. Small, since it probably encompassed five acres at the most, the Faraday Cemetery was neat and tidy. At least, neat and tidy for the Worchester District. The graves looked like they had been well maintained.

A line of cops stretched out in front of the gate, carrying shields and long batons. I could feel the energy shift as we drew near. The cops were afraid and they were looking to us to help. It always daunted me when I realized that to them, we were the superheroes coming to save the day, and usually we had no idea what the fuck we were doing.

They silently parted as we walked up to the gates. Beyond the gates, a mere ten to twelve feet away, the vrykos had gathered and were shuffling in our direction.

I wondered if they were communicating with one

another. Were they like a hive mind? Were they individually controlled by whoever had dragged their spirits into the bodies? I had no clue how this actually worked.

"Wait for me!" The voice was familiar, and when I turned around, Raven dashed up. She was wearing a short skirt over heavy leggings, boots, and a heavy jacket over a tank top. "Cripes almighty," she said, staring beyond the gate.

Behind her, Kipa led a group of stalwart men. They all had a keen look to them and felt on the wild side.

"I've brought members of my SuVahta. Herne? Oh, there you are," Kipa said, picking Herne out of the group. "We're here. Let's go in. My men have been warned."

Relief washed over me. These were men out of Kipa's elite guard. They were wolf shifters, on point, fearless, and loyal. At least we had a decent number to go up against what seemed like a swarm of the hungry ghosts.

I dashed back over to the medics' station and handed Angel my bow. "Please hold this for me." I didn't want to go back to the car, and it seemed foolish to encumber myself with the extra weight and bulk. After she took it, I withdrew Brighid's Flame from its sheath. The blade glinted against the light penetrating the clouds overhead. It was razor sharp, and could cleave through metal when need be. The sword had more powers to it than I fully understood, but it was up to me to discover them.

"Ready," I said, returning to the others.

"Ready," Viktor, Yutani, and Raven chimed in. She looked luminous, as though her magic was filling her aura. I had no idea what spells she had lined up to cast, but whatever they were, she was positively pulsating with energy.

"The others will have to catch up. Let's go." Herne motioned for the officers to open the gates and—with him leading the way—we charged in. The police closed the gates immediately after we were inside and I realized their primary function here was to prevent the vrykos from breaking through the gates into the streets.

We eased toward the creatures, eyeing them carefully. There were several groups clumped together, five over to one side, four to another, another six beyond. And then there were strays, wandering through the cemetery, ignoring the central hive.

Herne motioned for Viktor and me to move to the right, while he and Yutani took the left group. Kipa and his guards split off to take the center grouping, and Raven moved off to one side and quickly laid out a skull on the ground, two candles, and a few other tools. I quickly lost sight of what she was doing as the vrykos facing us began inching forward, the light in their eye sockets growing more malevolent with each passing moment.

I caught the gaze of one of the creatures. I could swear it was thinking—*If I move here where will she move...what kind of weapon does she have...what are my chances of eating the flesh off her bones?* Things of that nature.

Feeling all too scrutinized, I caught my breath and rushed forward, sword high, thinking on the go about which way I should turn. At the last moment, I swept Brighid's Flame down and around, twisting in midair to swing from my left rather than from my right.

I made contact with the vrykos, my blade biting deep into its flesh. I had managed to clip the creature at his knees, and Brighid's Flame was sharp, with a polished edge. The blade bit right through the flesh, stopping only briefly at the bone, but the force I had put into the swing carried through and pushed the blade through the knee joint, separating the lower leg from the rest of his body.

I was startled when no blood appeared, but then remembered he had been dead beforehand, and so there was no blood to spill out. However, magic couldn't preserve a corpse in its entirety, or at least whoever had cast the reanimation spell couldn't, and so a thick ooze of green juices slimed out of the wound, splattering on the ground. There was a hiss as it fell and I suddenly remembered that the blood of the vrykos—such as it was—was also toxic. It was burning the grass, which immediately withered up and turned yellow.

The creature hopped forward on the other leg. He had his arms stretched out in front of him and was aiming for me. I jumped back. He swiped at me again, remaining surprisingly steady on one leg. A low hiss came from his throat, scaring the fuck out of me. In the time we'd been fighting, the vrykos had been silent. I stepped back again as it kept coming toward me. I was trying to decide from what angle to attack again.

A shriek diverted my attention and I swung around. Oh shit, one of the SuVahta had been hit. He had stabbed his opponent through the heart but must have forgotten that wouldn't kill it, because the creature had hold of him by the ankle, and had pulled his feet out from under him. The vrykos was biting down on his flesh, ripping at the wolf shifter's shin.

"Crap!" I was the closest one to him.

I darted away from my own opponent, dodging around him to race over to the guard's side. As I came near, the guard screamed again as the vrykos bit down hard on his shin again, tearing further into the flesh. Blood splattered everywhere.

I raced forward, bringing my sword down across the creature's shoulders. I had first thought to behead it, but if I did that, I'd chance catching the guard's foot.

The guard kicked hard, dislodging the vrykos from his leg and rolled out of the way. I brought Brighid's Flame up again and then brought it down hard, right across the neck of the creature. There was the sickening sound of flesh rending, and then a crunch as my blade carved through the top vertebrae. A moment later, the head rolled to the side, teeth gnashing harmlessly.

I leaned on my sword, panting, but the next moment, I saw that the body was on the move, headless, dragging itself toward the decapitated head. The vrykos's eyes blazed, staring at me. It seemed that it was still in control of the body, even though the head was no longer attached.

"Freaking hell, what kind of horror show are you?"

I jumped over the body to get to the head before its torso did. Turning Brighid's Flame point down, I drove it through the skull, pinning it to the ground. The next moment, Viktor appeared by my side. He began hack-and-slashing his way through the corpse, tearing it to bits with his sword. I yanked my own sword out of the head, grimacing as I brought the blade down again, this time cleaving it in half. I managed to slice through it, then before I could think, I did so again, quartering the pieces. Finally, the light in its eyes died, and I glanced over to see Viktor doing the same to the body. We finished up and I pointed to the guard.

"He needs help. Take him to the medics."

"Will you be all right?" Viktor asked.

I nodded, leaning over, my hands on my knees. "I have to be. Just go and then get back here as soon as you can."

The half-ogre grunted, then swept up the guard in his arms and began jogging back toward the gate. I picked up my sword again and turned back to my first opponent, who was crawling toward me, using the grass to pull himself along. Taking a deep breath, I steeled myself and headed over to repeat the process, as dusk fell and the fight went on.

CHAPTER EIGHT

THE SOUNDS OF METAL AGAINST FLESH, OF GRUNTING AND shrieking and curses blurred into a tangled cacophony of unending noise. I ignored the shouts and shrieks, trying to focus on keeping myself alive as I plowed through corpse after walking corpse. The scent of blood was noticeably absent, except for the few guards who were getting caught. Whether Kipa hadn't warned them about the dangers or they were just getting cocky, I wasn't sure, but I saw Viktor carrying at least four men out of the graveyard.

The vrykos seemed like they'd never stop coming and their exhausting, nonstop attempt to break free into the city seemed like it would never end. Everything blurred into a haze in which only we and our enemies existed.

For a moment I wondered if we tried to talk to them, would they hear us? If we stopped and requested a truce, would they listen? But then reason took hold of me again. The vrykos weren't vampires. Their souls had been recalled into rotting bodies, and they were angry and confused. They were also being controlled. There was no chance they could—even if they wanted to—make any sort of pact with us.

By the fourth corpse, I was getting tired. They weren't easy to kill and I had almost been bitten twice. But I forced myself to keep going. I was fighting a smaller one —in life he had been a small man, thin and spindly—and I swung, trying to undercut him at the legs. At that moment, a shriek overhead jolted me out of my thoughts. It was so loud it set the air to vibrating. Both the vrykos and I stopped and looked up.

There, winging overhead, was a misty form of a dragon. Long and sinuous, like a serpent with wings, the creature shimmered as it sailed by, luminous against the sky.

I froze. "Dragon!" The word came ratcheting out of my mouth before I realized I was screaming.

I stumbled back, looking around frantically for a bush or tree to hide behind. My opponent took the opportunity to grab hold of my leather jacket. He flailed, trying to catch hold of my arm, but I quickly darted back before he could get a good grip on me. I slammed him with the flat of my blade, knocking him back.

"Run for cover," Herne was yelling.

Cover? From what? was my first thought, but the next moment, a trail of fire blazed down, strafing the graveyard. I dove out of the way, dodging the flames as they raked the ground like a Gatling gun. The next moment, every one of the vrykos froze, pulling back and turning tail.

What the hell?

They shifted direction and headed toward the back of

the cemetery, where I caught a glimpse of a large van near the sidewalk at the opposite gate. The cops had pulled back, and now I saw why. The back doors of the van were open and two tall men jumped out, shoving the vrykos inside as they stumbled toward it. I recognized the men—they were also dragons, Aso and Variance, twins who were on Typhon's side.

Then who was that? I thought, glancing up to where the long dragon had been. It couldn't have been Typhon—could it?

But the dragon who had flamed the ground was gone. There was no sign of him. *Crap, and double crap.* Where had he gone? As I turned back to the van, Aso and Variance closed the doors and vanished, disappearing down the street with the rest of the vrykos.

I slowly leaned on my sword, unable to fathom what had just happened. A moment later, Herne was by my side. "Are you all right?"

I nodded. "That van...Aso and Variance were there loading in the surviving vrykos. But who the fuck was the dragon overhead? It couldn't have been Typhon, could it?"

He shook his head. "If that had been Typhon, we would all be dead. But I *can* tell you that it was a shadow dragon and they're among the most dangerous of all. Any dragon can be problematic, but shadow dragons are particularly deadly." He glanced down at me. "It looks like they cleared the park of the creatures. How many were destroyed?"

I shrugged. "I have no idea. I waded through the sea of flesh without counting. I think I'm shell-shocked."

"You have every right to be." He slowly put his arm

around my shoulders, pulling me to him. "Come on, let's regroup and see what's happened and who's hurt."

Leaning into his embrace, I allowed him to lead me back to the front gate. I was exhausted and all I wanted was a hot shower and something to forget that tonight ever happened. We passed a group of officers milling around, instructing clean-up crews to go in and wipe up the carnage we had left behind.

"What if the dragons decide to strafe Seattle—randomly destroy it?"

"I don't think they will," Herne said, leading me over to where Angel was packing up her supplies. She looked dazed as well, but where I was covered in dirt and mud and liquids that I really didn't want to think about, she was clean. Wet from the rain, but clean.

"Why wouldn't they?"

"They want to regain the world, not just randomly destroy us. To do that requires strategy. No, Typhon has some plan in mind. Otherwise, the dragons would have already started to destroy the cities. But he's holding back and I'm not sure what his scheme is. I know we have a committee working on figuring it out in Annwn." He paused, then motioned to Angel. "Can you drive? Ember's exhausted and I don't trust her behind a wheel."

"I'm perfectly capable of driving," I protested, though I felt like a limp noodle.

"I'll drive. Just let me finish up here. I'll be back in a moment." Angel turned back to help out with the last of the victims.

I watched her for a moment, then said, "You know what scares me? How rough this fight was, and *all we did* was fight back a band of vrykos. What happens when they really hit hard? What do we do then?"

"That's why it's so important to bring in the Fae and shifter militias," Herne said. "We need them for backup. They're used to taking orders and fighting on the front lines." He paused. "I happen to know that a number of officers in the Fae militia were brought over from Annwn when Saílle and Névé first started up the militia. There, the Fae wars are real, not petty hissy fits. When Saílle and Névé decided to call a truce last year and pull together a militia, they didn't just recruit from their cities here. They called in reinforcements from the older city-states."

Something about his tone of voice sent shivers down my back. I mostly knew the Fae as petty and vindictive. But whenever Herne talked about TirNaNog and Navane in Annwn, I could feel the massive energy that surrounded the ancient cities, and their equally ancient wars. Some of the soldiers had to be walking weapons in their own right.

"That scares me almost as much as the dragons," I said.

"It should. While I don't think any of the mortals can take on Typhon, the Fae and shifter militias shouldn't have a hard time taking on his children. We also need to explore another avenue—Raven's people. The Ante-Fae. Granted, they tend to be solitary, but the Morrígan has enlisted her Bean Sidhe in the fight, and they're all Ante-Fae."

"Like Raven's mother, Phasmoria," I said. "She's freak-show scary, and I'm sincerely grateful she's on our side."

Phasmoria, Raven's mother, was Queen of the Bean Sidhe, directly in service to the Morrígan. She was no-

nonsense, kick-your-ass strong and she seemed fearless. That appealed to me. I didn't like running scared.

"I wish I could be more like Phasmoria," I muttered.

Herne stared at me. "What? Why?"

"She's not afraid of anything. Remember? She went against the Lykren with us and we saw how she fought. I wouldn't ever want to be on her bad side." I shrugged. "I just envy her sense of sureness and the way she dives into things without worrying about the end result."

Herne frowned, stepping back. He placed his hands on my shoulders and gazed into my eyes. "Ember, for one thing, Phasmoria's a queen. Of the Bean Sidhe, no less. She's practically one of the Immortals. For another, Raven takes after her and you've seen the mishaps that can happen. Raven tackles challenges with the same savoir-faire attitude that her mother possesses and she lands herself in hot water almost every time."

"True," I said, feeling like I should stand up for my friend.

"I really do like Raven and I'm grateful she works with us on occasion, but the girl's managed to almost get herself killed a dozen times. She doesn't have her mother's experience. Phasmoria can get away with being fearless because she knows exactly what she's doing. Raven can't, and you can't either. Not yet."

I didn't want to admit that he was right, but the fact was he *was* right and I grudgingly acknowledged it. Like Raven, it was easy for me to get myself in scrapes I couldn't resolve.

"I suppose you're right. It's just that you and Viktor and Yutani...even Talia...you're all so experienced and I feel like I need to catch up, to prove myself around you."

"You're *thirty-one* years old. You've been with the Wild Hunt for about a year and a half. I'm a god, Viktor's over two hundred, Talia's close to a couple thousand years old. Yutani is over two hundred years old. Give yourself some leeway. You'll catch up as you gain more experience and as you become accustomed to the work. Right now, you and Angel have barely scratched the surface of what we do here." He paused, glancing over his shoulder to make sure she couldn't hear. "But Angel's human and that—"

"Don't say it. I don't want to think about it." I was all too aware that Angel was on a tight timeline because she was human. I was also determined to figure out a way to extend her life because the thought of losing my best friend when I had barely even begun to explore my own options hurt so much I could barely even acknowledge the feeling.

"Someday you're..." Herne stopped. "Never mind. Leave that for another time. Right now, you need to go home, take a bath, and eat cookies. Or something along those lines. I'd come with you, but I have to wrap up business here."

I nodded, turning to Angel, who had just finished stowing her gear. She slung her backpack over her shoulder and joined us, taking one look at my face before turning to Herne.

"What happened? Did you two have an argument?"

He shook his head. "No, Ember's just exhausted. As are we all. Tired, frazzled, and ready for bed."

At that moment, Viktor, Talia, Charlie, and Yutani joined us. Talia looked chipper, but then, she had been able to hide in her car. Viktor and Yutani looked about as banged up as I felt.

"Raven and Kipa took off," Viktor said. "She asked me to let you know they're headed back to the Eastside."

"Thanks," Herne said. "I wish Kipa could have stuck around but hey, given the spells I saw Raven throwing over by the mausoleum, she must be exhausted."

"I missed that," I said. "I was so focused on my own little corner of the fight."

"I think we were all focused on saving our own skins while taking out the vrykos," Viktor said with a faint grin. "Raven put on quite a show. She must have got three of them with fireballs and this time, the creatures didn't walk out of the flames."

"What about the van that sped off with the rest of the vrykos?" Yutani asked. "Was that Aso and Variance I saw?"

"One of the cops caught the license plate. There's an APB out on them, though we've instructed anybody who sees the van to follow at a distance and not make themselves known. We just want to know where they're going. Right now, anybody who tried to stop that van would get mowed down." Herne let out a sigh. "All right. Tomorrow morning, I mediate a truce between Saílle and Névé. Then I'll be at the mayor's office for a press conference at nine."

"Do you need us at the office?" Talia glanced at the calendar on her phone.

I yawned, suddenly so tired I could barely remember my name. "Please don't ask us to come in at eight. I don't think I'll be able to make it to the breakfast table by then."

"Sleep in. But we have a lot of work to do so yes, tomorrow's another work day. Everyone, meet at the office around eleven. But watch the press conference at home. That way I won't have to go over it again. And Happy Lughnasadh. I'm sorry it wasn't the evening we had planned." Herne glanced around at everyone. "All right, get moving." He pulled me to him and pressed his lips against mine.

I melted into his kiss, feeling ready to pass out in his arms. His lips were warm against mine, taking the chill off the rain that streamed down around us. A crash of lightning split the sky, followed by a low roll of thunder almost directly on top of it, and I reluctantly pulled away.

"We should get moving. Lightning is too close and might decide to hit one of the trees here in the park," I whispered.

"I'll take my chances," Herne murmured, kissing me again.

I wanted nothing more than to just drift along with him, letting the world spin on by. But after a few seconds, he let go.

"Go home, my love. Bathe and sleep. Rest easy. We'll manage through this. Though the world seems like it's on fire, we'll navigate through the flames. I promise you that." His voice was soothing, and I took a deep breath, letting it filter out between my teeth.

"I love you, so very much," I whispered.

"I love you, too." He patted me on the ass. "Go home now. Angel, drive safely. The roads are probably slick due to the hail."

"What hail?" she asked as we began to walk toward our car.

At that moment, the skies opened up and a sheet of hail descended, pounding the pavement around us, bouncing like pebbles on the rain-soaked surface.

"That hail!" Herne called back, heading to his car with a laugh.

"Smart ass," I said, but I was too tired to say anything else.

Angel made sure I was bundled in the car and that my seat belt was properly fastened before sliding into the driver's seat and locking the doors. She turned on the ignition and, as the car idled for a moment, she fumbled in the glovebox in front of me. She came out with two Caramel-Crunch bars, handing one to me.

"A night like tonight calls for chocolate," she said.

Laughing, I took the candy and bit into it. "I think that's an understatement," I said as we pulled out onto the street and headed for home.

WE BARELY MANAGED to drag our asses up the stairs and into our respective showers. By the time I was clean, I felt like I had been pummeled black and blue. I had more bruises on me than I had managed in a long while, even with the workouts I was putting in at the gym. Yutani was training me in martial arts, and he didn't pull his punches.

When I slipped into my robe, I smelled some sort of wonderful aroma from downstairs. Amazed that Angel had the strength to even work a microwave at this point, I padded down the stairs to the kitchen, my stomach rumbling.

"Hey, what are you doing?" I asked as I popped into the kitchen.

Angel grinned. She was sitting on one of the stools by the island counter with two plates in front of her. They were heaped with corn bread and smoked salmon, and artichoke dip and the rest of the peach pie also sat on the table.

"Oh my gods, how on earth did you find the strength to make all of that?"

"Grab a plate and sit down." She handed me one of the plates, and—carrying the other—joined me at the table.

My stomach suddenly realized it was famished and began protesting with a vengeance. It rumbled so loud that Angel started to laugh.

"For heaven's sake, eat. These were my contributions to the Lughnasadh potluck. I was going to take the artichoke dip and the cornbread. We just happened to have some smoked salmon in the fridge, so all I had to do was pull everything out and fix us a couple plates. The peach pie is left over from last night, remember?"

"Well, I appreciate it. I'm so tired I'd probably just stick my head in the fridge and scarf down the first thing I laid my hands on." I slumped forward. "It was rough, Angel. It was *more than rough*. I'm really afraid what things will be like in a few months if the dragons keep this crap up. And it's not just here—it's all over."

Angel stared at her plate, picking over her salmon. "I want to warn Cooper. I don't want DJ in danger. I'm going to ask Herne if I can tell him everything that's going on."

"Well, you can bet tomorrow morning the news will be full of what happened. And if anybody managed to catch a glimpse of that dragon except us, you know that's going to be hitting the air waves. They can't keep things like this quiet." I spread the dip on my cornbread and added smoked salmon.

"What do you *really* think's going to happen?" Angel

asked after a moment. "Do you think... Will we lose the world to Typhon?"

I wanted to tell her no, that everything would be fine. But I didn't know. I had no idea what was going to happen over the next few months. If the gods could get their act together and figure it out, we had hope. If not, then I had no clue what we'd be facing.

"I don't know, I really don't. I want to say yes, because I really want to believe that we'll be okay. But so many things depend on whether the gods can figure out his weaknesses and how to drive him back into stasis." I paused to eat for a moment.

Angel sliced the remainder of the pie and handed me a plate. "Ember, if the world falls to Typhon, you'll be moving to Annwn, won't you? With Herne?"

I looked at her, frowning. That thought hadn't even occurred to me. "I have no idea. I guess...that might happen, but I would think we'd be needed more than ever over here. If we do go to Annwn to live, you and DJ are coming with us. That's just a given."

She smiled, a look of relief sliding over her face. "Thank you. I wondered, but I felt awkward asking. If things get really bad, I want to bring DJ up here to live with us. I can find my own place, if need be—I wouldn't want to inconvenience you."

"DJ could stay here. We have a third bedroom. I don't have a problem with that." I polished off the cornbread and started in on the pie. "But don't you think he'd be safer down at Cooper's? The dragons will probably focus on the bigger cities where the population is larger."

"I guess we'll cross that bridge when we come to it."

She finished her pie and leaned back in her chair. "It's two A.M. I'm beat and you look totally exhausted."

"I am, and I'm covered with bruises, thanks to that fight. Herne wants us to watch the press conference at nine, but we can watch from bed. Why don't you come in my room in the morning? We'll curl up under the blankets and watch from there." I helped her carry the dishes over to the sink.

"That sounds like fun. Like when we were in college."

"Those days seem so long ago," I said, thinking back to the days when we roomed together in school. Angel had left college early to help her mother. I had lived with Mama J. and Angel from the time I was fifteen, when my parents were murdered, until both Angel and I left for college.

"They do, but you know what? I'll bet when we're fifty, this time will seem just as far away to us." She slipped her arm through mine and we headed toward the stairs, waking Mr. Rumblebutt up from where he was sleeping on the bottom stair. He followed us up the rest of the way. As I peeled off toward my room and Angel headed into hers, Mr. Rumblebutt joined me, jumping on the bed and kneading the blankets as I pulled off my robe and crawled beneath the light sheet.

Outside, the thunder and lightning continued. We didn't often get massive thunderstorms, but when we did it electrified the air, charging it like a battery. I slipped back out of bed to open my window a crack. There was a screen on the outside so that Mr. Rumblebutt couldn't get loose. As I watched the rain pour down, beating a tattoo against the side of the house, another fork of lightning split the sky, lighting up the night with a brilliant pink flash. A white flash followed, and thunder rolled through the air, shaking the house.

Mr. Rumblebutt meowed anxiously, so I returned to bed where he curled up in my arms, burrowing his head into my armpit to hide from the storm. I petted him gently, trying to soothe him.

"It's okay, Mr. R.," I said. "Everything will be okay, little man." I just wished I could believe my own words.

CHAPTER NINE

Morning brought with it fresh air, and the thunderstorm had passed, disappearing around three in the morning. As tired as I was, I had found it difficult to sleep. Finally, as the storm abated, so did my anxiety and I dropped into a light slumber and then, fully to sleep.

I squinted as the alarm went off. It was eight forty-five. I forced myself to sit up, groaning against the morning light that streamed through the window. It looked like August was going to be typical—a day or so of rain, but mostly dry and sunny. It was generally Seattle's hottest month of the year. At least the air smelled sweet and fresh, and there was a briskness that the storm had left in its wake.

I stumbled out of bed and went to the bathroom, then pulled on my robe and climbed back into the tangle of sheets. I stared at the bedframe for a moment, thinking I might want to buy a new one, but then it occurred to me that within a little over a year, Herne and I would be married. Maybe I should wait until we could choose one together.

Lost in the world of window-shopping for furniture, I didn't notice the time was ticking by until Angel tapped on my door.

"Come in," I said, shaking the thoughts of four-posters versus sleigh beds out of my mind.

Angel was still in her nightgown, too, but she was carrying an iced latte for me, and an iced tea for herself. She handed me the drink and motioned for me to scoot over. I saw that she was also carrying a bag of half a dozen doughnuts, along with a handful of napkins, so she must have been up early to go out. I held her drink as she climbed into bed, then flipped on the remote.

"Here's hoping the news isn't a mega-mess today," I said.

"Here's hoping the world isn't a mega-mess today," Angel answered.

She handed me a doughnut and took one for herself as I flipped around to find the local news station. A glance at the clock on my phone told me we had another three minutes before the press conference was due to be held. I muted it until the mayor came on.

"How did you sleep?" I asked.

Angel leaned back against the headboard. She was wearing a sleep shirt and a pair of pajama shorts, pale pink against her rich brown skin. "Okay, I guess. The storm was hard to ignore but when I did fall asleep, I slept deep."

"I wish I had. I'm still groggier than a tranked elephant. Which is why I'm so grateful you brought the caffeine." As I sipped the ice-cold latte, the announcement flashed on the station that the mayor would be speaking. I raised the volume.

A moment later, Mayor Neskan appeared on the screen. She was wearing a white pantsuit with a pale blue shirt beneath the blazer, and her hair was neatly pulled back into a tidy bun. She was wearing sunglasses, and looked every inch a successful, hip politician. She launched into her introduction, which we mostly ignored.

"Last night, there was an incident in Faraday Cemetery in the Worchester District. A full contingent of police officers along with members of the Wild Hunt Agency were battling a brigade of creatures called 'vrykos.' As reported, these are reanimated corpses. They are not—we repeat *not*—vampires. While most of the creatures were subdued, several vanished in a van with the license plate of B14DRC89C. That's a white Toredoro van with a side-loading door and two doors in the back. Members of the community are urged to avoid this vehicle if you see it, and to immediately call the police.

"Meanwhile," the mayor continued, "we must discuss a difficult situation. We have confirmation that the invasion of vrykos *is* spreading across the continent. We have some idea of why this is happening, but until we know for certain, we don't want to spread unnecessary rumors. I'm joined today by Herne the Hunter from Annwn." Her expression took on an almost dreamy look and I realized she was heavily in crush. I snickered.

"Yeah, she wants to jump his bones, that's for sure." I took a long swig of my drink.

"Does it bother you?" Angel asked.

"No. I trust Herne, and let's face it, he's a god and he's

gorgeous. If I got upset every time some girl or woman mooned over him, I'd be unhappy the rest of my life."

Herne stepped up to the microphone. Several other members of the camera team backed away, as though they thought he might flatten them or something. He was handsome, yes. But he could also be intimidating when he chose to be.

"Lord Herne, what can you tell us about this situation?" Mayor Neskan turned to Herne.

"Just this: If you see one of the vrykos coming toward you, get the hell out of the way. They are *dangerous*. Their bite is as deadly as a Komodo dragon's bite and the infection from their saliva is contagious. If you are bitten by one of these creatures, get away at all costs or you may forfeit your life. Immediately go to a hospital and tell them what happened."

"What do the vrykos want?" the mayor asked.

Herne let out a sigh and he took the microphone from the mayor. He turned back to the cameras, his expression serious. "The vrykos themselves don't have an objective—they are being controlled by forces beyond our ability to contain at this point. We will be working with members of the United Coalition to do our best to track down and destroy the vrykos, but we expect to miss a number of them, and the forces controlling them are probably going to continue to reanimate more of them. If you see one, run. When you are a safe distance away, phone the authorities. We need every citizen to be on their guard. I cannot stress how dangerous these creatures are. They *will* kill you if you get too close."

"What about reports that someone saw a low-flying

plane over Faraday Cemetery last night?" a member of the press corps asked.

Herne closed his eyes for a moment, then glanced at the mayor, who gave him a nod. "That was no plane. I will be discussing this with the United Coalition. Look for a statement within a week or so. Until then, please don't feed into rumors. Unverified rumors and patently false information will only lead to harm. For now, please stay away from cemeteries. Keep alert. Again, if you encounter one of the vrykos, get away and alert the authorities. Thank you."

He shook his head, refusing to answer any more questions. As the press hounded him, he followed a police guard through the crowd, out of sight. The mayor had a few closing remarks, but she was just reiterating what had been said before.

I turned off the television. "Well, that was uncomfortable. You *know* that wannabe ghost hunters and monster hunters are going to be heading toward the cemeteries in full force now."

Angel leaned her head back and groaned. "You're right. And that's just going to cause more headaches for all of us." She stretched, yawning. "All right, up and at 'em. I'll go make breakfast. Why don't you take those bruises for another run under a hot shower? I can't imagine how you feel this morning."

I eased out of the other side of the bed as she stood, and slid off my robe. Angel and I were used to seeing each other naked and it didn't faze us in the least.

"Look." I turned, holding my arms out so she could see the array of bruises that covered my body.

"Damn, girl, you're literally black and blue." She shook

her head. "Do you have anything Ferosyn might have given you? I know most human meds are off limits, even the topical ones."

The Fae and shifters needed specialized medications. Most of us couldn't take the drugs formulated for the human community. They either didn't work, or they produced unwanted side effects, one of which could be death. Either way, they weren't worth the risk.

"Yeah, I think I have some salve he gave me for muscle aches. I'll use some after I shower. But man," I said, looking in the mirror at the massive black-and-blue splotches across my body. "I look like the poster child for the clumsiest person on Earth."

"Get into the water, woman. I'll make waffles. We have enough time."

"Don't forget the—"

"Bacon," she said, interrupting me. "Don't worry. I won't leave you dangling without your crispy pig." But she was laughing as she headed out my door. She liked bacon just as much as I did, though I could easily eat a pound of it and she kept it down to six or seven rashers.

BY THE TIME we finished breakfast, it was ten-thirty. After making sure Mr. Rumblebutt had plenty of food, we headed out for work, taking both our cars in case something came up.

As I drove into the heart of the city, the sun broke through the high, thin clouds, burning them off. The storm had left the air clear and charged, and looking around at people going about their business as usual made

Typhon and the vrykos feel a million miles away. Of course, I knew they weren't, but I let myself drift in the feeling of hope for as long as I could.

I eased into the parking garage, finding a spot near the door. Angel was right behind me and parked three cars down. I waited for her before heading across and down the street to the office.

The Wild Hunt was located in downtown Seattle. Known as the Emerald City, Seattle was a complex organism, with vast swaths of greenery interspersed among the old brick buildings and the new chrome and glass. Some skyscrapers looked like mile-high mirrors. Their windows were reflective. I found it a wonder that, on the few hot days we had in Seattle, the glass didn't reflect a beam somewhere to start a fire.

The city was a mixture of old and new. Red brick walkups mingled with modern concrete. Residential zones hopscotched with businesses and mini-malls. The UW—the University of Washington—formed its own district, adding to the kaleidoscope that was the city. There was a buzz to Seattle, a busy-ness that was wired on coffee and high tech. But beneath the surface, Seattle had its dark, seedy sides. For one thing, the city was home to the Catacombs.

During the early days of the city, a fire had raged through, burning a great swath of it to the ground. As rebuilding advanced, the planners had decided that old Seattle was too low—well below sea level. Indeed, it was often flooded by high tides on Puget Sound. So new buildings were built on streets that covered the remains of old buildings below.

Underground Seattle still existed in the dark and

gloom that came from being entombed. But what most of the residents back then hadn't realized was that the vampires had gotten there first. The vamps had built catacombs below the ground. Once the surface of the streets had been raised, the vampires broke into Underground Seattle and claimed it as part of their territory. Now the entire underground structure was simply called the Catacombs.

The Wild Hunt Agency was downtown, on First Avenue, a wide street lined with trees. The brownstone walkup was five stories high, with both a series of steps and a ramp leading up to the main floor. The first floor was made up of the lobby and the urgent care clinic that catered to Cryptos and to the streeps in the area—the street people.

The second floor was a combined daycare and preschool for low-income families. On the third floor, a yoga and dance studio held their lessons. The fourth floor was ours—the Wild Hunt. And the fifth had recently been rented by the Stone & Needle, offering chiropractic services, acupuncture, a nutritionist, and several massage therapists. Unlike the brothels along the other side of the street, they actually did offer massage.

Across the street, delis and vintage shops intermingled with the fetish boutiques, where you could find specialized kink in just about any flavor you chose, running the gamut from vanilla to chocolate to rocky road, depending on how bent your tastes ran.

Angel and I strolled along the street, greeting the streeps as we went.

I was grateful to see that Pain and Shayla were no longer around. A young couple, they had been living in a cardboard box. But Shayla had been pregnant, and Pain wanted to do better for her and the baby, so we had hooked them up with a shelter where Shayla could stay while he continued to look for a job. A few weeks ago, Pain had contacted me to let me know he had found a good job. They could afford an apartment of their own. As I watched the jugglers and buskers on the street corner, I could only hope they would manage to keep the gains they had found.

As if reading my mind, Angel said, "I heard from Pain last week. Shayla had her baby. They found an apartment and he's doing really well at his job. I'm cautiously optimistic that they'll manage to pull themselves out of their old life."

"That makes me happy," I said. "And I can use happy news. The day seems so bright, and everything seems so normal that it's hard to remember what we're facing. And truth be known, I don't want to remember it."

Angel slid her arm through mine as we headed toward the stairs leading up to the agency. "Ember, one thing I've learned through all that's happened, is sometimes you just have to go about your daily routine even though it feels like everything's fallen out from under you."

"Yeah, it's not easy, but you're right."

"When Mama J. died, I *really* didn't want to deal with all the fallout. But I had to put a roof over our heads and food on the table and keep DJ going. So I did what I had to. I got up in the morning, I sent DJ to school, and I went to work. I couldn't think about my mother too much because so many things were weighing on my shoulders."

I nodded. When my parents had been murdered, I wanted to curl up in a ball in the closet and stay there. But

I couldn't. Mama J. had offered to take me in, so I had picked myself up and continued my life, even through the pain.

"So, buck up, smell the roses, and deal with life as it comes?"

Her eyes twinkled. "Something like that."

We were at the bottom of the steps, and we dashed up to the door. Inside the building, there was an elevator to the right, a few yards before the door leading into the urgent care clinic. We opted for the elevator and I pushed the button for the fourth floor.

The doors opened into the waiting room, which meant that someone had made it to work before we did. If the doors hadn't opened, Angel would have had to use her key to unlock the stop at the fourth floor.

Angel headed to her circular desk directly across from the elevator. To the right was the seating area for clients. Directly behind Angel's desk was Herne's office door, and the hallway behind her desk led to the break room and the rest of our offices.

There were sounds coming from the break room, so I headed down to see who was there while Angel settled in at her desk and checked for any messages.

Herne and Talia were in the break room, talking.

Talia waved her hand to the counter where a fruit tray, a cookie platter, and the coffee awaited. "I brought snacks," she said. "How are you doing this morning?"

"The extra sleep helped." I eyed the goodies and decided that one waffle and bacon for breakfast hadn't been quite enough. The Fae had faster metabolisms than humans, and our appetites showed it. As I loaded up cookies and fruit salad onto a paper plate, Yutani, Viktor, and Rafé joined us. Angel was last.

"The elevator is locked and I armed the bell outside the stairs so we'll hear if anybody wants in that way." She fixed herself a cup of tea and we all gathered around the table.

Herne was just about to bring the meeting to order when my work phone rang—we all had two phones, our personal cells and our work cells. This helped avoid any clients getting hold of our private numbers. I pulled it out, frowning, and glanced at the caller ID.

Ashera.

"Whoa...I need to take this." I jumped up from the table and walked over to the counter so they could keep on talking. "Hello?"

Ashera answered, her voice low and sensuous. She was a blue dragon—one of the Celestial Wanderers. The Dragonni were divided into several types. The Celestial Wanderers were the blue, silver, and gold dragons. They were generally friendly to mortal-kind. The Mountain Dreamers were also human-friendly, and they were made up of the green and black dragons. But the Luminous Warriors took after their father, Typhon. The white, red, and shadow dragons had little use for any form other than dragon. They were the ones who we had to worry about at this point.

Ashera had helped us out when Pandora kidnapped Raven, and she was currently living over on Bainbridge Island with several other dragons who were determined to keep their father from destroying the world.

"Ember, we've heard about the vrykos, of course. You know that this is Typhon's doing."

"Yes, we figured as much."

"Well, I was planning on coming over to talk to your agency tomorrow at four, if that's convenient. I have some information that you'll want, but it's not something I'm comfortable talking about over the phone." She paused, waiting.

"Let me talk to Herne and make sure we aren't already booked." I turned to Herne. "Ashera wants to meet with us tomorrow at four, here."

He looked up from where he had been poring through an article on his tablet. "Angel, we don't have any appointments then, do we?"

Angel checked her tablet and shook her head. "All clear. Shall I put her down?"

"Yeah, do," I said, returning to my phone. "Ashera, we'll see you here at four P.M. Thanks. By the way, I was thinking we needed to run something by you that we saw last night during a fight in a graveyard."

"I think I know what it is, and we'll talk tomorrow. Meanwhile, tread carefully. I can't say more than that, but tomorrow—I'll tell you everything." And with that, she disconnected.

My stomach knotted as I stared at the phone. The very tone of her voice had chilled me to the core. I knew—as sure as I knew my name—that it had to do with the dragon we had seen flying overhead. A shadow seemed to fall across the room, and suddenly the sunshine outside seemed too harsh. The brighter the sun, the darker the shadow, I thought.

CHAPTER TEN

AFTER I TOLD THE OTHERS WHAT ASHERA HAD SAID, THE speculations flew high and thick. Herne listened for a few minutes then put his fingers to his mouth and whistled the meeting back to order.

"We'll find out tomorrow exactly what she means, but for now, back to business. So, I want to go over this morning, first, and then we'll talk about what happened last night. Today, Jana Wildmere arrives at four to discuss forming a Shifter Alliance militia." He gently tossed his tablet on the table. "First, about the parley with Névé and Saílle."

"Oh that's right," I said, suddenly remembering he had been scheduled to meet with the Fae Queens early. "How'd that go?"

"Just about what you'd expect. Long, tedious, aggravating. But in the end, we hammered out a truce for six months. They refused to look beyond that, but frankly, I consider even six months a win, given those two. They will not wage war—outright or covert—against one another until Imbolc. And the parley included assigning me control of both their militias, which will be combined into one, again. I did have to make one concession, however." Herne looked over at me. "You aren't going to like this."

I stared at him with trepidation. "What did you agree to and why do I have a feeling that a target's just been painted on my back?"

"I had to promise to lend you to them over the next few months if they need an outside eye on anything going on. Essentially, you're on call—no more than once a month for each—if they have some case their investigators can't, or won't, handle."

"What?" I stared at him. "You pimped me out to them?"

Herne grinned, leaning back and folding his arms over his chest. "Essentially, yes. I made them agree that whatever they call you in on won't be too dangerous. And your work here comes first."

I glowered at him, fuming. I wanted as little to do with the Fae Queens as possible. They might be clamoring to get on my good side now that they knew I was headed for Annwn, so to speak, but that *didn't* mean they liked me and it sure as hell didn't mean I liked them.

"It's for the greater good, love." Herne held my gaze.

One look into his eyes and I realized he had done everything he could to minimize their impact on me. The Fae Queens were wily, and they were smart. They knew how to get what they wanted and in this case, they seemed to want me.

"All right. I just hope that we're always too busy when they do call." Frowning still, but feeling somewhat mollified, I let out a sigh and darted a glance over to Yutani, who was suppressing a laugh. "Oh, go ahead, you yappy coyote. Laugh it up at my expense. I'll probably need help when I go out there and you know who I'm going to take with me?"

"Whoever made the most fun of you?" he asked, his eyes still dancing.

"Right."

"Okay, that's enough, you two," Herne said. "Now, to the press conference. I met with the mayor. The city council and the governor were also there. We've formed a special task force. We'll have to have a member of both Fae Courts to sit on it, a member from the Vampire Nation, and a member from the Shifter Alliance. Also... unfortunately, from the Cryptozoid Association, since they're now part of the United Coalition. Governor Elkins informed us that every state is forming a special task force like this to handle dealing with the dragons."

"What does the UC think? We have to release the information about the dragons soon, or somebody's going to snap a picture and then it will be too late to stop the rumor mills," I said.

"I think the rumor mills will play havoc even once we let the info out."

"So, you don't think the United Coalition will try and bomb the dragons, are they? That might take out one or two of them, but it would only antagonize the situation." I could see that happening, but I hoped that, for once, level heads would prevail.

"I hope not. That would be a mess. I'll talk to the governor again as soon as I can." Herne shrugged. "But we can't regulate what other countries intend to do."

Yutani was tapping away, taking down notes. "Do they know about Typhon in particular?"

Herne nodded. "I talked to my mother and father and *they* already talked to the Council of Gods and it was agreed that the leaders of the world needed to know how far reaching this whole matter is. They held a worldwide conference of all the top leaders, and at this point, everyone's agreed to leave matters up to the gods when it comes to Typhon."

"So the Wild Hunt and its sister agencies are to be the go-betweens?" Talia asked.

"We are, in the cities we're in, but the Council of Gods is forming more agencies similar in nature, just for the time we're dealing with Typhon. They won't handle Fae matters, however." He paused, then added, "I do know that not all members approved. There were a number of arguments, but after Zeus and the Dagda gave their word that we aren't trying to turn the world into a theocracy, the protests died down." He looked worried, though.

"You're afraid the government will revoke its approval?"

He shook his head. "Not particularly. But one thing that *does* concern me is that some of the gods—not all, by a long shot, but some—might actually see this as a chance to take over power over the world again. As it is, most of my kind have accepted the rise of mankind and their desire to rule themselves, but some still feel usurped."

I hadn't even thought about that. At one time the gods held sway over the world, but now they worked in conjunction with it, and their powers here were limited by treaty and agreement. What if a few power-hungry gods decided to break the treaties, under the guise of trying to help fight against Typhon? Would that lead to a war? Going up against the dragons was hard enough. Going up against a group of gods intent on taking over the world would be suicide.

"All right, so does this mean we have authority over the police?" Viktor asked.

"Not unless it directly relates to Typhon, the undead who follow him, and the rest of the dragons. What concerns me is this. What if the Luminous Warriors convince the UC they're on our side and ask for membership for the Dragonni in the United Coalition? Once they established themselves, it would be so easy for them to con people into complacency. Then, when the world wasn't expecting it, they could easily rise up and smash down everyone else." Herne leaned back in his chair, staring at his tablet. "I've warned the governor about it. She promised she'll fight against their inclusion, should that happen."

His thoughts were worrisome, but could dragons really be that subtle?

"Do you think they could possibly manage the reserve to achieve that? I mean, they aren't exactly low-key." I poured myself another cup of coffee and held up the pot. "Anybody want any more?"

Talia raised her hand. "I wouldn't mind another cup."

I refilled her mug, then Viktor's, before setting the coffee pot back on the warmer. Then, snagging a couple of cookies from the plate on the counter, I returned to the table.

Herne waited until I sat down to answer. "You have only seen a small side of the Dragonni. Do you know why Typhon was sent into stasis?"

"I don't," I said, biting into the peanut butter cookie. "Why?"

"Long ago, when the world was very young and the Titans ruled, back when humans were barely beginning to establish civilization, Typhon grew jealous. His mother, Gaia, was having more children. She left Tartarus and slept with Uranus, who fathered with her, among others, Cronus. Typhon managed to keep his disgruntlement to himself until his half-brother Cronus fathered Zeus. When Gaia announced that her grandson Zeus would become the father of the Greek gods, Typhon felt cheated. He saw that this new breed—the gods—were displacing the Titans."

"So he wanted to lead the gods?"

"Not exactly, but he sure didn't want the gods to grow in power. So he made his move. Now, this part isn't documented in the history books, but we know it happened. Typhon kidnapped Zeus when he was a baby and was about to sacrifice him to Tartarus in exchange for more power when he was caught."

"Uh oh," Talia said.

"*Uh oh* is right. The Fates realized that Typhon's greed could disrupt the entire progression of history, so they ordered that he should be bound into stasis. Now, here's the part that we're having trouble with. We don't know who actually forced him into stasis or how. We have to find out in order to return him to that state. But when he made his plans, Typhon was careful. No one expected him to move against Zeus, and nobody knew what he was planning. Not even his wife, Echidna."

Herne shrugged. "So Typhon managed to kidnap his half-brother away from the gods who were caring for him. No one knew how he did it, and he almost succeeded in disrupting the balance. It's believed Echidna helped the gods bind her husband-brother away from the world, and to banish her children to the Forgotten Kingdom."

"How did he break out of stasis?" Viktor asked.

"We don't know that either. There's so much we *don't* know. Most of the gods weren't hanging around Olympus or Greece at that time. For those of us who aren't a part of the Greek pantheon, this is a fight we never reckoned on, but we have to deal with it anyway because it involves the entire world."

Herne looked rattled. He really didn't want this fight, but it had been dumped in his lap.

"Is there any way *we* can do research?" Angel asked.

"I wasn't born when that happened," Talia said, "but when I was young, I do remember hearing stories about 'Be good or Typhon will rise and eat you up.' He was the bogeyman of the era."

"Frankly, it doesn't matter *why* he was driven into stasis." Yutani shoved his laptop back on the table. "The fact is, we have a power-hungry Titan—don't forget, he's not *just* a dragon—out there, sending his kids to do his dirty work. And that brings up another question: Why doesn't Typhon just come in himself? Why's he hanging out in the astral? What's he afraid of? Because nobody that powerful and that stifled for so long is going to just idle in neutral."

Herne stared at him. "What did you say?" A light in his eyes told me that what Yutani had said had sparked off some thought.

"I'm just saying, with Typhon's power-hungry nature, why is he hiding out on the astral? If he's so pissed about what happened, you'd think he'd be ripping the world to pieces by now. Is there some reason he's sending his children over in his place? I mean, it could be what you say—he could be going about it subtly. But maybe he actually needs their help?" Yutani frowned, tilting his head. After a moment, he added, "Think about it. When you've slept a long time, when you first wake up, you're just not ready to jump out of bed and go powerlifting or run ten miles. Your muscles usually need some warming up and you have to clear your head."

"You mean...maybe Typhon needs to strengthen himself? Maybe he grew weak over the eons of being locked into stasis?" Herne looked excited. "My father actually has been wondering about Typhon and why he's hiding, too. I need to talk to the others about your theory. Why didn't *we* think of it?"

I stared at him. "Why didn't the gods think of it? I'll tell you why. Because you're *gods*. You seldom feel exhausted or in pain, and when you are, you can usually shake it off. Yutani may have a father who's a god but he's lived his life among mortals, and he's half shifter." What Yutani had been trying to say finally clicked. "Typhon might not be at full power. Now would be the time for you to go after him, while he's weakened."

"*If* he's weakened," Talia said. She had a cautious look on her face. "It's a good theory, but it's just that—theory. If the gods go after him and he's at full strength, then..."

"Then what? They can't die. He can hurt them, but he can't kill them. Just... Oh." I stopped, realizing the folly of my plan. "They can't kill *him*, either. And they don't know how to drive him back into stasis—yet."

Herne grimaced. "Yes, that's our weakness right now.

And a good reason for finding out who actually forced him into stasis in the first place."

"Because they might be able to do so again," Rafé said. "Can't Zeus and Hera just question everybody who was around at that time? What's the issue there?"

"We asked them that," Herne answered. "Apparently, there were several Titans and gods there who have vanished off the map. Nobody knows where they are. And everybody who's been questioned so far seems to have no recollection as to what happened."

"All right, let's focus on what we *can* do," I said. "What's left on the agenda for today?"

"Jana Wildmere will be in at four, and we'll all want to be in on that meeting. Until then, let's get caught up on paperwork, shall we? I'm sorry you're having to work through the weekend, but..." He paused. "Okay, back to your desks. Ember, can I see you in my office?"

Yutani let out a low whistle and snickered. Angel and Talia laughed, while Viktor snorted before heading out the door.

"Oh, shut up," I said, glaring at Yutani. But I wasn't really mad. Herne and I had managed so little time together lately that it felt like we hadn't gotten down and dirty for months.

I followed him into the office and shut the door behind me. He turned, then immediately pulled me into his arms for a long, steamy kiss, his hands smoothing over my back, my ass, my hair. His chest was firm against my breasts, and his urgency caught my own flame. I leaned my head back as he began to trail kisses down my neck, along my throat. The warmth of his lips against my skin fired my senses and I let out a moan. His hair tickled me, trailing to mix with my own, and he pulled me tighter, tugging my shirt out from beneath the top of my jeans and sliding his hands beneath it.

"That feels so good," I whispered into his ear. "Do we have time?"

"We'll make time," he said, his voice ragged.

I turned to lock the door as he flipped off the overhead light, leaving the lamp on his desk on. His office was large, with no window to the outside. A large room painted sky blue with a white ceiling, Herne's office was filled with lush plants, their vines trailing everywhere. A large weapons case sat against one wall, filled with bows and knives and a gleaming sword. A mini-fridge sat on a table along with a microwave, over near a daybed. Herne's desk was dark walnut, gleaming under the lights, and his chair was black leather. Two matching wing chairs sat on the other side of his desk, and two more against the wall by the door. Over Herne's desk was a massive rack of antlers.

After locking the door, I turned back to see him standing by the daybed. He had stripped off his shirt and his chest gleamed, the muscles rippling down to his six-pack. His waist narrowed, and as he stepped out of his jeans, my eyes were drawn to the narrow V leading to his erect cock. He straightened his shoulders, his wheat-colored hair tousled and silken against his back.

"Come here, wench." He held out his arms.

I pulled off my shirt as I crossed the room, unbuckling my belt as I approached him. I shoved my jeans down, kicking them off, and in one fluid move, he caught hold of the sides of my panties and yanked them down. I barely had time to step out of them before he tossed them to the side. My nipples stiffened as the hunger rose within me.

"I need you," I whispered, my voice feeling gravelly. "Take me."

In a blur, he swept me up in his arms and laid me down on the daybed, his eyes gleaming. His lips began a trail down my throat, down to my breasts where he tugged at one nipple with his teeth, growling low in his throat. With my left hand, I cupped my other breast, squeezing hard, while with my right, I reached down, grasping him in my palm. He was hard and firm, pulsing as I held him tight. I reached down to slide my fingers inside me, getting them wet with my own juices, then went back to rubbing his cock again, holding him tight as I slid my hand up and down his length.

"Oh, stop," he moaned. "It's been too long."

"It's been far too long," I murmured.

He lowered his head between my legs and sought out my center, tonguing me gently, swirling around my clit. I let out a squeak, trying to keep as quiet as I could. Of course the others knew what we were doing, but I didn't want to embarrass them, so I bit my lip as he began to bathe me with his tongue, fluttering it back and forth as he slid two fingers inside of me.

Unable to help myself, I moaned. "I can't take it—"

"Oh, you'll take it, and more, my love. You'll take everything I give you." He worked me harder then, grabbing hold of my hips as he ate me out. The tension rose in my stomach. My lips were feeling tingly as I panted. Then, as I began to come, unable to hold back my cries, I grabbed hold of the daybed covers beneath me and let the wave of orgasm wash over me. It carried me up, spinning me around, but before it could subside, Herne was between my legs, driving into me with a fire that only sparked my own hunger more.

He was thick and hard, long and warm, and he penetrated me, pinning me to the bed. I laughed, nervous and giddy and still caught in the throes of my first orgasm. Then, before I could catch my breath, he began to slide in and out, long, smooth strokes. I fell into his rhythm, bringing myself up to meet him. But before I could settle in, he shifted position slightly, driving in at an angle.

Once again, I bit my lip, trying to keep my cries low. But Herne was a god, and as he pressed himself against me, every inch of our bodies met as one. I felt myself losing myself in the passion, losing myself in the rhythm that mimicked the rolling waves of the ocean.

I closed my eyes, all thoughts fleeing as I let go and let the waves of his love sweep me under, tossing me about like a buoy lost in the ocean. A moment later, I began to come again, and I gave up trying to keep quiet and cried out loudly as he stiffened. He dropped his head back and roared. As he came, he looked down at me, holding my gaze.

"You're mine," he whispered, the light in his eyes alien and powerful and terrifying. "You're mine forever and always, Ember. You have promised yourself to me, and you are my kingdom." And with that, he stiffened again, coming hard, and I joined him, my heart singing with joy...and...a little bit of fear.

CHAPTER ELEVEN

I FELT LIKE I SHOULD TAKE A SHOWER AFTER, BUT I DIDN'T want to march naked down the hall to the bathroom. The agency's bathroom had a shower and two toilet stalls in it. The shower was in an inner room in the bathroom. It was small, about five feet by five, but it was great for when we came back from cases covered in mud and blood.

"I needed that," Herne said, wrapping his arms around my waist. He nuzzled my neck, kissing my shoulder. "I love you so much, Ember. And I am so happy you are wearing my ring. You're mine, you know."

"I know. You told me while we were making love." I laughed as I slipped out of his embrace to find my panties and bra. Herne had a possessive streak, but he had managed to get beyond the intense jealousy that had driven me crazy. A little jealousy might be flattering. A lot of jealousy bugged the shit out of me.

"I can't help it." He pulled his shirt on and zipped his jeans. "So, what did my mother say? We haven't had a chance to talk about her visit."

"She was happy—more than I expected. She told me a little about the Gadawnoin. I'm not exactly looking forward to it, but you know…it will be all right. I trust Morgana and she said she'll coach me for it." I paused, then added, "She also said it makes the Cruharach look like a walk in the park."

"You're afraid," Herne said, pulling me to him for a slow, gentle kiss. "You'll manage. I would never have asked you to marry me if I didn't think you had everything necessary to survive the ordeal." He let go and handed me my shirt. As I pulled it over my head, he picked up my jeans and held them, waiting.

I slid into them, zipping them up and buckling my belt, then sat down to put on my socks and my boots. "That sounds so grim. *Survive the ordeal.*"

"You have plenty of time for my mother to prepare you. You won't undergo the ritual until the week of our wedding. So, now's not the time to dwell. We have far too many other things to concern ourselves with." He let out a sigh, shaking his head. "Yutani might be right. Maybe Typhon is weak. But until we have a way to capture him, there's no sense in taking him on."

"Do you have anybody you could send into the astral as a spy?" I asked, pulling my hair back and up into a ponytail.

"Hmm, I hadn't thought of that. I'll ask my father and mother." He motioned to the door. "We'd better get back to work, as much as I'd love to just cuddle and take a nap."

I kissed him again, then unlocked the door and headed back to my office. Angel glanced up and I saw she had her earbuds in. I blushed, but then again, I heard her and Rafé at home, and she heard Herne and me. It wasn't like we didn't know all about each other's sex lives. She caught my gaze, smiled, and gave me a thumbs-up. I winked at her and started to head back to my desk, but she pulled out one earbud.

"Hey, what do you want for lunch? I thought I'd call in an order since we're going to be here all afternoon."

"Tacos sound good," I said.

"Viktor wanted a burrito, so Mexican food sounds like the order for the day." She picked up the phone and I headed back to my office.

I settled in, staring at the mound of paperwork. Luckily, Rafé now was in charge of most of the data entry, but I still had to make notes so he could enter them in the files, and my handwriting had to be legible enough to read. As I picked up the first file, a *ding* announced a new appointment coming through.

A glance at my email showed me that Angel had just made an appointment for a new case. Somebody named Henny Jessaphy wanted to meet with us about a problem with a repeat intruder. Angel had scheduled the meeting for ten on Tuesday. I noted it down on the calendar and was about to dive into documenting some work on a case from last week when my personal phone jangled. Pulling it out, I glanced at the caller ID.

Sharne.

Sharne was my great-uncle, and he had been brother to my grandfather Farthing. Farthing had tried, among other things, to kill me. He was behind the murder of my parents, along with my maternal grandmother. I couldn't get beyond the fact that both had willingly killed their children in cold blood, all because of the war between the Fae.

It would have been different if my father and mother had committed some unconscionable acts, but their only "sin" had been their bloodlines. My mother was Light Fae, my father was Dark Fae, and they had fallen in love. For that transgression, they had paid with their lives.

I had come home from school to find them sprawled out in pools of blood, stabbed to the point of where there wasn't a drop of blood left in their bodies. That had been all I needed to hate both sides of my heritage.

But Sharne had surprised me. I had expected to meet a clone of my grandfather. Other than his looks, I had been pleasantly surprised.

Sharne had welcomed me into his home, and apologized for not being able to stop his brother. We were building a tentative bridge I never thought I'd be able to build, and I was getting used to the thought that at least one family member had a conscience.

"Hey, what's up?" I didn't have to ask—I *knew* what was up, but I'd let him tell me.

"I gather you heard the news?" he asked. He sounded uneasy.

"Yeah, Saílle told me. So, when did you meet... What's her name?"

"Her name is Neallanthra. And I haven't met her yet." He paused. "Just a moment."

I heard him moving around and then when he came back on the phone, there was a muffled sound to his voice.

"I just triggered a magical silence zone—it dampens what I say from reaching any ears that might be listening through magical means. I've already turned the place upside down looking for bugs." He let out a sigh.

"You think Saílle is trying to listen in on you?"

"Well, I didn't until yesterday. After she told me about my upcoming nuptials, I decided I'd better check my apartment and I found one eavesdropping device. There may be more." He sounded grumpier than I felt.

"So, you had no clue you were getting married until…?"

"Last night. The news was delivered by one of her messenger boys. All of a sudden, I'm to be part of the nobility, married off to a woman I've never met. At least the woman's from my home clan—the Orhanakai band."

"I've met them," I said. "When I was in Annwn, we traveled with Unkai and his people for a while. So this happened very fast."

"Right, and I have no clue what brought it about. Saílle has never taken much notice of me."

"I can tell you," I said. Our conversation confirmed what I had suspected since the parley. "Saílle found out that I'm marrying Herne. When that happens, I'm to be elevated to goddess. Saílle's trying to get on my good side, but she must think I'm pretty damned stupid given her clumsy attempts. She tried to drag me into her court before Névé had a chance, but I can only join both courts on an honorary basis. Neither one wants me, but they're not going to let a chance go by to get in good with me before I have the power to smack them flat. So Saílle is using you as a pawn to get to me."

Sharne groaned. "You mean my bachelor days are being sacrificed on the altar of royal diplomacy?"

I couldn't help but laugh. Sharne seemed to prefer his own company to anybody else's.

"I'm afraid so. You know most marriages among the

Fae are made for power and prestige. I *am* sorry you got dragged into this. I imagine she'll treat you right in the court, given she won't want to make me mad. Boy, this must be a thorn in Saílle's side," I said, laughing. "That's the only joy this whole mess gives me."

With a snort, Sharne said, "Yes, I imagine so. Well, let me congratulate you and Herne. And that you'll be safe from both the Light and the Dark Courts pleases me. If I have to sacrifice my single status to help ensure that, so be it. I sure as hell didn't do anything to help you when my brother..." The laughter vanished and I could almost see his face. "I'm so sorry, Ember. I really wish... I just wasn't strong enough to go against Farthing."

I knew that he meant it. "Sharne, it's all right. For what it's worth, I don't think there was anything you could have done to stop Farthing. Even if you *had* found a way, he would have just waited until later, when you weren't there. He was determined to destroy my mother and father. And he tried to destroy me. My grandmother and Farthing were too smart and too cruel, and too determined. You can't fight a force like that. You would have had to kill them both."

Right then, I knew that I was right. No matter what Sharne might have tried, he wouldn't have been able to stop Farthing's plan.

"Thank you. I'll always blame myself. But I appreciate your support. Apparently, you're supposed to escort my blushing bride over to TirNaNog?" He sounded about as enthusiastic as a wet blanket.

"I guess. Saílle hasn't contacted me yet, but I remember her saying something about it."

"Let's talk about brighter things. Say, I wanted to come

visit you, if I could. And the sooner, the better. Do you mind if I drop by tomorrow evening? We can discuss this more then."

I glanced at my calendar. "I'm free tomorrow night, as long as I don't get called out. I want to tell you about a few things, too. There's something going on and I want you to protect yourself—"

"Does it have to do with the vrykos that are running rampant?"

"Yeah. You might not want to stay in TirNaNog…at least on this side of the portal…if we…well, I'll go into it more tomorrow. Come over for dinner? Eight P.M.? Angel will cook." I knew that would win him over. He'd been over to our house a couple of times in the past couple of months, and each time, he'd been won over by Angel's cooking. I thought he might have a little crush on her, but he was polite and kept it to himself.

"Eight it is. I'll see you then."

As I replaced my phone in my purse, Yutani popped his head through the door and startled me out of my thoughts.

"Hey, Ember? Can you come look at something? I need a second opinion."

"Hmm? Oh, sure." I stood, following him into the office he and Talia shared. Talia was nose-deep in research. She had her headphones on, and it appeared that she had been printing out documents she found online. I tried to peek over her shoulder to see what she was researching, but it was all text and no pictures to give me a clue, and by the focused look on her face, I didn't want to interrupt.

"What's going on?"

Yutani pulled a chair over beside his desk and motioned for me to look at the site he had pulled up on his laptop. It was a story about a murder over on Whidbey Island. The victim had been found with marks all over his body in what sounded like an eerily familiar pattern.

I scanned the info. "That reminds me of…"

"Straff?"

"Right." Frowning, I read through the article again. "But he's in Cernunnos's dungeon, I thought. Surely he couldn't have escaped. And Blackthorn is batshit crazy, but not in the same way his son is."

Blackthorn was one of the Ante-Fae, the King of Thorns whose son had committed a series of murders over on the island. We had managed to catch Straff. Cernunnos had dropped him deep in his dungeon for… well…as long as Cernunnos thought he should be there. But the case Yutani was looking at sounded exactly like the one we had faced.

I shook my head. "We might want to bring this to Herne's attention. He can ask his father to check, to make sure Straff's still where he's supposed to be." I paused, then asked, "Do you know if Blackthorn had any other children?"

"I don't remember, but I can check. Maybe Raven knows?"

"Just because she's one of the Ante-Fae doesn't mean she knows all of them. I guess it couldn't hurt to ask, but don't tell her why. We don't want her going over there alone to poke around." I really liked Raven, but Herne was right. She could be reckless at times.

"Raven mostly pokes around where ghosts are involved. And this is a corpse, not a ghost." Yutani let out a sigh. "I think I'd rather be chasing down Straff again instead of dealing with dragons. This is a hell of a mess."

"I know what you mean." I glanced over at Talia, who was still absorbed in her work. "I feel like we've been under a massive weight ever since this business with Typhon started. It's like a rock hanging over our heads."

"The sword of Damocles," Yutani said. "Hanging by a single thread and once that thread breaks, we're so much cannon fodder." He leaned back in his chair, crossing one leg over the other. "So you and Herne are actually tying the knot?" He examined my face with a dark gaze.

Yutani was an intense man, and I could feel the chaos of his father's blood swirling around him. It had grown stronger as time passed. The Great Coyote's magic seemed to fill Yutani's aura and he walked on the path of chaos. Yutani was magnetic, and he ran on a spectrum that I chose to avoid, but there was no denying how attractive he was. But Yutani liked control, and whoever he ended up with would have to bow to his leadership.

"Yeah, we are. I decided that I can handle life as a goddess. Though even the sound of that is so absurd that I still can't quite believe it. Herne's a powerful man, but I often forget he's a god. And now…"

"Now you'll join him in that realm. You're going to kick ass as a goddess, Ember. And I hope to be around to see it." He grinned at me, breaking the mood. "Okay, I'll go show this to Herne. I just wanted to make sure that I wasn't imagining things. I'm not sure what we can do about it, but at the least, we need to make sure Straff is still locked up in that dungeon."

"He wouldn't go back to the same feeding grounds, though, would he? Maybe it's a copycat killer?"

"Could be, but if it's not…" Yutani stood, following me out the door.

I headed back to my office while he went to talk to Herne. I hoped it was a copycat. The last thing we needed was to go up against Straff and Blackthorn again. Once had been enough.

AT FOUR O'CLOCK, we met with Jana Wildmere from the Shifter Alliance. She was a short woman, about five-four, sturdy and solidly built. She looked like she probably was a bodybuilder, but in a weird juxtaposition, she was wearing a short pleated pink skirt, a cream-colored V-neck tank top, a pair of heels that showed off her impressive calf muscles, and her purse was covered with silver sequins. Her blond hair made her look like a short, athletic doll.

"Won't you have a seat?" Herne said, ushering her into the break room where Talia, Yutani, Viktor, and I sat.

Rafé was busy entering data at the desk that Herne had crammed into the storeroom, and Angel was still at her desk. Given Rafé and Angel were in a relationship, Herne had decided it would be better for both if they had some distance between them.

"I'd like you to meet Ember, Yutani, and Talia, three other members of our team."

Jana smiled pleasantly, though there was a predatory air about her. I chalked it up to her being a wolf shifter. They always had a competitive *size-up-the-opponent* vibe to them. I reached out and she shook my hand, then offered her hand to Yutani, Talia, and Viktor in turn.

"Let's get down to business, shall we?" Herne said.

"Yes, please. The council members on the board of the Shifter Alliance are curious as to what this is all about." She leaned back, waiting.

Herne let out a long breath. "You know about Typhon? I assume you were there when my mother and father talked to the United Coalition?"

She nodded, her smile evaporating. "Yes, I was there."

"Well, we've come to the conclusion that, given all the attacks from the vrykos lately, and there are likely to be more incidents in the future, we need resources to fight them. My agency can't take care of every uprising, and the police aren't equipped for it. The mayor agrees that we need a militia we can call on when skeletal walkers or vrykos or zombies are on the move."

A light flickered in her eyes. "I think I know where you're going with this."

"We've already spoken to TirNaNog and Navane and have forged a truce between them for the present. We've also received their permission to call up the Fae militia. We'd like the Shifter Alliance to create a militia and give us access for the same reasons." Herne motioned to Viktor and pointed toward his coffee cup. "Jana, would you like a cup of coffee and something to eat? I think we have cookies?"

"Doughnuts today," Talia said.

Jana smiled at Viktor. "Thank you, yes. With cream." She turned back to the rest of us as the half-ogre crossed to the counter where he poured her coffee and carried both it and the doughnut platter over to the table.

"So, do you think the Shifter Alliance might agree?" Herne asked, pressing gently.

Jana accepted the coffee and took a sip, then set her cup down. "I think we might, though I can't speak with certainty until I talk to the others. I may be the president of the Shifter Alliance, but I'll have to take a vote of the council. But I *can* say that I, for one, will be pressing for a *yes* on this. Typhon poses an incredible threat to everyone."

Visibly relieved, Herne let out a sigh and leaned back in his chair. "I can't tell you how happy I am to hear that. Typhon's the biggest threat to this world right now that I can think of, and we need everyone on board in this."

She arched one eyebrow, turning to Yutani. "Pardon me, I don't mean to be rude, but do I sense coyote medicine around you?"

He shrugged, giving her a long look. "My father's the Great Coyote, and my mother's a coyote shifter. So, yes." He held her gaze and I detected a subtle challenge.

Jana stared back at him, until he suddenly flinched, which was totally uncharacteristic for Yutani. I grinned. He had met his match. Jana was no beta bitch—she was an alpha for sure.

But a smile played over her face as she dragged her gaze away and turned back to Herne. "I'll meet with the council today—I can convene a special meeting under our emergency treaty rules. I'll get back to you with our decision either tonight or tomorrow."

Herne let out a long breath. I wondered if he had expected to have a fight on his hands. "Thank you," he said. "For once, something might go smoothly."

"Just promise my people that we'll only have to deal with the Fae if we're all called out to a fight." She glanced at me and blushed. "I'm so sorry," she said. "I didn't mean…well, I guess I did but I didn't…" Her voice drifted off and she shook her head. "I'm not going to even try to talk myself out of this one. I apologize. I seem to have lodged my foot in my mouth and I really don't know what to say."

I decided that being gracious was more important than being offended. Besides, my own opinion of my people was pretty much at the bottom of the barrel when speaking in generalities. "Not a problem," I said, and the tension faded as we hammered out the details of what we were looking for.

CHAPTER TWELVE

Angel and I were curled up on the sofa with Mr. Rumblebutt, watching a movie and eating pizza when the phone rang. It was Raven, calling my work phone. *Uh oh.* Something was up.

"Raven, are you okay?" I motioned for Angel to pause the movie as I put Raven on speaker. "Angel's listening too. What's up?"

"More than I bargained for. I could use your help."

I frowned. Raven wasn't one to ask for help unless she really needed it. "What's going on?"

"I'm in a bar. I was called out on a case and it's not at all what I thought it would be," she shouted in my ear as the sound of crashing echoed behind her. "Cripes!"

"What the hell? Are you hurt?"

"No. A chair just flew past me, but I ducked. I honestly don't know what I'm dealing with. They thought it was a ghost but I don't think so. Or maybe it *is*, but it's crazy physical and I'm having trouble protecting myself long enough to even set out my gear. I wasn't sure who else to call. I don't think Llew is the best answer." She yelped and I heard another crash in the distance.

"Raven!"

"I'm here. I told you, this thing is getting physical. I can't handle it by myself." She paused, then shrieked and I heard yet a third crash.

"Raven, where are you? We'll be over there ASAP." I motioned to Angel, who had already set down the popcorn bowl.

"I'll text you the address," she said. "If you could hurry, I'd appreciate it." She hung up and I jumped off the sofa.

"Raven's in trouble. She's fighting something she thought was a ghost but it's throwing things around and she's not sure what it is." I punched number 2 on my speed dial and Herne picked up almost immediately.

"Hello?"

"Herne, Raven's in trouble. She apparently went out on a job to clear a ghost or something and whatever the damned thing is, it's throwing things around the room and she's in trouble. She's texting me her address. Can you come?"

"I'm on my way. Text me where to go."

My phone jingled and Raven's text came through. I glanced at the address. It was on the Eastside, so not the Worchester District for once. But it was in the UnderLake District, another hot spot for spooky stuff. Raven *lived* in the UnderLake District, and every time Angel and I went over there to visit, I had the feeling something was watching us as we entered the neighborhood.

I jammed my boots back on, grateful I hadn't changed out of my clothes yet. Angel turned off the TV and made sure the stove was off, then handed me my purse and we headed out to my car. As I started the ignition, I handed her my phone.

"Text the address to Herne, would you?" I thought about calling out the others, but decided that we should wait until we knew what we were up against.

Angel tapped out a text, then snorted as he immediately texted back. "Herne enjoyed this afternoon. Should I answer for you, *sweetcheeks*?"

"Oh good gods, no. Just text him—"

"I'm texting him that it's me who has your phone right now and we'll meet him there," she said. "I'm not about to catfish him." She chuckled as the chime sounded again. "He very politely asked me to ignore his prior message and says that he'll see us over on the Eastside."

I laughed. "Yeah, that's Herne, all right. Pretend it never happened and everything will be all right." I took a right onto West Government Way, following it till it turned into Gilman Avenue West. I followed Gilman Avenue to Dravus Street, where I took a left and headed over the freeway. Once we were in the North Queen Anne District, I navigated to Westlake Avenue North, which took us down to a cross street that led to I-5, and then to the 520 floating bridge.

Traffic was fairly sparse. By the time we pulled off the bridge and turned left onto 116th Avenue Northeast, we had been on the road about ten minutes. Another fifteen minutes of clear roads and we were headed north, near UnderLake State Park. The address that Raven had texted us led up to the north end of the park, not too far from Raven's house. I turned right onto 148th Place and pulled into the parking lot of what looked like a dive bar.

Tracy's Tab was a small hole-in-the-wall tavern that

was one of those bars where you went to get drunk. The outside was nondescript, but the surrounding shops—a tobacco shop and a weapons shop—gave it a distinctly seedy feel and it occurred to me how dangerous it was to have easy access to weapons when people had had too much to drink.

We parked. Herne hadn't arrived yet so Angel and I headed in. I was packing my daggers—sheathed and strapped on both legs—and Angel had done her best to muster up the protection spells Marilee had been teaching her.

As I opened the door and entered, I froze. Angel bumped into me and I quickly stepped to one side. The bar was dimly lit, dark paneling covered the walls, and the booths were covered in a garish red and gold upholstery. But what stopped me was the teetering stack of bar stools that were precariously balancing on one another, forming a tower that almost reached the ceiling.

The stools must have been three feet high each, and there were five stacked atop one another, but they were each balancing on one leg, at a skewed angle that looked impossible to achieve. Another bar stool was upside down, spinning in midair.

Knives were embedded in the walls, and broken liquor bottles covered the floor and counter. One man was splayed flat against the wall, four feet off the ground, his arms and legs spread as if he had been chained there. A look of terror filled his face and I didn't blame him in the least.

Two men and a woman were hiding beneath tables. In the corner near the cash register, Raven was ducking as various items sailed toward her—a glass, a plate with a half-eaten hamburger on it, somebody's purse.

"What the hell?" I said slowly, catching my breath as the purse suddenly switched direction and came barreling straight for me.

Raven let out a shout as I ducked and it bounced off the door behind me.

Angel shook her head. "This is bad, Ember. Really bad."

"Well, it ain't good," I said, trying to pinpoint the source of the energy behind the activity. But the psychic ooze that filled the bar seemed to flow from everywhere, a tidal wave of currents washing over me.

A deep laughter emanated from behind the bar and two more liquor bottles went flying across the room to smash on either side of the man pinned against the wall.

"Damn it, that's my best scotch!" a voice shouted from behind the counter.

The man on the wall said nothing, but I could see his mouth move and I realized that, thankfully, he was still alive. I crouched, scurrying toward Raven, with Angel right behind me.

She motioned to a nearby table. "Grab that and turn it so we have a shield, for all the good it will do."

I managed to grab hold of the table and began to tip it over when something felt like it was grabbing it from the other side and pulling. "Damn it, something's trying to yank it away from me. Angel, help me."

Angel grabbed hold of the central leg and together, we yanked as hard as we could. What ever had hold of the other side let go. We tumbled back, the table almost breaking my foot as it landed on my boot. I groaned, pulling my foot out from beneath it.

"What the hell is going on?" Angel asked.

Raven was keeping a close eye on the objects flying around the room. "My friend Rachel asked me to come over and help her out—she owns the bar. Apparently the past couple days something's been mucking around, scaring the help and the customers. Then tonight, it let loose and she called me. I thought it was probably just some ghost that was pissed off, but this is beyond anything I've dealt with in a while."

"Poltergeist?" Angel asked.

Raven shook her head. "It doesn't have that energy. Poltergeists usually don't manifest with laughter and cursing, and this force has done both tonight. You heard it laughing when—" she paused as a large framed picture tore off one wall and came sailing toward us. We all ducked, hiding our heads as it crashed against the wall in back of us so hard that the pane and glass shattered into a thousand pieces, raining glass and wood. The pieces of glass and wood began to spin, as if caught in a twister, and before I could say anything, the funnel cloud of debris headed our way.

At that moment the door opened and Herne stepped in, right into the path of the debris cloud.

"Watch out!" Raven and I shouted at the same time.

Herne immediately dropped, and the debris paused, raining sparkling shards of glass down onto his back. As he stood, shaking off the splinters, his expression told me he had just joined the fight.

"Fuck this," he said, raising his hand. "Show yourself,

you coward." His voice reverberated through the bar, ricocheting off the walls.

There was a pause—a brief silence during which I felt the energy shift. Something had heard and was accepting his challenge.

"Look," Angel said in a hushed voice, prodding me in the ribs and nodding toward the arch leading to the restrooms on the opposite wall.

There, a crimson glow began to flicker. It wasn't the light of fire or flames, but it sputtered before it grew stronger. There was a thickness to the air that almost made me gag—the feel that if you just opened your mouth, slime would flood your throat and suffocate you.

"What the hell is it?" I whispered.

Raven slowly inched her way up and peeked over the edge of the table. "Holy fuck… Ember, have you ever seen anything like that?"

I shook my head, my gaze glued to the light. It was taking form now, a cloud of crimson mist shaping into a robed figure. All we could see was the flowing cloak and the piercing white eyes from within the hood. It emanated so much energy that my body was tingling, setting the hairs on my arms on end. A current of fear electrified the room, and Herne pointed to the door.

"Everybody who isn't one of us, get out while you can."

The men and the woman hiding beneath their booths crawled out, then scrambled for the door. The man against the wall suddenly came crashing down face first, landing with such an awful thud that I swore I could hear bones breaking. He lay still, unmoving, and I wondered if he were playing possum, or if he was really dead.

"Bring it on," Herne muttered, striding forward.

Raven crawled out from behind the table, following him. "What is it, do you know?"

"A Reaver. They're created by several ghosts that have been merged into one creature. They only appear when there have been a number of murders nearby. The ghosts are unaware of what's happening when they're absorbed." He glanced back at her. "Do you have any War Water on you?"

She nodded. "Ember, my bag's back there. Can you bring it to me?"

I glanced around, my gaze falling on a black and silver bag. I grabbed it up and darted up to her side. "Here. What can this thing do?"

"What *can't* it do?" Herne asked. "But even though they're powerful, they aren't indestructible."

All the while, the Reaver was watching us. As Raven handed Herne a bottle of black water, it streaked past us so fast it was a blur. As I turned, Angel let out a shriek and then stumbled forward, her eyes glowing.

"Die, idiots," she said, holding out her hands. The Reaver hovered behind her and I could see the strings of energy connecting it to her.

"Angel!" As I shouted, a sickly beam of red light flared out of her hands to catch me in the chest. It knocked me off my feet, sending me sailing backward. I spun through the air at least ten feet, only to slam into a table. The force of my landing broke the table beneath me and both I and the splintered wood went crashing to the floor.

Herne snarled and leapt toward Angel.

"Don't hurt her!" Raven shouted. "She's possessed!"

"I'm not going to hurt her," Herne shouted. "But I'm

taking our red-robed friend out." He splashed the War Water across both Angel and the Reaver behind her.

Raven held out her hand, aiming at the Reaver. "Close your eyes," she shouted.

I turned, knowing what she was going to attempt, and hid my face as she began to chant:

Fire of heaven, I call thee down,
from top of cloud to kiss the ground.
Bolts to forks, forks to bolts,
I summoned thee, a million volts.
Strike to true, I set the mark,
jump from heaven, to Reaver arc!

Raven's voice rang clear as the bar began to shake and a swirl of mist and smoke formed. A lightning bolt ripped out of her hands, across the room, to strike the Reaver. There was an electric *snap*, and then the Reaver shrieked and froze into a blackened statue, shattering into pieces that fell to the floor, smoking.

"My bag—there's another bottle—Blessed Water. Sprinkle some on every piece of that thing," Raven shouted, collapsing to her knees.

Herne turned, frantically looking for the bag that I had been holding. I sat up, my entire side aching from having smashed the table.

"Crap, where is it?" Herne scanned the floor of the dimly lit bar.

I caught sight of the bag. "There—over there, beneath that booth!"

Herne dove for it, coming up with the bag. He dumped

everything out on the floor and selected one of the bottles filled with a clear liquid.

"Hurry, it's trying to re-form!" Raven called. She was trying to stand up, but she was covered in soot and looked dazed and confused.

The pieces of the Reaver were sliding toward one another and I realized that it was, indeed, trying to regroup. I tried to stand but something wasn't working right and I realized there was blood on my hands.

Herne managed to get the lid off and began sprinkling the water over the agitated pieces of charcoal. As he did so, they sizzled, snapping and popping like a blown transformer.

The pieces of charcoal began to melt. He pressed on. I made it to my feet and stumbled over to Angel, who was on her knees, shaking her head, looking absolutely bewildered.

"Are you all right?" I asked.

She squinted up at me. "What happened? I don't remember anything from when we first came in the door." She looked over at Raven, then at Herne. "What... did I do something?"

I winced as I tried to help her stand, but I was too sore for her to put weight on my shoulder, so I pulled over one of the bar stools that was now scattered on the floor.

"Here, use this for leverage."

She struggled, but managed to get to her feet. "What happened?"

"That damned thing possessed you and blasted me with a bolt of energy that sent me flying across the room." I winced again.

"Oh crap, oh Ember! I'm sorry—"

"Save it," Herne barked. "Let me make sure I get every piece of this thing. Go see how Raven is." He was peering behind the bar, trying to find any piece of the Reaver that he might have missed.

I groaned, leaning on the bar for support as I limped over to Raven, followed by Angel. Angel helped her stand and sat her down on one of the chairs that was still intact. A moment later, the room suddenly brightened—both in energy and literally as the lights flared up again—and Herne let out a sigh of relief.

"I think I got everything," he said, turning to the three of us. "You look rough around the edges."

"Which one of us are you talking to?" I asked, wincing as my side spasmed. "Oh gods, I hurt like hell. I must have bruised myself."

"All three. Man, you look like you had an all-night bender." He strode over to stand beside us, a worried look on his face. When he turned to me, he blanched. "You're bleeding. Ember, what's going on? Let me see your side."

"What?" I asked, glancing down. And then I saw where the blood on my hands came from. A piece of wood about four inches long was sticking out of my side. "Crap. Herne?"

He examined it. "We have to get you to a medic. Angel, are you all right?"

She nodded. "I feel a little out of it but I'm all right, basically. I'll stay with Raven, you take Ember to the clinic."

"No, you're all coming with me," he said. "Tell the bar owner to lock the front door and don't even bother with anything tonight. I'll check back tomorrow."

Angel trudged outside as Herne gathered me in his arms. "I'll carry you. Just relax."

"I can't do much else." I leaned my head against his shoulder and breathed a sigh of relief as we left the bar. Angel and Raven were talking to someone and then they caught up, Raven walking like she was eighty years old—at least eighty *human* years. We all looked ragtag around the edges, and we smelled like soot.

As Herne maneuvered me into the back seat, then helped Raven into the front, I wanted nothing more than to close my eyes and just go to sleep. With Angel driving my car, we eased out of the parking lot and off toward the nearest urgent care facility. All the way there, I kept slipping in and out of consciousness. By the time we got there, I let myself fall into a deep sleep, and I didn't even feel Herne carrying me out of the car and into the building.

CHAPTER THIRTEEN

By the time I was patched up—I needed twenty stitches, and got a warning from the healer to quit playing vampire hunter, and we didn't correct him—Herne had called for Viktor to pick up Yutani and meet us at the clinic.

"I'll take Raven home first. Yutani, if you would drive her car there, please? Viktor, stay with Ember and Angel until we return. Then I'll drive Ember and Angel home. Yutani, you can drive Ember's car and follow behind. Viktor, meet us at their house so you can take Yutani back home."

It was a quiet ride and I didn't remember much of it. Being slung across the room by the Reaver had not only knocked the wind out of me, but given me a mild concussion. The doctor had said I'd be fine with a good night's sleep, though for the next few days, I was off of active duty—no more bar brawls, whether it be with a ghost or anybody corporeal. I'd split the stitches if I got physical.

The traffic was light and we made good time. Herne

pulled into the driveway, with Yutani and Viktor behind us. Angel asked them all in, which I was fine with—I wasn't capable of playing hostess, but it was nice to feel there were people around who could pull my ass out of the fire. I wasn't sure whether it was the concussion, or the fight, or the energy of the Reaver, but I was feeling incredibly vulnerable.

"We should probably go home and let you sleep," Herne said, but I stopped him.

"Can you stay for a while? You and the guys? I'm nervous."

He frowned. "Of course, love. Here, let me settle you in the recliner. The doctor wants you to prop up for the night."

Though my concussion was mild, the doctor was worried about me throwing up while I was asleep. So he had recommended sitting up on pillows. It would also keep me from stretching my side too much.

Herne lowered me to the recliner, then motioned to Viktor. "The girls are beat. Can you make a pot of peppermint tea? It will clear their heads and also relax them. No caffeine."

Viktor headed into the kitchen. Angel curled up on the end of the sofa, rubbing her forehead.

"I have a massive headache," she said.

"I'll bet Raven does too," I muttered. "Will she be okay? Was Kipa there?"

"Yes, he's there. He'll keep watch over her," Herne said. "He's nervous. Her father's coming to visit next month and you know...meeting the parents. Phasmoria likes Kipa, but she's not nearly as protective as I imagine Curikan is."

"Guess again," Angel said, smiling at Viktor as he brought in a plate of chocolate chip cookies he had found in the kitchen. He started to hand me one but I shook my head. My side felt like I'd been twisted in knots and I was queasy from the pain.

"What do you mean?"

"Phasmoria is incredibly protective of Raven. She just doesn't show it. I get the impression that Curikan is a lot more passive-aggressive." Angel winced. "My shoulders feel like they've been pummeled."

Yutani swung himself behind her. Sitting on the back of the sofa, he straddled her with his legs so he could reach her shoulders and neck. "Let me give you a massage."

She glanced up at him, a startled look on her face, but when he began to rub her shoulders, she closed her eyes and sighed.

"Oh, that feels so good."

"I'm good with my hands," he said, winking at me and laughing.

I laughed back—it felt good to have something to laugh at. But my side thought otherwise, and it spasmed right where the stitches were.

"Damn it, first time tonight I've had a chance to smile and my side goes and ruins it." I shook my head. "Herne, do you know if Reavers are summoned or are they just… Do they randomly form from ghosts in an area? What causes them to come into being?"

"I'm not certain. Raven might be able to tell us, though I don't think she'd even seen one before this. I've dealt with a few throughout my life and they're usually found in areas of tremendous psychic disturbance. I don't think they're actually a creature you can summon, though maybe a necromancer can *make* one, so to speak." He was sitting beside me in an armless side chair, stroking my forehead. "Drink your tea—and water. The doctor warned against you getting dehydrated."

Viktor stood. "I'll get her a bottle of ice water and a straw."

"The bendy kind?" I asked.

"Sure, the bendy kind."

Tears flickered in my eyes and I realized I was seconds away from crying. Everything felt so hopeless and I felt like crap. I gingerly leaned my head against Herne's arm and closed my eyes. He leaned down and gave me a gentle kiss on the forehead.

Angel's phone dinged and she picked it up, glancing at the screen. "Crap, it's DeWayne. I thought I'd managed to shake him."

DeWayne was DJ's father. Angel had refused to tell him anything about DJ, even as to whether Mama J. had borne him a son or a daughter. DeWayne was a mooch and out to get his hands on anything he could.

"What do you want?" Angel wasted no time on pleasantries. She paused, listening, then in a seldom-seen fit of anger said, "Get the fuck out of my life. You aren't even the father. My mother was having an affair and *he's* the father of her child. I know this because she told me."

Another pause and then, "You can believe it or not, but I guarantee you, if you try to make waves, I will hit you so hard you'll end up on your ass in the corner. You're not welcome in our lives, you have no place in our lives, and you can just go scam off somebody else who doesn't know what kind of a leech you are." She hung up, staring at the phone as it rang again. She turned it off and tossed it on the coffee table.

We were all staring at her, but I was the first to speak. "Is that true, Angel?"

She frowned, shrugging. "Who cares? Maybe it will shake him off. He's just so sure that Mama J. left money for DJ and he wants to get his hands on it. I will never let him near my brother. He doesn't give a flying fuck about his kid—he only wants to steal any inheritance that might have been left."

Herne cleared his throat. "Would you like me to look into DeWayne's background and see if I can find some way to put a stop to him bothering you?"

Angel frowned. I knew that she hated to ask for help, but DeWayne had been a thorn in her side for far too long now. "Yeah, could you? I'll email you all the info I know about him."

"Fine. We'll make sure he can't ever bother DJ...but... do you think DJ might ever want to know his father?" Herne asked the question slowly.

But Angel just shook her head. "No. DeWayne was trouble when he was with Mama J. and he's trouble now. He's a lone wolf—rogue from his pack, I believe. I think they excommunicated him and that usually means a criminal record or something equally as bad."

"All right. I'll get on to it as soon as you send me his info." He glanced at the clock. "We'd better get Ember to bed. Tomorrow's a full day, but the two of you don't have to come in until noon, given what you've been through. Ember, if you are still feeling queasy or sick, just call and we'll bring Ashera over here."

He stood. "I'll get you some blankets."

"Thank you. And another pillow?" I paused, then added, "Do you think you could stay the night and sleep on the sofa? I'm feeling so…vulnerable."

Angel glanced over at Herne. "I wouldn't mind if you stayed, either. The Reaver really threw me. I've never… been possessed…before."

"Of course I'll stay." He turned to Yutani and Viktor. "Vik, could you drop Yutani off at home? Thank you both for your help."

Yutani slid off of the sofa from behind Angel. "Better?" he asked her.

She nodded. "Yeah, thank you so much. You really are good with your hands." She laughed. "I'd better not let Rafé hear me say that. He might not understand."

Yutani smirked. "Never hurts to give them something to think about. Anyway, come on, Viktor. Let's head out. I have a program I'm working on that I need to check. I left it running to test it and I want to see what's happened, if anything. I'm working on a way to penetrate the Dark Web with absolutely no trace-back. I have the feeling we may need more access to it as the months go by, and I want to put as many layers between it and my computer as possible."

They headed toward the door. Herne followed them, locking it behind them.

Angel groaned as she forced herself to stand. "I'm going to bed. I need a shower, but I'm too exhausted to stand up."

"Use my bathroom. I've got the walk-in shower with a bench. You can sit down and just let the water stream over you." It sounded good to me, too, but I was too sore and the stitches too fresh to subject myself to a stream of water.

Angel waved, hauling herself up the stairs, holding onto the railing like a lifeline. Mr. Rumblebutt looked confused but decided that my lap would make the perfect bed, so he jumped up onto the arm of the recliner.

"I'll get you a sleep shirt and some pajama shorts," Herne said.

As he vanished up the stairs toward my room, I struggled to sit up and gingerly eased my shirt over my head. My side screamed as I raised my arms, but I managed to undress. By the time Herne returned with my nightclothes, I was sitting in my underwear on the ottoman near the recliner. He rubbed my back with a liniment I had gotten from Ferosyn for aching and bruised muscles, scrupulously avoiding the gash. As he helped me dress, he kissed my shoulders and neck.

"I love you and I worry so much about you. At least, once you're married to me, I won't have to worry about you dying in some godawful fight." He started to wrap his arms around me but then froze. "Crap, that would have hurt. I'm sorry."

I turned around, feeling ragged and sore and ready to cry. "I just need a good night's sleep," I said. "The doctor gave me a sleeping draught that works for the Fae. I didn't want to take it while everybody was here. Can you get me some water?"

He nodded, darting into the kitchen and returning with a glass of cold water. I poured the potion into the glass and then, after staring at it for a moment, I drank it down. Herne tucked me back into the recliner and I leaned back, but was still upright enough so that I wouldn't choke if I vomited.

As Herne bedded down on the sofa, Mr. Rumblebutt rejoined me, curling up on my lap. I closed my eyes, wondering if the ghosts who had once inhabited my house would ever return. This had been a murder house, with a double murder taking place. We had cleansed it and evicted the spirits. But if there were any spooks waiting to pounce, they kept to themselves for the night. I dozed off, thanks to the sleeping potion and Mr. Rumblebutt's churning motor—he kept up a steady *purr-PURR-purr-PURR* until I fell asleep. I slept through the entire night, not even waking once.

By the time I opened my eyes, Herne was gone, and Angel was in the kitchen making breakfast. She must have heard me stir because she peeked into the living room, a smile on her face.

"You need help?"

I started to say no, but as I brought the recliner to an upright position and started to stand, I realized I was sore as shit and that my entire body felt like it had been run over by a semi.

"Yeah, I think I do."

She came over and helped me stand. As I straightened, the stitches on my side pulled and I let out a groan. I pulled up my sleep shirt and took a look. My body had already been bruised up from the last go-round, but now my entire side was black and blue. I couldn't see the stitches—they were under the bandage—but there didn't appear to be any seeping blood, so that was good.

"Let's get this changed and then I'll help you shower and get dressed." She wouldn't take no for an answer, so I let her help me up the stairs and into my bedroom. While she set the shower temperature to warm, I stripped out of my clothes. I felt grungy and grubby and covered with a layer of grime.

"Can you scrub my back for me? I think I'm going to need some gentle stretching for a couple days to get back to full strength."

"A couple of *days*? Woman, you're dealing with a row of stitches and a body covered in bruises. I think it's going to take more than a couple days. Now come on, get in there and sit on that bench." She made me sit on the shower bench. "What 'smell-good' do you want me to use for your back?"

I grinned. That was Angel's term for all the various body washes, gels, soaps, and lotions we had accumulated.

"The wild lilac." I loved the smell of lilacs. While I also liked the scent of roses, lilac was one of the only floral fragrances I liked. I loved the smell of most flowers, but when they were made into a body wash, so many of the floral scents were pungent and unnatural.

She poured a stream of the gel onto the bath poof and gently began scrubbing my back for me as I leaned forward, letting the water stream over my head.

"You'll get wet," I said, feeling a little guilty for needing her help.

"So what? I'm wearing a T-shirt and jeans. I can change." She finished scrubbing my back and then handed me the poof. "Here. I'll just sit on the vanity bench outside and wait for you. I don't want you to get dizzy and fall."

I finished washing, lathering up as she pulled out her phone and began reading a book. I washed my hair, too, and when I finally felt clean, I eased my way out of the shower and she draped me in a large bath sheet. I toweled off, wrapping my hair in a smaller towel, and she examined the bandage, easing it off and grimacing.

"Well, he did a good job on the stitches and it doesn't look infected but dang, woman, that's a nasty gash. That piece of wood hit deep, but at least it didn't hit anything vital." Angel slathered it with the cream that the doctor had given me the night before, then affixed a new dressing over the top. "There. At least you heal fast. I wish I could say the same."

The Fae healed faster than humans. That was yet one more perk we had.

"I'll make it down to the office, though it would help if you drove. I'm not going out in the field today, even if I wanted to." I frowned, staring at the bandage. "I should keep a running tally of all the wounds I've gotten since I started working at the agency."

"Granted, they're worse than before, but you already had a number of scars when you and I came into the Wild Hunt." She followed me into my bedroom, where she handed me a loose gauze sundress. "Here, wear this. It won't irritate your side. If you put on a close-fitting shirt today, I guarantee you're going to regret it."

I nodded, accepting the dress. Angel fastened my bra for me because reaching around my back hurt, but I couldn't go without one because my boobs were just too big to leave swinging in the wind, so to speak. As I pulled the dress, an olive gauzy shift—over my head, Angel found a pair of slip-on sandals.

"You don't want to chance any residual effects of the concussion unbalancing you, so wear flats today." She handed them to me, then began to comb my hair, carefully untangling the wet locks. "Sit in front of the mirror and I'll dry your hair for you."

"Yes, mother hen." But I grinned as I said it. Truth was, Angel was a born nurturer. It struck me that if she and Rafé were ever to have a child, things might be just a little easier on the kid due to the fact that I was setting a precedent with the Fae Courts. Oh, the child would still be regarded as an abomination, but perhaps I could instill enough change so that the bigotry would be lessened by some degree, if only legally.

I closed my eyes, enjoying the play of warm heat as she dried my hair. It was naturally wavy, long to my mid-back, black with a blue sheen in it. My eyes were deep green and I hoped that wouldn't change when I went through the ritual. I still wanted to be me, even if I was a becoming a goddess.

When Angel finished drying my hair, she braided it back for me, tying it off with a pretty bow over the hair tie.

"There, you're set. Well, makeup but...you finish your face and I'll go start breakfast. You call me before you come down the stairs. I don't want you to chance tripping or losing your—"

"Balance. I know." I sighed. "I'm really okay, but yeah, I will call you." I knew she wanted to help. It made her feel good and Angel was the type of person who needed to feel useful.

She hugged me gently, then headed out of the room.

As I sat there, staring at my makeup-devoid face, it hit me once again that I was going to miss these moments. There was something about a platonic close friend—a *best friend*—that couldn't be replaced by a spouse. Yes, most people thought their spouse was supposed to be their best friend, but the truth was that I liked having separate categories. I liked having a best friend who wasn't my lover, and a lover whom I didn't share quite everything with. It felt like it made life more bearable, and by not relying on just one person to meet all my needs, I would never feel totally adrift if I lost one of them.

I glanced over at the sun shining through the window and, trying to shake off gloomy thoughts of death and loss, I quickly finished my makeup and texted Angel that I was on my way down for breakfast.

CHAPTER FOURTEEN

We made it to work by eleven-thirty, and found everyone there except Rafé, who had a dentist's appointment. As we stepped out of the elevator, Talia, who was sitting at Angel's desk, let out a loud whistle.

"Well, thank you, but you've seen me in a dress before," I said with a grin.

She snorted. "That wasn't for you. Herne wanted to know when the two of you arrived." She straightened some papers, then yielded the chair to Angel. "I fielded several calls already. Mostly just inquiries about how much we charge, things like that. Also, one former client who's worried that their goblin problem has returned. I took their name and number so that you can return their call and do whatever it is that you do."

"Thanks," Angel said, sitting down and glancing through the notes. "I'll call them back in a while. Do you know if we're going to have a morning meeting as usual, considering it's almost noon?"

"Herne said no—we'll be meeting with Ashera at four,

and we might as well just use the time until then to get organized and finish up paperwork." Talia glanced over at me. I was slowly headed down the hallway. My head wasn't hurting anymore, but I was still a little dizzy and my side burned. "You really got the stuffing beat out of you, didn't you?"

"Yeah, I did."

Herne popped out of his office at that moment. "Hey, love." He kissed me quickly, but there was a distracted light in his eyes and he looked concerned about something. "Talia, we're having the morning meeting after all. I just learned something that is...rather disconcerting."

I groaned. "We don't want disconcerting. We don't *need* disconcerting. The world is disconcerting enough."

"Toughen up, cookie," Herne said, kissing me again. "I wasn't the one who brought this issue to light, by the way. It was you and Yutani, so blame yourselves."

Frowning—for the life of me, I couldn't figure out what he was talking about—I slowly inched my way to the break room. As I sat down, Talia immediately veered toward the coffee pot. Without asking, she poured me a cup of coffee and brought the cookie tray over to the table.

"I know you probably just ate, but...here." She winked at me.

"Hey, how's that boytoy of yours? What's his name? Tanjin?"

She smiled and that told me about all I needed to know. "He's good. We're good. Nothing serious, but I have to admit, I'm having a lot of fun and he seems to be, as well."

"Are the two of you exclusive?" Viktor asked, leaning

over my shoulder to snatch a cookie off the tray. He gave me a pat on the head. "How you doing today, Ember?"

"Sore but alive. That's the most important part."

"The stitches pulling on your muscles?"

I nodded. "They're right where I bend to the side." I motioned to my waist. "So they hurt like crap every time I turn."

"That sucks," Yutani said, coming into the room. "I'm glad to see you up and around, though."

"Me too. By the way, Herne's blaming you and me for whatever it is he has to tell us." I gnawed on my lip, trying to figure out what it could be.

"Uh oh, that doesn't sound good." He sat next to Talia, who was nose-deep in a magazine that she pulled out of her tote bag. I leaned closer and saw that it was *Dog Health Monthly*.

"Rema and Roxy all right?" I asked.

She glanced at me over the top of the magazine. "Yeah, they're doing fine. I just like to keep up on new treatments for their health and whatever, especially since they're rescue dogs, and greyhounds tend to have a myriad of problems."

When we were all seated, sans Charlie and Rafé, Herne cleared his throat and set down his tablet. "I wasn't going to bother with a meeting this morning, but something's come up that we have to talk about. Yesterday, Ember and Yutani discovered a murder case out on Whidbey Island that sounded suspiciously similar to the ones committed by Straff, Blackthorn's son."

I groaned. "Please don't tell me we're actually onto something?"

"I'd like to just gloss over it, but I can't. I looked into

the case and you were right—the wound marks are all too similar to the murder victims in the Straff case. So I called my father to ask him if Straff was still in the dungeons, or if he has any siblings around."

"And—?" Yutani asked.

"And, turns out, someone helped Straff escape. Since he was in solitary in the darkest, deepest part of the dungeons, there were only a couple staff members who checked on him and brought him his food. Each guard takes shifts for three or four days. So when Tokkberry—the guard who discovered him missing—found out he was gone, he reported it to his commander. The *shoya*—the leader of the prison guards—investigated. Turns out the guard who had been on duty the days prior had vanished, along with Straff. It was an anti-magic zone, which negates personal and innate magic as well, so he couldn't have charmed her. But the pair are gone, and nobody knows where they went. From what we can tell, this happened a few weeks back and nobody thought to tell my father. Heads are rolling, you can be sure."

I grimaced. Knowing Cernunnos, heads could literally be rolling.

Herne shrugged, tossing a file on the table. "We don't know that this murder was committed by Straff, but we can't rule it out. I've alerted Rhiannon to be on watch. She'll keep an eye on the news and let us know if anything further happens."

I stared at the table. Straff had been a gnarly opponent, and his case had been my first realization that punishment in the world of the gods had a very different nature than it did here. The thought that Straff was out in the world again, at large, unnerved me. His father had been a freak. But Straff was psycho-crazy.

"Just what we need. Straff at large again." I glanced over at Yutani, who gave me a faint nod. "Although, given Typhon's nature, I think I'd rather face Straff and his father again."

"Well, that was a good catch, and my father thanks both of you. He's pissed out of his mind and I have no clue what he's going to do now. If he ever finds that guard, I pray she has time to slit her own wrists, because anything my father does will be worse."

The thought of being on the bad side of Cernunnos was terrifying. He was massive, with the primal nature of the forest behind him. It occurred to me that as Herne aged, he, too, would grow into that power. Grateful I'd met him when he was young—relatively—I hoped that I could grow with him once I turned into a goddess, so I wouldn't feel so overwhelmed as time went on.

Herne must have noticed my expression, because he said, "I know, love. And I truly meant what I said. Death would be far preferable to my father's anger over something like this. The forest isn't a gentle place when it's angered."

That darkened the mood of the room.

Yutani cleared his throat. "Do you think we'll end up over there again? On Whidbey Island?"

"I hope not," Herne said. "But I can't promise we won't."

"Wouldn't he get as far away from there as possible, given that's the first place Cernunnos would likely look?" Talia asked.

"I thought that too, but then again, Straff has a disease that drives him to seek energy and blood. His father allowed him to feed on his victims without stepping in. Blackthorn might cover up for his son again, even though he allowed us to drag Straff off without protest." I shook my head. "The island is probably the only place Straff was familiar with."

"It's not that large. Surely we could find him again," Talia said.

"Maybe. But there's something else. Remember, Straff's condition was still in a sporadic stage. The disease hadn't advanced to where he was pushed to kill on a frequent basis. But that doesn't mean it hasn't gotten worse. I wonder if there's a way to contact Blackthorn without going over there. He might give Straff up if he thought his own neck was on the line, and I doubt he wants Cernunnos on his back."

Herne shook his head. "Unlike Raven, Blackthorn's not carrying around a cell phone. He's far more primal. As I said, I asked Rhiannon to stay in touch."

Rhiannon was head of the Foam Born Pod—a pod of waterhorse shifters, or hippocampi, as was their proper name. I had enjoyed getting to know her and her people.

"Okay. Anything else until Ashera gets here?"

"Yes, actually. Rhiannon mentioned they're having another problem now. She wanted to know if we might be able to come over and check it out and I told her we had to see how things were going here. She hadn't heard about Typhon, and actually, her issue might tie into his return. There are unusual goings-on in their compound and she's getting worried members of the Pod coming up to her right and left. I'm going to call her back and ask for more details later—she was on her way out to an appointment when I called her to ask about the murder."

"Does *she* think Straff's back?" Viktor asked.

Herne shrugged. "*That* I don't know. All right, people. Let's get to work. Ember, how's your side?"

"Sore, but manageable. It shouldn't take long to heal. I think the bruises will last longer than the cut, so I'm going to look pretty beat up for a while."

My legs and arms were covered with bruises, as was most of my body. When the Reaver had thrown me across the room, I landed against the edge of the table. Added to the bruises I had from the fight in the graveyard, and I was one walking shiner.

"Take it easy. Hopefully we'll be able to avoid another fight today. I don't think any of us are up to it, to be honest," Herne said. "Physically, I can handle it, but I'm really tired of beating dead bodies over the head. After a while, the gore gets to you, you know?"

"Boy, do I know," I muttered, with Viktor and Yutani seconding me.

We broke up and I headed to my office, where I opened the window to let in the fresh air. My office was four stories above the dumpsters, but that wasn't far enough to avoid the stench of garbage. However, the trucks had been through two days ago, and the air was still relatively fresh. I eased into my chair and turned my attention to the paperwork, sighing.

This was my least favorite part of the job. I flipped open the first file and glanced through it, looking for sections that needed documentation. The "Actions Taken" box was empty. I was supposed to fill out all of the forms the day after we went out on a case, but that seldom happened for any of us. We were just too busy. Rafé could fill in most of the information, but he wasn't there for the fights, and so that was up to each of us.

As a crow cawed outside, followed by the screech of a seagull, I picked up a pen, sighed, and began to jot down what I could remember for the archives.

I HAD BEEN FILLING out paperwork for almost two hours when my work phone rang. I pulled it out and glanced at the caller ID, raising my eyebrows when I saw Eldris's name. So he was actually calling back, was he?

"Ember Kearney speaking," I said as I punched the speaker button.

"Hello, Ember," Eldris said, his voice smooth and sensuous. He was definitely a pretty-boy, charming in a way that was hard to ignore.

"Hey, Eldris, I'm glad you called back. Do you have good news for me, I hope?"

I had already resolved that I wasn't about to strike a bargain with him. I wasn't putting myself in his debt, or within arm's reach of him without a guarantee he'd keep his fangs to himself. Vampires were almost always out for their own agendas.

"That depends. I suppose it could be considered good news, but I'm not envying you the privilege. Dormant Reins, the regent, will see you tonight at ten P.M. in the Catacombs. I'll text you the directions. You and two other members of the Wild Hunt may come, but only the three of you. Dormant will guarantee your safety if you meet me at Wager Chance's office at nine forty-five. I'll escort you to the regent's chamber. *No silver. No stakes. No pointy daggers that could double as a stake.* You bring any one of those and you lose the chance. And I guarantee you, he won't reconsider once he's closed the door. You *will* be patted down." He made it sound like an invitation.

I cleared my throat, trying to focus on what I was saying. "As I figured. All right, we'll be there. Are you coming with us?"

Eldris sniggered. "Me? I'll escort you from Wager's office, but once we're at the regent's door, you go dancing down the yellow brick road on your own, girl. I'll wait and escort you out, but I'm not hitching myself to your star." Even when he was being snarky, he sounded sexy. I hated that I responded to even his voice, but I kept telling myself it was because he was a vampire, and the vamp glamour affected just about anybody.

"All right. See you at Wager's at a quarter to ten. Sans pointy objects and silver." I hung up before he could say anything else. Staring at my phone for a moment until the pull of Eldris's glamour faded, I went to tell Herne.

"WHO'S GOING WITH US?" I asked.

"You're not going." Herne shook his head.

"I *have* to go or my guess is Eldris won't follow through. I'd suggest Yutani. He knows how to approach this, where Viktor might get in a snit or something. Yutani plays with one foot in both shadow and light. He understands the vamps and their customs." I eased myself into one of the leather wingback chairs in his office.

"I don't want you down there, injured as you are."

Herne stood, crossing his arms across his chest. "That's all there is to it."

"Beloved of mine, get it through your head. I don't go and I doubt Eldris will lead you anywhere but to the exit." I wasn't quite so sure on that, but we couldn't afford to take the chance. "Ask Yutani. If he says he thinks I can skip the meeting, I'll stay home. If he says I need to go, then you have to quit bitching about it."

Herne let out a little huff and I thought he was going to argue some more. Instead, he walked over to the door to his office, opened it, and shouted, "Yutani, get your ass in here."

A moment later, Yutani appeared, looking worried. "What have I done now?"

I laughed. "Nothing, but Herne and I need you to settle an argument. Eldris called. Dormant Reins will see us tonight. Eldris wants us to meet him at Wager Chance's office at a quarter to ten. He'll lead us to the regent's chambers. Herne doesn't want me to go. *I* think I'd better go. What do you think?"

Yutani rolled his eyes. "More testosterone wars? Dude, I get it. You don't want Ember there because she's your fiancée and you think that Eldris wants to play hoochie with her coochie—"

"No, that's not the reason!" Herne's mood seemed to be shifting from bad to worse. "Or at least, not most of the reason. I'm worried about her wound. She'll still smell of blood and you know what the smell of blood does to vampires."

I blinked. I hadn't even thought of that aspect. "I'll wash and wear strong perfume."

"She has to go. I told you, I know Eldris a little too

close for comfort. He has his eye on her, you're right about that. But he won't make a move if I'm there with her. And he won't cooperate if she's not there. Just put it this way: If he can't buy, he likes to window shop."

Yutani turned back to me. "But Herne makes a good point about the smell. Even the scent of disinfectants and ointments point to a wound, and a wound means vulnerability. Tonight, I suggest you wear a strong spice-based perfume. Also, wear something that gives you side support so you don't twinge. One of your corsets would be a good idea, but cover up your shoulders and neck with a jacket."

"That works for me." I turned to Herne. "Are you okay with that?"

Grudgingly, he nodded. "Fine. But you better douse yourself to high heaven with that perfume." He glanced at the clock. "Not long till Ashera shows up. Let's get back to work until then."

He grazed my lips with his, then turned back to his desk. Feeling summarily dismissed, I turned to go. Yutani walked me back to my desk, and the only thing he said was, "Typical."

CHAPTER FIFTEEN

At four p.m., right on the dot, Angel escorted Ashera into the break room. The rest of us were there and waiting with the exception of Charlie, who was busy with an online class. Rafé was taking notes.

Standing over six-three, Ashera was lean and slinky, with pale skin that had a faint cerulean cast to it. Her hair tumbled down her back, the color of dawn when the first tinges of light illuminate the morning. Around her head, she wore a silver circlet, which I remembered from our first meeting, but this time she was not dressed in a flowing gossamer dress. Instead, she wore a white sundress splattered with a blue and purple hydrangea pattern, and white wedge sandals that boosted her height even more. Her eyes were the palest gray I had seen, and her lipstick was pale pink. She looked like she had stepped right out of a fairytale.

"Good meet, Sister Water," she said, addressing me first. "I trust you are well?"

I smiled, rising as gracefully as my injuries would

allow. "Ashera, it's good to see you again." Ashera was a blue dragon, connected with the water, and that had forged a connection between the two of us since my Light Fae side was Leannan Sidhe, one of the Water Fae.

Herne stood, also, as did Victor and Yutani. "Welcome. Please have a seat. Would you like anything to drink?"

She held up her cold cup. "I have lemonade, thank you. One of the delights I've discovered since coming into your world."

Viktor pulled out her chair for her and she settled herself gracefully at the table, greeting everyone with a smile and a nod.

"So," Herne said after all the niceties were out of the way, "you said you have important information to share with us?"

Ashera nodded. "I didn't want to broadcast this over the phone since you never know who's listening and I know these devices aren't foolproof. As you know, a group of us who are the Celestial Wanderers and Mountain Dreamers have gathered over on Bainbridge Island. We're one of a number of such groupings who have chosen strategic spots around the world in order to keep watch as the Luminous Warriors arrive. The Luminous Warriors are, almost to a dragon, in league with our father, Typhon."

Yutani cleared his throat. "Would you mind clearing something up for me?"

"What do you want to know?" Ashera asked, accepting a cookie from Talia, who passed her the tray.

"Your father—Typhon—did he sire all the dragons? I mean, are you all his actual children?"

Her eyes grew wide for a moment, then a look of

understanding crossed her face. "Oh! No, Typhon isn't my *literal* father. But he is the ancestor of us all—Typhon and Echidna were the beginnings of the Dragonni. So, in essence, we all bear his blood. But the first hatchlings—there were sixteen of them, a pair to each color. And Echidna cast a spell that they would breed true and free from genetic issues that often plague inbreeding. So, while all blue dragons spring from the original pairing, we evolved and mutated over the years. If you were to test our DNA, there would be differences."

"Magical genetics?" Talia asked.

Ashera nodded. "Echidna was brilliant. She had an eye for the future. She and Typhon fought tooth and claw over many an issue. Echidna believed in evolving, in cooperation and diplomacy and compromise. Typhon had his sights on conquest and keeping the status quo."

It was hard to know what to say to that. But after a moment, Angel asked, "What happened to her? We know what happened to Typhon, obviously."

"Echidna vanished, shortly after Typhon was driven into stasis. Nobody knows where she went, but we always keep hope that she might return one day and lead us against the Luminous Warriors. We wish she could return and take up the throne, as a good queen should." Ashera's expression grew dreamy, and it occurred to me that was one thing that the dragons lacked.

Oh, the Luminous Warriors followed Typhon, but there was no true monarch, no true council. The Dragonni were a race without a clear leader. That made me sad. It was hard to live under a leadership you hated—under someone who was a despot.

Herne cleared his throat. "I wish for that, too. Very much. She seems to have been an extraordinary woman...dragon..."

"*Queen*," Ashera said, smiling at him. "I suppose, there is always hope. Anyway, to matters today. I wanted to tell you about a dragon who has been spotted around Seattle. I believe he's the one responsible for the vrykos rising. And we think this is happening all over your country, if not the world. You see, the shadow dragons have a firm grasp over the dead. And one in particular has been seen in your city. He's dangerous. I remember him from before we came through the portal, back in the Forgotten Kingdom. His name is Gyell."

She pronounced it with a hard "G."

"Gyell? Would he possibly be working with white dragons?" I asked. "We saw Aso and Variance out at the graveyard, loading the vrykos we hadn't managed to destroy into a van."

"Yes, from our network we've been developing, we found out the three of them are assigned to the Seattle area. They're all dangerous, all deadly, and Gyell is an ancient dragon compared to most of us. He's cunning and brilliant, and he's ruthless. Aso and Variance might as well be common thugs compared to him." Ashera shuddered. "The white dragons act pretty much as the brawn for the red and shadow dragons. They seldom rise to prominence. My guess is that Pandora was put in charge of all three, and she and Gyell are most likely the ones hatching the ideas."

I let out a sigh. Pandora, again. Part of me had ridiculously hoped she had gotten bored and meandered off.

Last we saw her, we had been out on Mount Bracken, rescuing Raven from her clutches. The goddess, a wayward daughter of Zeus, had chosen to throw her lot in with Typhon. She had proven a sadistic and ruthless servant for the Father of Dragons.

"Do you have any idea where Pandora escaped to? She's not on the mountain anymore," Herne asked.

"She's not? You checked?" I asked, swiveling to look at him.

"Yes, I checked for my father and mother. Pandora packed up and got her ass out of there after we found her." Herne frowned.

"Pandora has moved into the Seattle area, so she's hiding out somewhere. We aren't sure where. She's very good at keeping out of sight." Ashera sighed. "She'll rear her head again soon enough."

"The murders she was committing seem to have stopped," Talia said. "At least, we aren't getting any more reports. That doesn't mean she's no longer targeting necromancers."

Ashera gracefully crossed one knee over the other. "My thoughts are that they've moved onto bigger plans. But think about this: They could be flushing out those who work with the dead. Who else would you call to combat an army of ghosts and vrykos and zombies?"

A light went off over my head. "Bone witches, necromancers...mediums."

"Right. And when you engage them to help you, it makes it easier for Aso and Variance to pinpoint those you've called on. They can then target them at leisure, while disrupting the town with the creatures that Gyell's set free. Two birds. One stone." Ashera shrugged.

A knot in my throat made it hard to speak. We had called in Raven to help, and she had already been under Pandora's thumb once. Would they be targeting her a second time? Add to that, Pandora knew where Raven lived, so it wouldn't be hard to find her.

"We have to warn Raven," I said.

Herne gazed at Ashera, a contemplative look on his face. "I have another question and maybe you can answer it."

"I'll be happy to help, if I can."

"What's Typhon's end game? That's one thing none of us can figure out. It can't just be domination or he would have sent the Luminous Warriors in force, to drive the world into submission already." Herne shook his head. "The gods have discussed this ad nauseum and we can't seem to come to a consensus."

Ashera smiled, then, and a cold light filled her eyes that made me shiver. "We captured one of the shadow dragons who's high up in the ranks of the Luminous Warriors. After we found out what we wanted to know, we stripped his memory and sent him back. The other side will find him, and he won't be able to tell them anything. By the marks on his body, they will assume he had an accident that left him wounded in both body and mind."

The room seemed to darken. The strength behind her words made me feel very much like a dust speck next to her. It was as though her true nature—her dragon self—filled every inch of the building and beyond. And at that moment I realized that, one of the Celestial Wanderers or not, Ashera was far more than deadly.

"What did you find out?" Yutani asked, and even he seemed subdued.

"Typhon isn't out to kill the mortals of this planet, but to enslave them under his rule. Even in stasis, while he slumbered, images and information from the outer worlds crept in, and he watched as civilization evolved. There's much that could benefit the Dragonni, including melding magic with technology. And with so many people…let's just say the food supply is far more likely to support a larger dragon population." She shifted uncomfortably.

I took a breath, not quite understanding what she was saying.

But by the look on his face, Herne did. "Then it's worse than we feared." He pulled out his phone. "I need to text this information to my father and mother, so they can pass it on."

"What are you talking about?" Angel said. "What's this mean? My stomach feels like I swallowed a rock, and my psychic alarms are screaming."

Rafé looked worried, leaning over to stroke her arm. She gave him a wan smile as Viktor cleared his throat and turned to her.

"If I am hearing right, Typhon intends the mortal population—I assume humans, Fae, and Cryptos all inclusive—to become the food supply for a large and robust dragon community."

Ashera nodded, a grim smile on her face. "Yes, that's his plan. To take over this world, and to enslave humanity —Cryptos included—for work and for food."

I started to say *You have to be kidding me*, but the words died on my lips. She wasn't kidding. Typhon saw the world as one big hors d'oeuvres platter for the Dragonni. The old *Twilight Zone* episode—"How to Serve Man"—came to mind and I cringed.

"So, throw the world into panic, and when we're steeped in chaos, come in and take control?" Herne asked.

Ashera nodded. "Yes, that's about right."

"Question: If Typhon is so powerful, why's he hanging out in the astral realm right now?" Yutani asked.

"That I can also answer. Thousands of years in stasis has weakened him. He needs to regain his strength. Until then, he's vulnerable. That was another thing I wanted to tell you. Herne, if the gods go up against Typhon soon, they may be able to defeat him. Typhon is a Titan, yes, but if you can weaken him even further, perhaps you can find a way to permanently disable him. The Titans can't be killed, but they *can* be hurt. The Celestial Wanderers and the Mountain Dreamers will do everything they can to help you." Ashera leaned forward. "We would like to ask you to find Echidna. If you can find the Mother of Dragons, she will stand with us. She alone, of all the dragons, has the same strength as Typhon. At least when she vanished she did."

Find the Mother of Dragons? I blinked. "How are we to find her, if her children don't even know where she went?"

"You have the power of the internet. You have the power of worldwide communication at your fingertips. We can tell you everything we know about her, and maybe you can find out what happened to her." Ashera opened her purse and pulled out a thumb drive. "This has everything we have been able to dredge out of our memories, and from the LoreKeepers, who are our oral historians."

Herne looked at the drive, then slowly picked it up. "We'll do what he can." He handed it to Yutani. "You and Talia, get started on this. Meanwhile, Viktor, contact our informants and set them in search of Pandora, but warn them to hang back, avoid catching her notice, and to be careful. Pay them overtime and stress the need for secrecy."

"What should I do?" I asked.

"Warn Raven. Tell her what's going on. If she takes on any cases, she needs to verify who's actually offering her the job. Also, tell Kipa, but no one else. That way, she won't just think we're being overprotective."

"Will do." I leaned my elbows on the table. "Ashera, what's the name of the dragon network you guys have formed? What should we call you? Just referring to the 'Dragonni' relates to all the dragons, and we can't just say 'the good dragons'...that sounds ridiculous."

Ashera laughed, her voice musical. "We call ourselves the Spiral Web. The dagoids are such beautiful webweavers and they work as a hive mind, which is what we're trying to do—weave a web to trap Typhon as we work together."

"What's a dagoid?" Angel asked.

"In the Forgotten Kingdom—the kingdom of the Dragonni that exists beyond the mists, on the other side of the astral realm, in another physical world much like this one—there are spiders that are the most beautiful creatures you've ever seen. They have eight legs, like spiders here, and an exoskeleton, but they also have an internal skeleton, and they grow to about three feet in diameter. They're golden and white, with black tiger markings, and while they are poisonous, they're also intelligent, so they can be reasoned with. *Sometimes.* They live in the woods surrounding Miareta—the city of the Dragonni."

Visions of a vast city rose in my mind, and I wondered, did the dragons live there in their natural form, or in their shifter form? "If you don't have your queen, who rules?"

"A council—the Star Dragonni. They're descended from the Celestial Wanderers but somewhat different. They evolved into...think of a hologram in your world, but give it intelligence and vision and the ability to move about."

"Like a spirit?" Angel asked.

"Not exactly. The Star Dragonni exist between worlds, like ghosts, but they aren't just spirits. They're pure energy. They make up our Council. There are six of them, along with one dragon each from the Celestial Wanderers, the Mountain Dreamers, and the Luminous Warriors. Which means, the Luminous Warriors are almost always overruled when it comes to decisions. That's what drove them to move to their own city in the Forgotten Kingdom. They seldom even bother addressing the Council of the Dragonni now." Ashera paused, then laughed lightly. "And now you know much more about my people than I had intended, but no harm, no foul, no damage."

The last thing I wanted to meet was one of the dagoids, but I appreciated the fact that the Spiral Web took their name from one of nature's architects.

"If you have no more questions, I should be off. I have to return to the island tonight. We're meeting again to discuss—among other things—this meeting I've had with you today." As she stood, Herne and the other men stood with her.

"Thank you for being so open with us. We need all the help we can get," Herne said, holding out his hand. She extended hers.

Ashera regarded him solemnly. "You *do* need our help, and we need yours. Together, perhaps we can stave off the worst of the damage."

A vision of the future rose up in my mind, with humans and Crypto alike enslaved, forced to work for Typhon, and forced to die to feed the hungry dragons.

"Ashera," I said before she turned away. "We've established that the Luminous Warriors will eat humans... but...what do *you* eat? And the other dragons who make up the Celestial Warriors and Mountain Dreamers?"

She paused for a moment, then said, "Blue dragons eat mostly fish and seaweed and, of course, human food when we're in our *shiftings,* as we call our human shapes. We also gain a certain amount of energy from being in the water. All dragons gain sustenance from eating large animals—or small, though something like a dog would be a snack. Silver and gold dragons can gain energy from being under the stars or the sun, respectively. Green dragons gain energy from the forests—from living among the trees. Black dragons are able to breathe in life force from being underground. Red dragons from being near magma or large fires, white—from the upper reaches of the world where the air is thin and the snow is deep. And shadow dragons, from the underworld."

"So, humans, for example, would fall under the..."

"Large animal category. One of the reasons that the dragons are not nearly as numerous as we could be is the lack of food in the Forgotten Kingdom. There is food to go around, but we have kept to a strict protocol when it comes to laying eggs, and there are a number of hoops to jump through in order to be permitted a birthing license. But here..." She ducked her head. "Here, we could breed without end—humans breed so quickly, there would be an unending supply of food. Yet, regardless of that temptation, the Celestial Wanderers and the Mountain Dreamers do not yield. We will not help the Luminous Warriors enslave you, nor will we feed off your kind unless it's in self-defense."

With that, she turned and left the room. Angel silently followed her out to unlock the elevator for her.

I stared at the table. Typhon's end game could spell the end of life as we knew it. If we didn't stop him and the Luminous Warriors, we'd all be under enslavement and we'd not only provide free labor, but our very lives for the Dragonni's continued existence.

"What do we do?" Talia asked. She stared at the table, unmoving. "Even when I had my powers, the harpies were never this deadly. We preyed on people, I admit that, and as a harpy I ate more than my share of..." She paused, looking miserable. "As a harpy, we fed on humans as well. But we never set out to enslave them."

"Ogres seldom forage for humans, though I won't say that's never happened." Viktor rubbed his temples. "Herne, when will you tell the others about this? They need to know."

"I texted my mother and father while we were sitting here, but I'll go...I can't tonight, we have to meet Dormant Reins in the Catacombs. I'll go tomorrow. Ember, will you and Yutani do the intake on Henny Jessaphy?"

I nodded. "Yes, of course. When will you leave?"

"After we talk to Dormant Reins, I'll go. This will take a little time. I'll text for Morgana to gather the gods to meet at dawn." He looked preoccupied. "All right, back to work. Given the severity of the issue at this point, I think we need to devote most of our time to finding Pandora, Gyell, Aso, and Variance. Also, we need to start the search for Echidna and find her, if at all possible."

"Since she disappeared about the time Typhon was forced into stasis, there's a good chance she knew how he was defeated," I said.

Herne nodded. "Yes, I've thought of that. And I'm sure Ashera's thought of that as well. All right, we should get busy."

As we broke the meeting, Herne gently embraced me, taking care not to hurt my side. "I'm afraid we don't have time for an afternoon tryst, my love. And with your side..." He looked pained. Herne was lusty and passionate, and I knew that days without sex wore on him, probably more than they did on me.

I kissed him back, lingering in his embrace. "I know. It may be several days. But when we do, it will be all the sweeter. At least, it helps to think that way," I added.

He laughed, patting my ass. "I love you, wench."

"I love you, rogue."

And with that, he went back to his office and I returned to my desk.

Sharne was supposed to come over for dinner at eight, but I didn't think that with meeting Dormant Reins at ten, I would have time. I put in a call to my uncle, asking if he could reschedule and come over the next night instead. He agreed, and I went back to my paperwork, my thoughts replaying the conversation with Ashera over and over. The gloom was thick, and I wanted nothing more than to go take a dip in the ocean to wash away the tainted film that Typhon's looming presence had spread across the entire world.

CHAPTER SIXTEEN

I STARED AT MY CLOSET, WONDERING WHAT TO WEAR.

No silver. Keep my throat covered. Something a little sexy, but not too inviting.

Also, I had to douse myself with perfume to cover the smell of the wound. Feeling like this was just a little too complicated, I steeled myself and flipped through my clothes. One dress would have been good, but it was too short for my comfort level, at least among a bunch of vampires. Another was a little too tight and would be hard to run in. Then I remembered Yutani's advice and brought out a leather corset top that I could zip up the front, and a pair of nice jeans. I paired them with knee-high boots and my leather jacket.

Angel had me sit at the vanity while she brushed my hair into a high, tight ponytail, fastening it with a gold band. I had cloisonné combs that I fixed on the sides, and then I put on my makeup, going heavy on the smoky-eye look and cat wing eyeliner. As I picked up my bottle of

Autumn—a spicy-scented perfume—I motioned for her to stand back.

"You might want to stand downwind," I said, laughing, as I began to spray it on thick. After a moment, I smelled like I'd walked through a fog bank at a fragrance counter. I coughed, wrinkling my nose. "How do I smell?"

"Like you spilled a bottle of perfume all over you." Angel waved her hand in front of her face. "But I doubt if they should be able to smell the blood beneath that."

"Good." I draped my purse over my shoulder, after sorting through it to make sure that I didn't have any pocket knives or anything else in it that would be objectionable. "Okay, downstairs. Herne and Yutani will be picking me up soon."

Angel made sure I made it down the stairs without problem. I wasn't as woozy or as in as much pain as I had been during the morning, but I was still leery. The stitches pulled, but I could tell the most immediate pain of the wound was starting to die down and Yutani was right, the corset helped shore me up.

"I think I'm on the mend. Thank gods I heal quickly." I sat down at the kitchen table to wait. "Got any cookies?"

"We're out, but I made scones. You want one?" She moved toward the fridge.

I shook my head. "No, I wanted something lighter. A few chips, maybe?"

She brought over a bag of Fritos and set them on the table, sitting down beside me. "I wish I healed up like you do. I'm black and blue from the gym. My trainer is teaching me how to street fight—you know, down and dirty. It goes against my nature, but I think, as I take on more responsibility with the Wild Hunt, I need to get over it."

I nodded. "I have a feeling that eventually Herne wants to move you into more of an investigative position, while letting Rafé take over your job. While he has the advantage of strength, you have the advantage of your empathic abilities, and coupling that with the magic you're learning, you'll be a lot of help."

"I never believed I'd be saying this, because the thought scared me shitless last year, but I think I'm going to enjoy that. I don't like facing down ghosts or other critters but I have to admit, it's nice feeling like I can contribute more than just typing up reports or making appointments." She popped a handful of chips into her mouth. "Yum, fat and salt. I'm PMSing horribly."

"I don't envy you that." Among the side effects of the herbal birth control that Ferosyn had given me was the fact that my periods were much lighter and lasted only a couple days. The herbal concoction I took once a month also reduced PMS to where it was almost nonexistent. I wondered if it would work for Angel. She couldn't take the pill due to nasty side effects, so she had to rely on other methods with Rafé. "What if I ask Ferosyn if the Monthly-Eeze that he gives me would work for you?"

"Hey, if it won't hurt, I'm willing to try it." She glanced out the window. "I think Herne's here."

"Nine-fifteen, right on the dot. That will give us time to get downtown, park, and meet Eldris. I wish to hell that I could take something to protect me against vampire glamour. I hate being attracted to someone whom...I'm not attracted to, if you know what I mean. It feels all date-rapey, to be honest. And I'm sure the vampires make full use of that with people they're attracted to."

"That's a question I wondered about. If they use their glamour to lure someone in, is that considered rape under the law?" Angel asked.

"I think one of the women's rights groups is spear-heading a proposed law about just that. Right now, it's only if they go for blood. The United Coalition still leans heavily in favor of men, but I know several groups are working to change that too." I stood as the doorbell rang. "Okay, I'm off. Don't wait up. I don't know how late we'll be." As I headed for the door, Angel followed. She saw me off, and then shut the door behind her.

Herne kissed me, then looked me up and down. "That's a good look on you. I like the leather corset," he said, his eyes shining.

I could tell he was turned on, and I grinned. "You want me to wear it more often?"

"Only if it's comfortable," he said, but the gleam in his eye said otherwise. He opened the door for me and I slid into his SUV. Yutani was sitting in the back seat, staring at his tablet. Both of them were wearing black leather jack-ets, dark jeans, and no-nonsense button-down shirts with ties.

I pointed to Yutani's tie. "Going for formal, are we?"

"Yeah. The regent makes Eldris look like a schoolboy. Unfortunately, from what I've been able to read about Dormant Reins, he's a hard nut to crack. And he prefers dealing with men over women."

Frowning, I shrugged. "Par for the course. I assume he'll have bodyguards there?"

"No doubt. And possibly, his wife."

As Herne turned on the ignition, Yutani brought up a picture. "Here she is." He handed the tablet over the back seat to me.

I glanced at the image. Beneath the photo was a caption that read: EMELIA REINS, WIFE OF DORMANT REINS. The woman in the picture was striking. Her glamour came through the photo loud and clear. She wasn't what I would call classically beautiful. If anything, she was more along the lines of what they used to call a "handsome woman" rather than pretty. Tall, with a smooth retro-flapper haircut that would now be called a euro bob cut, her hair was smooth and black and precisely razored so every strand seemed to be in place. Her eyes were wide and eyeliner made them wider, and her bowed lips were colored with a matte black lipstick. She wasn't curvy, but instead looked more athletic. She was wearing a long dress, red and black with a sequined diamond pattern.

"She reminds me of the 'it' girl from the old glamour girls of the early cinema days." I handed the tablet back to Yutani. "She's a vampire too, I gather?"

He nodded. "No vampire that I know of would even think of marrying a living woman. Vampires are fairly strict about interacting with their own kind. It's both cultural as well as practical. You can have human concubines, but wives? Vampire only. And they have both written rules and a host of unwritten ones that go with every aspect of belonging to the Vampire Nation. Woe to those who decide to disregard them."

"Charlie would never make it up the ladder, would he?" I asked. Even though he was far more sophisticated now than when we had first met him, Charlie didn't have the heart to live within the confines of the Vampire Nation and we all knew it. Most of all, Charlie knew it.

"No, he wouldn't. We've talked about that a few times," Herne said. "He recognizes that he may have to harden himself a little to interact with the VN, but he realizes that he's just not cut out for the life style. It would be far worse if he wasn't part of the Wild Hunt. He belongs with us. Without us, he'd be a rogue, on his own, and that's never good when you're a vampire. Too easy to slip into madness as the centuries go by."

I thought about Charlie, and how he'd been so geeky and lost when we first met him. In the space of a year, he had turned his life around and he seemed truly happy.

We arrived near the entrance of the Catacombs that was closest to Wager Chance's office. Raven had told us about it. As we stepped out of the car, Herne set the alarm on the vehicle. It would take a picture of anybody trying to break into the car, as well as sound an alarm.

We entered the Viaduct Market—years ago it had been called the "Pike Place Market"—and headed through the throng of evening shoppers. The market was open until midnight most nights, but we were headed toward one shop in particular. An art studio that catered to nobody. There were always a few students in there, but Raven had told us they were shills, fronts so that the studio seemed on the up-and-up.

Herne led us up to the woman behind the counter, who glanced up from her magazine with a bored expression, smiling a fake smile.

"Yes? May I help you?"

Herne leaned on the counter. "Hi, Vivian. I'm Raven's friend, and I run the Wild Hunt Agency. Did she call?"

Vivian dropped the smile and stood. Even from across the counter I could feel the magic tingling around her. She nodded and pulled back the curtains that were covering the doorframe behind her.

"Take the elevator and press S2, for 'Sub-Level 2.' If you're not back before midnight, you'll have to use another exit." She held up her hand before we swung around the counter. "Raven asked me to give you these. I trust her. Don't make me regret that trust." She handed over three keycards with the name "Art Shack" stenciled on them. "Next time, just show these to me and you can go through without a problem. But I need your names so I can log them in."

"Ember Kearney," I said, and she took my picture with a digital camera, then typed in my name next to the photo and the number of my corresponding badge on her computer. Herne and Yutani followed suit before we headed through the curtains.

We found ourselves in a small alcove with a door to the left, and an elevator straight ahead. Herne punched the button and the elevator doors opened. He tapped the S2 button and the car began to move.

A moment later we came through the doors and found ourselves facing a sign on the wall that read S2-SECTOR 6. A sign to the left read S2-SECTOR 5, with an arrow pointing left. A sign to the right read S2-SECTOR 7, with an arrow pointing right. We turned to the left.

Without the signs, we would have gotten lost within minutes. The Catacombs stretched out, a vast labyrinth below Seattle, and they interwove and interconnected in dizzying loops.

Sub-Level 2 was oriented toward tourism. We passed a

branch of the Vampire Nation Worldwide Financial Institution, or VN Worldwide for short. There were restaurants geared toward tourists, given vampires didn't need to eat food, though they could if they wanted to, and souvenir shops, along with clothing boutiques and shops of that sort. We passed through the wide corridors, skirting groups of humans, Fae, and vampires alike. This level of the Catacombs was relatively tame. It wasn't till you descended farther into the labyrinth that the danger for outsiders grew.

We received a number of looks, but nobody approached us as we neared shop 223—Wager Chance's place of business. As Herne opened the door, standing back to let me enter first, I felt a sense of relief. I hadn't realized that the Catacombs made me feel that tense, but apparently they did.

The walls of Wager's shop were painted in a pale cream and muted sage. There were three rooms to the suite, and we found ourselves in the reception room. A bell on the desk instructed clients to ring it when they entered. Herne did so, and one of the other doors immediately opened.

Wager Chance stepped out. He was around five-eight, with hair as black as mine, and eyes as green as mine, but his skin was a rich golden hue, and he was wearing a pair of jeans, a sportscoat, and a lightweight sweater beneath the coat. Wager was half Dark Fae and half magic-born, and like me, he was considered a tralaeth.

"Herne, Ember, Yutani, welcome to my humble shop." He looked relieved to see us. "Eldris is waiting for you."

I frowned, starting to roll my eyes, but Herne

squeezed my elbow and I plastered a smile on my face. "Hey, Wager. Thank you."

"You can use my office. I'll just wait out here." He seemed more than eager to avoid joining our discussion.

We filed into his office, and sure enough, there was Eldris. He looked every inch as handsome as he had the last time we had met. Long blond hair flowed down his shoulders, his blue eyes so sharp that it felt like they could look right through you, and his lips were full, showing just the tips of his fangs. He had a trim but athletic body, and he wore the same outfit I had remembered: leather pants, no shirt, a tangle of gold chains around his neck, and a salacious grin on top of everything.

"Ember, you're looking lovely," he said, making it sound as dirty as anyone possibly could. He arched his eyebrows and grinned.

As he held out his hand to me, totally ignoring Herne and Yutani, my stomach lurched as his glamour hit me full force. I forced myself to stand still—I wanted to squirm—and accepted his handshake, pulling my hand back as quickly as I could without being rude. He held my gaze for a moment, then turned to Herne.

"So, you are the illustrious Herne I've read so much about?" Again, he reached out, though this time, I noticed his handshake looked firm and professional. Damn him, he really was trying to make me as uncomfortable as possible.

"Eldris, thank you for meeting with us." Herne's voice took on a hard edge, and I knew he was responding to what he saw Eldris doing to me. "You know Yutani?"

"Yes, we've met. This time, you're not holding Ember's leash, are you?" Eldris said, sliding his gaze back to me. "I notice a piece of jewelry I didn't see before," he added, pointing to my finger. "Who's the lucky man…or woman?"

Eldris knew perfectly well that I was Herne's girlfriend, but he was still pushing the boundaries.

"You know perfectly well that Herne and I are together. And yes, Herne's my fiancé."

"Congratulations," he said, laughing. "Well, then, you're here to see Dormant Reins. I'll take you to meet with him in a moment. First, I must examine you all to make certain you are carrying no weapons, no silver."

We agreed, and he subjected us to a pat down, though Herne glowered the entire time Eldris had his hands on me.

Then, when Eldris stood back, suddenly the lecher was gone and he was all business.

"The do-nots, first. Do not move quickly around the regent. Do not address him as anything but 'Regent Reins.' Do not speak first—wait for him to speak. Do not threaten him. And an extra piece of advice that I'll throw in free, and you would do well to heed my words—even *you*, Lord of the Hunt," Eldris said.

"And what would that be?" Herne asked.

"Be cautious asking favors of the regent. There's always a price, and usually a steep one, and once a bargain is struck, it's expected that you will fulfill your part." Eldris looked at me. "Also, as much as I enjoy toying with you, Ember, for me it's a game. But the regent entertains little regard for women. I advise you to let Herne handle the details of negotiation. The only woman the regent listens to is his wife, and the Queen."

He stood, leading us to the door. We passed into the

waiting room, where Eldris nodded to Wager as we left the office. I gave Wager a little wave. With a look of relief on his face, he shut the door behind us as we left.

"ARE you taking us to the regent's office?" I asked as we followed Eldris down the hallway. We were heading for an elevator, and as we entered the car, he pressed the button marked S4.

"No. I'm taking you to a conference room. No one ever enters the regent's private offices unless they are part of the Vampire Nation." Eldris glanced around Herne, who had placed himself between the vampire and me. "Ember, I know you're a strong-willed woman, but let me give you some advice, and I mean this in all sincerity: Do not, under any circumstances, correct the regent. He has a short temper and very little time for those who offer unrequested advice."

I glanced at Herne. "I'll let you speak. Why did you insist I come, when you knew the regent doesn't care for women?" I asked Eldris.

He smirked. "I enjoy your company?"

Herne gave him a steely gaze.

Eldris cleared his throat. "All right, then. No jokes. The regent may not care for women but he needs to know that you speak for the Wild Hunt. He needs to know that if it's necessary, you can command authority for your agency."

He fell silent as the elevator doors opened and he led us out. We were on sub-level 4, at sector eight. He turned to the right, leading us toward sector nine.

The fourth floor had a different feel. There were fewer

shops here that catered to the living, more clubs and bars, few restaurants. There were still clothing stores and boutiques, but I also saw a number of kink clubs and they didn't look as wholesome as those aboveground. In fact, the energy that oozed around this floor was slimy and damp, like a slug when you accidentally stepped on it barefoot. I shivered, drawing closer to Herne, who started to put his arm around my waist then stopped as I let out a moan as his fingers closed over the wound.

Eldris noticed. I saw him glance at me, then at Herne, then back at me. But he said nothing, just adopted a faint smile and turned back to the hall. We paused in front of a plain door with "4-A52" stenciled on it. Eldris tapped on the door and a slot at eye level opened. A moment later, the door opened.

There, guarding the opening, was a large, burly guard. I could tell he was a vampire—his eyes were shining and the tips of his fangs seemed unusually long, extending along the corners of his mouth. He was joined by a second man, equally as large and threatening. The first guard motioned to me.

I glanced at Eldris, a question in my eyes.

"He's going to search you." Eldris looked half delighted, half nerve-wracked. That the owner of Fire & Fang looked nervous was enough to make me skittish. But I had no choice, and Herne was here. So I stepped up, expecting to be patted down.

Instead, the guard pulled out a metal detector and wanded me. He stopped by my corset top and my coat. The wand beeped.

"Zippers," I said.

He ran the handheld gadget around me and it beeped

in all the right places, apparently, because he nodded and moved on to my boots, which also beeped at the grommets for the laces, but he ignored that. After a moment, he nodded for me to stand to the side.

When he had finished scanning Herne and Yutani, he looked at Eldris. "Wait for us in the lounge. I'll notify you when it's time to retrieve them." The bouncer nodded to the nightclub across the corridor.

Eldris's smooth demeanor vanished and he gave the bouncer a single nod before turning away and heading across the corridor.

The bouncer glanced at the three of us. "The regent awaits. Follow me."

And so, falling in behind him, with the second guard behind us, we followed the vampire into the lair of Regent Dormant Reins.

CHAPTER SEVENTEEN

THE FIRST THING I NOTICED WAS THAT THE ROOM WAS brighter than I expected, especially compared to the dim corridors of the sub-level. An overhead crystal chandelier illuminated the small but elegant chamber. It looked well used—rooms often had an abandoned feel to them when they weren't used very often.

The floor was a black and white checkerboard, and the walls were a pale gray with black trim. In a totally non sequitur way, it reminded me of a retro diner. But instead of booths and a kitchen and the smell of food, the conference room was set out like a living room, with a black leather sofa, chrome and glass tables, several wing chairs matching the couch, and a desk to one side, with a rolling office chair behind it. The desk was neat, with a laptop on it, what looked like an appointment book, and a landline telephone. For a moment I was surprised, but then I realized—we were several floors below the surface. Cell phones might not get such great reception here.

A man sat in one of the wingback chairs, his knee casually draped over his other leg. He was wearing a designer suit—I couldn't tell what label, but there was no mistaking the quality of the material. He was sturdy, though not husky in any sense of the word. *Athletic* would be more appropriate. And his coppery-colored hair was shoulder length, pulled back in a neat ponytail. With a chiseled jaw and eyes that were almost turquoise, he was a striking man. The two guards moved to flank his sides as he motioned for us to sit on the sofa.

"Lord Herne, you honor me with your visit. I am Dormant Reins, regent of the Vampire Nation, the Pacific Northwest Division." He glanced at Yutani, nodded, then his eyes slid over me and passed on without acknowledgment. Part of me bristled, but given the immense sense of power behind the stare, I was almost grateful to be ignored.

"May I introduce my fiancée, who is also an agent with the Wild Hunt, Ember Kearney." Herne seemed determined that Dormant give me some sign of recognition.

Dormant shifted just slightly enough to signal to me that he really didn't want to respond, but he inclined his head. "Ms. Kearney."

I wasn't sure what to say, so I stuck with the familiar, "How do you do?"

Herne slid in immediately, saving me from trying to make small talk with the vamp. "And this is Yutani, another one of my agents."

"Yutani, welcome to my world." Dormant motioned to one of his guards. "Drinks." He turned to us. "What will you have? My bar is stocked with just about anything you could hope to order."

Herne answered for all of us. "Café mochas would be good. We're on duty, so we'll forgo the alcohol."

Dormant snapped his fingers and the guard immediately disappeared through the door. My guess was he was headed across the corridor to the club that Eldris was waiting in.

"So, what might I do for you?"

Herne cleared his throat. "I assume you are the local liaison with the United Coalition?"

Dormant shook his head. "My right-hand man is. Elliot Cordova. Why do you ask?"

"Did he fill you in on the situation with Typhon?" Herne went straight to the point, which made me breathe easier. I really didn't feel like hanging around here any longer than we had to.

"Yes, I know about the Father of Dragons." Dormant's eyes narrowed. "What of him?"

"We are trying to create a united militia. The dead are rising, and not in the way of your people. I know this might be a delicate subject, but—" Herne paused as the guard returned, carrying a tray with three to-go iced mochas, and one glass that looked like it might be bourbon or scotch. He held the tray out to me first and I took one of the mochas, murmuring a thank-you. Herne and Yutani followed suit, and then Dormant accepted the glass.

He raised his glass. "Here's to dispensing with pleasantries. Be blunt, Lord of the Hunt. It's better to state the facts than tiptoe around them and risk miscommunication."

Herne saluted him with the glass. "Thank you. All right, someone has been raising the dead in the form of vrykos, and we also know that there have been incidents with skeletal walkers, ghouls, and an inordinate amount of ghost sightings. I don't know if we've seen zombies yet, but they're sure to come. Typhon is waiting in the astral, sending in his emissaries. Did you hear about the incidents with Pandora?"

Dormant sipped his drink, then contemplated his glass for a moment before speaking. "Yes, actually. I have my finger on the pulse of most of what goes on in this city. I heard about that, I heard about the serial killings, and of course, the incidents of the other day were broadcast far and wide. I saw your press conference with the mayor. What do you want from the Vampire Nation?"

"We've made arrangements with the Fae Courts and the Shifter Alliance to outfit militias to help tackle the problem with the undead. Humans can't handle them—not without weapons. And bombs and hand grenades aren't the answer for crowded city streets." Herne shrugged. "So we come to you, seeking a similar agreement. We realize that vampires cannot come out during the day, but we're wondering if you can create patrols to walk the city at night, to help keep the rising dead at bay. And if we need reinforcements at night, to help back us up in case of a fight. The police were forced to stand back and let us take care of things since they weren't prepared."

Dormant took another sip of his drink. "So you want a vampire militia? Who would have authority to call them out?"

"The Wild Hunt, or if something should happen to us, then Mayor Neskan. But most often, it would be me. This would cover the entire greater Seattle metropolitan area." Herne paused, then added, "You said to speak bluntly.

This would go a long way toward cementing relations between the city and the Vampire Nation. And I know there are several vampire rights issues that are floating around the political arena. This might be a good boost toward passing them."

The regent smiled, looking even more fierce than when he was stone-faced. The tips of his fangs appeared at the corners of his mouth, but instead of feeling pulled toward him, I felt terrified. Vampire glamour could be used in a multitude of fashions, and he obviously wasn't trying to charm us.

"You make an excellent point. Very well, I'll give the orders and contact you when we're ready." He straightened up, uncrossing his legs. Motioning to his guard, he set the glass on the tray and stood. "If that's everything?"

Herne looked as surprised as I felt. We had discussed the possibility of rejection, or of the regent stalling us, but we had never expected an immediate agreement.

"You're agreeing?" Herne blurted out.

"Of course. It makes sense and, as you say, it would show...that we're *good neighbors*. Now, if you'll excuse me, I'll begin work on this tonight and contact you within a couple of days. Expect a call from me by Thursday." He turned to the guard who was still holding the tray. "Fetch Eldris and see them safely out." And with that, he followed the other guard out of the room.

"Wait here," the guard said, carrying the tray with him as he headed to the door. As soon as he was gone, I turned to Herne.

"Can you believe that went so smoothly? Do you think it was too easy?"

Herne shook his head. "He might be many things, but

from what I understand, once he makes up his mind, that's the end of a subject. We'll have the vampire militia working with us, and I suspect it will be far sooner than we expect. Now, quiet until we leave the Catacombs."

The guard returned at that moment, Eldris behind him. Eldris motioned for us to follow him and we retraced our steps. Within ten minutes, he had led us back to the elevator leading to the exit through the art studio.

He turned to us before we stepped into the elevator. "You must have impressed the regent. The guard told me that Fire & Fang is receiving a bonus from the VN, which means things went well and I'm getting a commission out of it."

I glanced at Herne, who shrugged. Turning to Eldris, I said, "We came to a mutual agreement, yes. Thank you for playing intermediary."

Eldris smiled then, once again the glamour hitting me full force. "You're welcome, Ember. Any time. And whenever you feel the need for a jaunt on the wild side, you know where to find my club." Before Herne could warn him off, the golden-haired vamp turned and vanished into the crowded corridor. We silently rode the elevator up to the main level of the Viaduct Market and, given it was barely eleven, managed to leave the way we had come, through the art studio.

When we were on the streets, I took a deep breath, holding the fresh air in my lungs. Regardless of what anybody said, vampires made me nervous, and I suspected one day, we might regret letting them into the United Coalition. But for now, they were acting as allies, and we needed all the help we could get.

THE NEXT MORNING, I headed out back while Angel was fixing breakfast. We had both gotten up early. I slept like the dead, which surprised me after the meeting with Dormant, and woke up with my side aching far less than it had. Angel changed my bandage for me, and the wounds were starting to heal quickly, though I was still a mass of bruises.

I was wearing a loose shift again, to avoid pinching the stitches with a waistband, and a pair of flat sandals as I walked out to our side yard to check the kitchen garden. The tomatoes were ripe and hanging on the vines, the lettuce was growing like weeds—everything was flourishing. The mums were starting to flower, though the roses were almost done for the season.

I made my way over to one of the benches and sat down, breathing in the early morning air. A light breeze fluttered past, tossing my hair in its wake. I closed my eyes and tilted my head up. The sun had already risen, but it had yet to heat up the day. Light clouds drifted through the sky, a blur reminding me of a wide jet trail. But there was something beneath the August morning—something that I usually didn't feel until later in the month. There was the slightest tang in the air, a faint prescience of autumn, still distant, but it was a hop and a skip beyond the horizon, warning me that it was on its way.

A crow landed on the bench beside me and I reached up to touch my crow necklace Morgana had given me. It signified our bond, and I wore it like an amulet. The crow let out a caw, then hopped closer, staring up at me.

"What is it? Do you have something you want to say to me?" I very slowly held out my hand. The crow regarded it for a moment, then hopped on. I held my breath, waiting, but it seemed comfortable. After a moment, I raised my hand, trying to hold it steady, and the crow remained perched on my palm. As I brought it to eye level, it met my gaze and then opened its beak and let out one raspy *caw* and flew away. I watched it go, wondering what that had been all about, as the crow circled me three times and then flew over to perch in the oak.

"Breakfast!" Angel called from the sliding glass door.

I gave the crow one last look, then headed back to the house.

FIRST AVENUE WAS HUMMING when I pulled into the parking garage. Angel had left a few minutes before me so she could stop and pick up a package that the Parcel Service Unlimited—PSU—had inexplicably refused to deliver. As I made my way to the office, all around me were buskers and jugglers, streeps playing guitar and street artists. It was then I realized that it was Urban Street Fair week, and all over the city, artists of all sorts were hustling their services and wares.

I stopped to listen to a girl who couldn't be more than fifteen as she sang a traditional Celtic ballad, and her voice was scintillating. Pulling out my wallet, I tossed a fiver in her guitar case and smiled, waving as I moved on. She waved back, and I wondered who she was and where she lived. I didn't recognize her, but the streeps came and went, a continual flow of all ages.

Some slept in the alleyways, some in flophouses run by slumlords who turned over the beds on a shift-by-shift basis. Others chose to live in the tent cities that lined parts of the freeways. The city was beautiful—but Seattle was like a jewel surrounded by a tarnished setting, the grace and elegance of the port city glossing over the underside where the poor had no place to live, and even grandmothers were turned into beggars, asking for handouts because there weren't enough jobs or affordable housing. But a fraction of the streeps were actually happy in their life style, and they tended to gather in the downtown area, forming a culture of their own.

I passed through the throng on the street, carefully dashing up the steps to the door of our building. As I pushed through into the hallway, the noise miraculously vanished. The building had been soundproofed long ago. The landlord might not be fully on top of things, but he had built an accessible ramp up to the building, and the elevator seldom broke down anymore.

As I stepped into the waiting room, I saw Talia behind Angel's desk. She gave me a cheery wave. "Did you see the crowd out there? It's like a party."

"It is, in a way. Remember? Urban Street Fair Days? That's this week." I glanced around. "Angel still not here? We took separate cars."

"Nope, she hasn't come in yet. Herne's been here and left again. Yutani and Viktor are waiting in the break room. Rafé called, he'll be in when he can. Herne sent him on a post office run and there's a huge wait because there was a bomb scare and the police are just now clearing the area."

"Bomb scare?" I froze. We had been through far too many bomb scares with the Tuathan Brotherhood.

Talia picked up on my thoughts and shook her head. "Random psycho, false alarm. They caught the guy and they're just checking to make sure that there really isn't any bomb. But since he's down there with all the packages, Rafé didn't want to come all the way back, just to have to go again later." Talia glanced at the calendar. "Remember, Herne has to meet with the mayor this morning, so you and Yutani are supposed to do intake for the Jessaphy case."

I nodded. "She's coming in at ten, right?"

"Right. So it's up to you to run the staff meeting as well." Talia paused as the elevator opened and Angel appeared. "Here she is. Why don't you head to the break room and I'll lock up and we'll meet you there."

"Sounds good," I said. Slinging my purse over my shoulder, I headed toward the break room.

"LET'S SEE." I looked over the notes Herne had left for me, scanning the checklist. "Henny Jessaphy will be here at ten. Yutani, you and I will field that one. How are the research efforts on locating Echidna? Anything new?"

Talia glanced at her tablet. "We've uncovered a few things. Legends have it that she vanished shortly after Typhon was put into stasis and the dragons driven into the Forgotten Kingdom. She was last to go—she was actually working with Gaia at that point to corral Typhon, a little-known fact—and it's unclear where she went.

There's no record of her being consigned to the Forgotten Kingdom like her children."

"Hmm...all this took place near Greece, right? Because...well...Olympus and the Greeks and all that?" I asked.

Talia snorted. "And the Greeks...and all that. Right. Remember, that's where I hearken from, missy." But she was laughing as she scolded me. "Honestly, nobody's quite sure where the actual battle against Typhon occurred. It might have been Greece, it might have been somewhere else in Europe...who the hell knows at this point."

"Gaia...wouldn't Gaia have information on all this? Why can't the gods just go ask her?" As far as I was aware, Gaia was still aware and active.

Talia shook her head. "No, they can't. For one thing, the Titans...well...they aren't like the other gods. They were primal forces, embodied into form. Gaia is literally the soul of the planet, and when she takes form, it's for appearances only. She doesn't act or think like the rest of the gods at this point. Same with the other Titans. Every one of them is a primal force, and every one of them is so far away from humanity—or the gods they engendered—that you can't predict how they'll act when approached."

"Which means, we can't have Herne just ask her to meet with the gods and grill her on what she remembers from that time period." I sighed. "Is there any way of contacting her? I suppose that's a question for Herne to look into."

"Yeah, because none of us is going to be the best choice for that investigation." Talia shrugged. "We think Echidna left Earth after Typhon went down, and after her children were banished."

"But you're not sure?"

Talia shook her head. "No, we're not."

"Maybe she went into hiding?" I frowned. "Think about it—she helped trap her husband. She helped drive her children out. Maybe she decided that the day might come when she would be needed again."

"You mean she might be hiding out in some ancient cave? Or someplace like that?" Yutani scratched his chin. "I suppose she might be. We can run a search on any mentions of dragons over the past few hundred years... see what we come up with. A number of dragon sightings will just be hallucinations or maybe large birds or something like that, but it can't hurt to look."

"I'll get on that as soon as the meeting is over, while you and Yutani talk to the new case." Talia jotted down a few notes.

I looked at Herne's list again. "All right, let's see. Oh!" I jerked my head up. "Angel, this is for you. It seems Herne has located where DeWayne is and he's going to pay a call on him today on his way back from the mayor's house."

Angel giggled. "Hopefully, that will be the end of DeWayne bothering DJ and me."

"I hope so," I said, glancing back at the list. "Other than that, Herne says he'll be back around lunchtime and he's bringing lunch today, so don't order anything." I leaned back. "So, Yutani and I went with Herne to see the vampire regent last night. Surprisingly, Dormant Reins jumped on board immediately with the idea of a militia. So we're waiting for a call from him—he said he'd call on Thursday."

"How were the Catacombs?" Talia asked.

"Spooky, as usual. Dormant is an efficient man...

vamp…I'll say that much for him." I glanced at the clock. It was eight-thirty. "Yutani, meet me in Herne's office a few minutes before ten. Until then, back to work, everybody." And with that, I ended the meeting and headed back to my office to face the never-ending pile of paperwork that just seemed to grow and grow.

CHAPTER EIGHTEEN

It felt odd, sitting in Herne's chair, behind his desk, though I rather liked it. There was definitely a "seat of power" placement to the desk and the chair. Yutani pulled one of the wing chairs over beside the desk and took my usual spot, taking notes while I talked to Henny Jessaphy.

As Henny entered the room, escorted by Angel, I sized her up. She was strong, short, solidly muscled, and by the scent that filled the room, I realized she was a very nervous skunk shifter. She blushed, groaning as she sat down.

"I'm sorry. It's not my retaliatory scent, but I know it's still unpleasant." She didn't even try to cover up the fact that she was the reason for the pungent odor filling the air.

Angel quietly turned the air cleaner up to high before retreating through the door.

"Don't worry about it," I said, standing to hold out my hand to her. "We know it's just a natural response." Privately, though, I was wondering how she could hold a job with such an uncontrollable problem. But she answered that, as though she were reading my mind.

"Most skunk shifters have their scent glands altered so they only keep the defensive mode ones. But I chose not to. My scents are part of who I am, and there's a large movement among younger skunk shifters to keep the glands intact instead of deactivating them."

"Well, either way, welcome to the Wild Hunt," I said, sitting back down. Yutani gave her a graceful nod as I glanced over the file that Angel had given me. "You're here due to…I'm not exactly sure what's wrong. Why don't you tell us? And do you mind if I record the meeting, for clarity's sake?"

She shook her head. "Please, feel free. The problem is that my husband and I run an urban farm. Our whole family works on it, and we make a decent living selling our eggs and honey and artisan goods. However, something's been messing with our chicken coop and also, we think, our beehives, during the night. I'm not sure what's going on. The chickens have stopped laying eggs, the bees seem agitated, and we're worried they're going to fly off and create a new hive."

"Problems with the neighbors?" Yutani asked.

She thought for a moment, then said, "No, we haven't had any squabbles with the neighbors. I can't find anything that points to what's going on. No dead birds, no tilled-over flower fields… We had the vet out to check out the chickens and physically, they're fine. I bought an alarm for the coop. It's gone off several times, but each time, we can't find anything there. As far as the bees go, they've been testy lately and honeybees are usually sweethearts. They won't bother you if you don't hurt them, and we've only ever gotten a few stings and those were our fault."

I frowned. "How long has this been going on?"

"For several weeks now. At first, I thought maybe that it was just something in the air—you know how sometimes things just get off-kilter, but they usually self-correct. This hasn't."

I glanced over at Yutani. "What do you think?"

"We could check it out this afternoon—at least have a cursory look."

Henny looked so relieved that I decided we needed to at least try to help her.

"All right. Give us your address. We'll need a retainer if we take the case, but I think we'll just start by charging you our usual service fee. We'll come out to look over the situation and see if there's anything we can actually do. If we take the case, then we'll talk about a retainer." I glanced at the clock. "Are you amenable to us coming over to your house now?"

She nodded, looking so grateful that it gave me hope. We might not be able to solve every case, but we could at least solve some of the world's problems.

"All right." I buzzed the intercom and asked Angel to come in. She did and I handed her the intake form. "Can you please take a service fee from Ms. Jessaphy? Yutani and I will be heading out to her place to look over her problem, and if we think we might be able to solve it, we'll talk about a retainer."

Angel took the form from me. "Herne called. He wants you to take care of anything that comes up. He's still bringing lunch but it will be a little later."

"Sounds good to me. Ms. Jessaphy, please follow Angel

to the front desk. We'll meet you in the waiting room in a few minutes. Angel, text us her address, if you would." As Angel led Henny out of the room, I turned to Yutani.

"You have any clue of what it might be?"

He shrugged. "It could be anything from a goblin to a ghost. You should remember from your freelance days that goblins are notoriously tricky and clever. They're talented at avoiding security cameras."

"Yeah, I do remember that."

Goblins were members of the sub-Fae, and they were supposedly banned from entering Seattle city limits, but that was a hard law to enforce, given how tricky they were. They, along with most other forms of sub-Fae, weren't welcome in either TirNaNog or Navane. They were trouble all the way around, nasty creatures who had the decency to melt when you killed them. I never figured out what it was about them, but every time I took down a goblin, their bodies began to decompose at such a rapid rate that within less than fifteen minutes, you wouldn't have known they had been there, except for a pile of goo.

I slid into my leather coat—it might be August, but if we ended up in a fight, I didn't want more skin exposed than necessary. Wearing a light shift dress wasn't ideal for the work, but the wound was healing enough that I could probably get away with pants by tonight.

"You want me and Viktor to check this out?" Yutani asked as he watched me. "I don't want you getting hurt. Herne would flatten me if you got injured again before you've even healed up from the last go-round."

I frowned, considering his offer, but my ego wasn't having any of it. "Nope. I'm going. If anything, I should leave you here to research with Talia, and take Viktor with me."

"Come on, knucklehead, let's get a move on," he said, laughing. He shook his head. "But if you end up in the hospital, I'm dropping the blame entirely on you."

Sticking my tongue out at him—Yutani was starting to remind me of the brother I never had—I followed him out the door.

HENNY JESSAPHY HAD an urban farm on the northside of Spring Beach, near the Sound. It was a beautiful spread—five acres that reminded me of a park. As we drove past her house down the graveled drive, I saw that it was a sprawling ranch. A moment later she parked by what was obviously the chicken coop. It was fenced in, with a large yard for the chickens to roam around in. But even in the sunshine, the chickens seemed skittish and as we watched them, they kept stopping their feed to look around, as though some noise had startled them.

Henny sat on a nearby bench made out of a half-log. She pointed to the gate. "You can go in there. I'll stay back. I don't want to make them nervous with too many people in the coop at one time."

We started by circumnavigating the coop from the outside, looking for any breeches, holes, or any other entry that would allow something to enter the perimeter, but there wasn't a break in the fencing. Not even a tiny one. Everything looked sturdy and well-mended.

As we started to enter the coop proper, the chickens began to clamor and run around our feet. They didn't seem to have any particular place they were going, but then one of them—a big, fat, white hen—came waddling up to me and promptly perched on my feet.

I stared down at her, and she looked up at me, and oddly enough, at that moment, a crow came swooping down out of the trees and landed on the edge of the henhouse, cawing at me. I stared at it for a moment, then slowly reached down to pick up the hen, not quite sure if I was holding her right. But she didn't struggle as I nestled her in the crook of my arm.

"So, what's wrong, chickie?" Slowly sitting down, I stared down at the beady little eyes that looked up at me. She looked almost as though she trusted me.

Yutani snorted. "Made a new friend?"

"She's trying to tell me something. I know it, but I don't speak...chicken." I looked up at the crow, who was still perched on the eaves of the coop. "Hey, do you know anything about this?"

The crow let out an echoing call, and then—before I could set the chicken down—I found myself standing in the yard of the chicken coop at night...

...The chickens were restless, unsettled on their nests. I could see them from where I was standing, through the mesh door that was open to let the cool night breeze sweep through. The entire area around the coop felt unsettled, and I could sense something creeping around the edges. It was dark and squat, and angry. Oh, so angry. Whatever it was, it couldn't overwhelm me like many of the creatures I had encountered.

I stared at the water trough where the chickens drank and suddenly it clicked. There was a tiny water spirit in there—one of the Water Fae, and she was sitting on the edge of the trough, sparkling blue in the dark of the night.

Kneeling beside her, I smiled. "Hello, my Water Sister."

Startled, she looked up at me. "Oh! One of the Leannan Sidhe." Her voice was melodic, faint like a tinkle on the wind.

"Well, yes. I am part Leannan Sidhe. And you are—a naiad?"

She shook her head. "I'm a Nixie."

I froze. Nixienacks were nasty creatures, but then I realized she had said "Nixie" and that was something entirely different. Nixies were water creatures, as opposed to carnivorous little sub-Fae.

"You live in the chickens' water trough?" That seemed like a pretty poor excuse for a home.

"I watch over them. I like them."

"Then can you tell me what's bothering them? I sense something out here that's very angry. I'd like to chase it away, if I can figure out what it is."

The Nixie clapped her hands and laughed. "There is something here, and if you could dispatch it, my feathered friends and I would be most obliged. It doesn't bother me, because it can't, but it's upsetting the chickens and the bees. It's a Gilding and it lives behind the coop in the thicket of ferns." She flew into the air and buzzed around my head, landing on my shoulder. "Thank you, in advance."

And before I could answer, I opened my eyes and was back in the yard, staring at the water trough, and it was midday.

"WHAT'S A GILDING?" I asked Yutani.

He frowned, watching the crow as it rose from my shoulder and flew away. "A Gilding? Is that what you think is bothering the chickens and bees?"

I nodded. "Yeah, the Nixie told me." I relayed everything that had happened, and he sat down on the log beside me.

"Okay, Gildings are creatures that cross from one dimension to another. They're physical when they come into our realm. They're...harbingers of bad luck and they curse any place that has too much good energy to it. They're the grinches of the astral world, so to speak. Their presence can cause crops to fail, milk to sour, and all sorts of nasty things. Often, when homesteaders have one bad season after another, it's because they were inflicted with a Gilding's curse. The only way to lift the hex is to banish the Gilding and protect against it coming back."

I frowned. "Banish it, huh? I take it we can't just kill it?"

He shook his head. "Gildings can be killed, I think, but it's a lot harder than just getting rid of them in the first place. What Henny needs is a witch or sorcerer rather than us. We should refer her to Raven's friend Llewellyn. My bet is that he'll be able to get rid of the creature without a problem."

I shrugged. "Sounds good to me. Let me call him up. I have his number." I pulled out my cellphone and called Llew at his shop—the Sun & Moon Apothecary, a magic shop on the Eastside. He answered on the first ring.

"Hey, it's Ember, from the Wild Hunt. We have a case that might be right up your alley." I told him about

Henny's problem and the fact that we suspected a Gilding. "Can I give her your number?"

"Sure. I can't come over right now, but I could make it after I close up shop." He seemed to be preoccupied, and I guessed he was dealing with another customer.

"I'll give her your number and tell her to call you. If you find out that I'm wrong and need us to come back, just give me a call. But I think we're right on this one." I hung up, then set down the chicken, who had made herself comfortable on my lap.

We stood and exited to where Henny was waiting.

"Your problem can be solved, but we can't do it. I'm texting you the number for Llewellyn Roberts, who owns a magic shop. He can take care of the hex that you're under."

Henny's eyes widened. "Hex? What hex?"

I told her about the Gilding. When we finished, we asked her to let us know whether the problem got sorted out and then returned to Yutani's car. He opened the door for me, and we headed back to the Wild Hunt.

"I'm glad that it wasn't a case for us," I said. "Right now, we've got our hands full with Typhon."

"Yeah, but I wouldn't mind having an easier case for a change. I'm so tired of running after ghouls and vrykos and all the other undead. And dragons aren't my first choice to head up my enemies list." Yutani paused as he stared out the window. "We're headed into a dark time for the world, Ember. I hope to hell that Talia and I can find some sign of Echidna and where she's at because I have the feeling she holds the key to locking Typhon back up."

"Me too, actually. I think she had something to do with his imprisonment. I don't have anything to go on other than instinct, but I have the feeling that she disappeared so nobody could use her to unseal his prison. Which brings me to another thought. I still think he had to have help getting out of stasis. You don't think she helped him, do you? And if so, is it a mistake to try to find her?"

Yutani eased the car onto the road and we headed south, toward the city central. "I don't think she would. Every account we've found has her acting against her husband."

"Then she might be in hiding because she fears Typhon going after her. Think of the revenge factor. He knew she was against him, and if he knew she helped the Titans to lock him up, then that anger would have festered all these years." I shuddered. "Ten to one, he's hanging out in the astral plane not just to strengthen up, but to keep out of her way until he feels he can fight her."

"That's a good point. If they're both playing cat and mouse with each other, then we have to contact her and convince her to work with us." Yutani veered off the street, into a drive-thru espresso stand. "What do you want?"

"Bless you. Iced large triple peppermint mocha." I looked around at the people milling through the streets. "What happens to them if we don't stop Typhon?"

"I don't even want to think about it," Yutani said. "So, if you were the Mother of Dragons, hiding away from Typhon, where would you hide?"

"Hmm...not in Greece. My thoughts are he's got his emissaries combing the Greek islands looking for her, since that's where they last parted. Somewhere high in the mountains, with deep caves. Does Everest have much of a cave system?"

"I know there are some around Tibet, but honestly, that seems a little extreme even for dragons. But...there are caverns all over the world. She could be anywhere. What else would she use as criteria for where she's hiding?"

"It would have to be safe from climbers, so I doubt she'd hide out anyplace where hikers routinely travel. Maybe we're looking at this wrong. Maybe she's not hiding out in the mountains. Maybe...what about some-place remote, where humans don't go but that dragons could withstand. Death Valley? Not a lot of people hang out in there and that's almost...let me see..." I brought out my phone and brought up a search engine. "Death Valley's almost three thousand square miles—that's a lot of land there and most of it uninhabited. It also has mountains, or at least big hills, and a dragon could hide out there and not be noticed."

"Why there rather than, say, the Sahara?"

"Simple. I'm guessing she knows Typhon broke free. She knows his emissaries are tackling the cities. She's not going to want to be too far from where she can gather information. The Sahara's a lot more remote than Death Valley."

Yutani frowned. "It seems a stretch, but it's worth checking out. As soon as we get back to the office, I'll get on it. We have contacts all over the states."

He pulled into the parking garage and we jogged through the street performers. I glanced around the crowd, looking for anybody that I might know, but none of them were familiar.

When we entered the office again, Angel shooed us toward the break room.

"Herne's back and he brought lunch. I'll be there in a moment after I lock down the elevator," she said.

We entered the break room to see Herne sitting there with Talia and Viktor, and on the table was a pile of Chinese takeout boxes. I washed my hands, with Yutani following suit. As I sat down beside Herne, I leaned forward and gave him a warm kiss.

"Hey, love, how are you doing today?"

"Side hurts, but it's okay."

"You weren't out there knocking about, injuring yourself again, were you?" He stared at me tenderly, and once again, my heart fluttered. When he looked at me, I felt like the most special woman in the world.

"No, I wasn't knocking about. The most strenuous thing I did at Henny's was to pick up a chicken and hold it."

Talia snorted. "You making friends with fowl folks lately?"

"Funny woman, *ha ha*." But it was funny, and I laughed. "Actually, it's not a case we can do much about. I referred her to Llewellyn and only charged her the service fee."

"What's the problem?" Herne asked.

"Chickens stopped laying eggs, bees are agitated. A Nixie told me that it's a Gilding. I had no clue what that was, but Yutani filled me in and so I called Llewellyn and put Henny in touch with him. They need a hex-breaker, not a head-basher." I sniffed the food, inhaling deeply. "That smells so good. I'm hungry." Pausing, I turned to Herne. "So, how was talking with the mayor and the United Coalition?"

Once we were settled with our food, Herne told us how it had gone.

"The UC is mustering up militias all over the states—the Shifter Alliance and Vampire Nation are helping. The Fae militia's focused here, but there are some Fae in other parts of the country who are willing to work with the shifters." He looked pleased. "Dormant Reins sent a note this morning that we should expect a vampire patrol call-list this week, and he's also reached out to other regents around the country."

"That's good news," I said, selecting an egg roll out of one of the cartons. I spooned some fried rice, orange chicken, and pot stickers onto my plate, and began to eat. "Yutani and I had a couple thoughts about finding Echidna."

As we told them about our speculations, I relaxed for the first time in a while. It felt like we were getting on top of the problem. I pushed aside my worries and focused on lunch and the conversation that buzzed around the table, once again thanking my lucky stars that I had found Herne—or rather, he had found me—and that I worked with people who felt like family.

CHAPTER NINETEEN

HERNE GAVE TALIA AND YUTANI THE GO-AHEAD TO contact any informants we had in Death Valley, but he also cautioned them to check out other avenues too. "It doesn't pay to focus on one theory and miss other viable ideas. Don't overlook anything."

They headed to their office. Viktor had already gone out—he was going to make sure all the weapons were polished, cleaned, and ready to rock before we were called out again.

"Before you go, Angel...Ember, too... I have something I need to tell you," Herne said.

"What's up?" I asked, sitting back down.

"Angel, as I mentioned to Ember, I found DeWayne's whereabouts." A fanciful smile played over Herne's face.

"Where?" Angel asked.

Herne ignored her question, continuing on. "I found out where he was staying and I paid him a visit. You were right. He had a lot of notes, trying to find out where you lived so he could spy on you. And he had somehow managed to pull the records of a half-dozen hospitals around the area, from the year DJ was born. He was trying to find out whether your mother had a boy or girl."

Angel shuddered, looking stricken. "Oh no. Then he might have already—"

"Relax. As I said, I found out where DeWayne was staying and he won't be bothering you again. I took him for a little walk and somehow, he landed over in Annwn, under the care of a good friend of mine."

She blinked. "What?"

"DeWayne's going to be working in Annwn, helping build a road through Y'Bain. I doubt you'll ever hear from him again, especially considering he has no clue of how he got over there—and probably no clue of where he is. I spiked his drink with a sleeping powder, and he was asleep when I took him through the portal. He's staying with Hoka, my friend who owns a contracting company. They're currently forging a trail through Y'Bain, as I said, and DeWayne's going to be…*working*…for him. He'll be well-treated, fed, and given a living wage, but I left strict orders that he's never to return through the portals."

I blinked. Herne followed his father's footsteps when it came to taking care of undesirable people. Throw them in a dungeon, kidnap them into a work force…but then again, they were gods, and it seemed better than letting DeWayne go on leeching off innocent women. He'd have a decent life. He'd just have to work for it.

"Well," Angel said after a moment. "I'm… Thank you. I don't know what to say. I sure wasn't expecting to hear that." She looked pensive. "Herne, I didn't want him in my life, but he won't be harmed, will he?"

"Not unless he does something stupid like provoke a

fight. Hoka's a good boss...and he will do his best to bring out DeWayne's positive side. We send a lot of troubled youth to him in Annwn, and he takes them in, shapes them up, and they leave as productive members of society. DeWayne may be older, but you have to figure there was something decent that your mother saw in him. Hoka will do his best to bring out that side."

Herne stood. "Now, to work, ladies. Ember, can you bring me the files on the MacCarris case? I think that you last had them." Angel smirked, but Herne waved her off. "No, it's not like that. I really do need to go over the files, so keep your mind out of our sex life, woman."

"Sure thing," Angel said, still laughing. "But just in case, I'll knock before I enter."

THAT NIGHT ANGEL and I arrived home at the same time. As we headed for the house, the sky began to cloud over. I glanced up, shading my eyes from the still bright light.

"Looks like we might have a bit of a storm coming up." I closed my eyes, reaching out. I could feel the rain droplets surrounding us, the moisture growing in the air. But they weren't ready to break loose. Soon, I thought, but not quite yet.

"Rain coming?" Angel asked.

I nodded. "Rain, and more thunder and lightning. I can feel the crackle in the air. The ozone is playing havoc with my senses." Ever since I had stepped up my magical practice with Marilee, I had become more aware of storms and the energies inherent within them. She said I had a natural bent for weather magic, and though I hadn't tried much of it yet, I could feel my connections growing when the clouds brought lightning with them.

"Have you ever tried to summon a storm?" Angel asked, pausing with me as I stared up at the clouds.

"Not in so many words, but yes, I've dabbled just a little in it. I wonder…it's been awhile since I've tried." I gazed at the rolling clouds overhead. My skin was jumping, tingling as though little shocks of electricity were running through me, tickling me from the inside out.

"Are you sure you want to do that?" Angel asked, breaking through my thoughts.

"Do what?" I asked.

"Summon the storm. I know you're thinking about it." She didn't sound entirely confident in my abilities.

"Well, maybe. I mean, what better time to try? We don't usually get many thunderstorms, and it just seems like it might be a good chance to flex my magical muscles." I stepped away from her, gauging my position. We had several tall trees in the yard and I didn't want to send one crashing through our roof. But the drive to try, now that I'd thought of the idea, seemed overwhelming, and I was determined to see if I could at least coax one measly bolt of lightning out of the sky. I wanted to be cautious, though, because I remembered all too well the shape Raven had been in when the lightning had forked through her body.

"Let's see…I don't want to call it down to the ground, I just want to jiggle it loose, to see it flash," I said to myself, frowning at I ran over how to do that. Raven did it via incantations, but she was a witch. I wasn't—not really. Not in the same way.

"I wonder…" I closed my eyes, reaching out, searching

for any water elementals that might be riding the winds, caught up on the currents of air. When it was pouring rain, sometimes you could find a rogue elemental, caught up by the energy. Usually, water elementals stuck to bodies of water, even though it might be one as small as a puddle. But the majority were found in rivers, ponds, lakes, and the ocean.

I searched, looking for any sign that an elemental might be nearby. And then, as I sorted through the various energies filling the airstream, I found what I was looking for—the signature of a water elemental. I snagged hold of it, searching, trying to follow it back to the source. Sometimes, finding the source of something meant that I'd be able to figure out how to manipulate it—especially anything to do with water.

The energy was thick on the clouds now, rolling through the atmosphere, approaching the tops of the trees. That meant the storm was close. I wasn't sure whether to call out, or just wait and see. But a sudden gust of wind caught me up and I found the thread of the elemental, the strand leading to its consciousness. It was riding a gust of wind, and the freedom made me want to jump aboard, to join it, and go gallivanting over the treetops.

Hello, I whispered. *Can you hear me?*

After a moment, a long slow breath answered. *Hello... Sister Water. Who are you?*

My name is Ember. I'm part Leannan Sidhe. I felt you nearby and wondered about the storm. Is it viable? Sentient?

Sometimes storms were sentient, in which case the best choice was to leave them alone, because a sentient storm usually brooked no interference and, beyond that, they were almost always dangerous and wildly unpredictable.

The storm is a storm. It holds no consciousness. It's simply passing through.

Well, that was good news. I frowned, trying to gauge how strong the lightning was. If it had not yet built up sufficient power, it would fizzle and I could disperse the storm altogether. If it *was* strong enough, then I could grab hold of the bolt and aim it.

I held out my arm. The hairs were standing straight up, and my hair felt all a-frizz. "All right, Angel, move back. Get out of the way because I'm going to try to call down a bolt."

She quickly backed away. "I still think you're crazy. Just be careful? Please?"

Nodding, I turned to face the street. I reached out, searching for the next bolt that was readying itself. There it was. I focused on it, trying to figure out how to trigger it. Then, I saw the structure of the bolt, and something very like a fulcrum. One side was weighing down, heavier than the other, and I understood that if I pushed just a little harder, it would overload it, triggering the lightning bolt. So I exerted all the force I could, focusing on pushing those scales beyond the breaking point.

The next moment, a brilliant light flashed as a loud rumble echoed through the air. Lightning split the sky directly overhead as the thunder sent me to my knees. Angel screamed and dove to the side, rolling away as the bolt hit the ground between us, plunging deep into the earth.

"Holy fuck, Ember! What the hell are you playing with?" Angel jumped to her feet as soon as the thunder stopped. "I didn't think you were going to try to fry our house. Or us."

I groaned as I tried to stand up straight. "I think I pulled a stitch."

"It serves you right. Get inside. No more goofing around." She marched me into the house, stepping around Mr. Rumblebutt, who was eyeing us both with a bright gleam in his eye that told me the thunder had scared him spitless.

"Now I feel bad," I said, wincing as I dropped my bag on the foyer table and hurried to the sofa, where I stripped off my jacket. "Mr. R., come here, boy."

He glared at me as though he knew I'd been the one to coax the lightning down, but finally jumped up on the sofa and mewed pathetically at me.

"I'm so sorry, little man. I didn't mean to scare you like that."

He allowed me to scritch his chin and then flopped on his side, rolling onto his back so I could pet his belly. I ruffled the fur, then leaned back, trying to decide if I needed to check my bandages. But Angel made up my mind for me.

"Get into the bathroom. I'll come look at your stitches." She pushed and prodded me to my feet and marched me into the downstairs bathroom, where I cautiously removed my dress. She carefully removed the bandages and grumbled, pulling out the salve and a fresh bandage.

"You ripped one stitch, but the others look intact. You're oozing just a bit, but the wound is healing quickly and I don't think you need to go back to the doctor. Let me put a new bandage on it for you."

"Thanks." I still felt awful for scaring both her and Mr.

R. "I'm sorry. I just wanted to see if I could make the lightning fork across the sky. I didn't mean…"

"Yeah, well, you could have shishkabob'ed us. And I, for one, am not ready to ride the lightning." She finished taping the new bandage in place. "I suppose you're going to want something to serve Sharne when he gets here."

I shook my head. "I'm not about to ask you to cook anything after that. Seriously, we can serve him chips and soda if that's what we have." I was feeling guiltier by the minute.

"I was going to make dinner anyway. I'm hungry, even after the lunch that Herne bought for us. What did you want to eat?"

I shook my head. "Just a snack will do."

"I know you better than that. How about tomato soup, grilled cheese sandwiches, and salad? And I have some frozen cookie dough left over from the last time I made cookies. I can bake up a couple batches for Sharne's visit."

"That sounds great," I said, staring at the floor, adding—as a peace offering, "I'll clean up after dinner."

"*Oh, yes you will.* Go on, why don't you change clothes while I make dinner? And straighten up the living room? I thought I saw a bowl of popcorn from a few nights ago still sitting out there." As she headed into the kitchen, I took the stairs, pleased to find that even though my side ached, the outright pain was mostly gone.

By SEVEN-THIRTY, I had cleaned the living room and Angel and I had finished dinner. Sharne was due in half an hour, and I looked around, trying to figure out what else to do before he got there. I felt slightly agitated—which could easily be due to the proximity of the lightning. I ducked into the hall bathroom and gave it a quick going-over, washing the counter and cleaning the toilet, then washing my hands and checking my makeup as the doorbell rang.

As I opened the door, Sharne's appearance took me aback, as always. He looked a lot like me in coloring and stature, but he also looked a hell of a lot like his brother—my grandfather. And Farthing was a memory I could do without.

"Ember," Sharne said, holding out a bouquet of roses. "For you and Angel. I know how much you love flowers."

"Thank you," I said as I handed them to Angel, who went to find a vase. I escorted Sharne into the living room. We sat on the sofa, and when Angel returned, she was carrying a tray with the freshly baked cookies and three glasses of iced lemonade.

"Oh that looks delicious," Sharne said, accepting a glass. He leaned back, then gave me a long look and let out a sigh. "So..."

"So...you're getting married."

"Right. As I told you, I had no clue that was coming. I really have no desire to get married, but there's no countering Saílle's decree. I live in her city, I'm one of her citizens, and if I know what's good for me, I'll just go along with it and do my best to suck it up. But this means my entire life's going to change."

I stared at my glass. "You know it's because of me, don't you?"

"Yes, I know it's because you and Herne are engaged. But that's the way it works in our world. I like living in TirNaNog, and I don't fancy being on the

Queen's shit-list, so I will make the best of it and just hope that my bride-to-be is even-tempered and not some harpy."

"She's a princess. She can't afford to be a harpy. Especially not when she's coming into a strange kingdom. Your marriage cements the bond between TirNaNog and Unkai's band, and inadvertently, paves the way for a stronger connection between Annwn and the TirNaNog here on Earth. I am not sure what Queen Pharial will think of it, though. I thought that Unkai's band answered to her."

Just because Saílle's TirNaNog was named for the original, didn't mean that Queen Pharial approved of everything the younger Fae Queen did.

"I'm not sure either, but I have no doubt we're going to find out. I have a message for you from Saílle. You are to escort my bride here tomorrow. She'll stay in a cloistered suite in the palace until the wedding. It's going to be in a week or so. I'm not sure of the exact date yet. I haven't been informed."

I blinked. "You have no say in it?"

"Do you have a say in your wedding to Herne? Oh, speaking of Herne, Queen Saílle specifically asked for him to accompany you over to Annwn to bring my intended back."

I frowned. "I know Unkai is the leader of the Orhanakai clan, but Saílle said that Neallanthra is royalty? Is he her father?"

Sharne shrugged. "I think he's her brother-in-law. How much do you know about your Autumn's Bane heritage?"

I shrugged. "Just that they're part of the Dark Fae, and

that Unkai is the leader of one of the clans—the clan my father came from."

"Yes. My father—and Farthing's—was a member of the Orhanakai band back in Annwn before coming over to Earth. My mother was also of that band. Within the Autumn's Bane—or Autumn Stalkers, as most people know them—there are five major clans. The Orhanakai are at the top—the nobility of sorts, if you can call it that. But there are four other clans, and the next in importance is the Lekanhika clan. Unkai's wife came from them, and she brought her sister with her when she joined the Orhanakai. They were both princesses, so to speak, of the Lekanhika. I did a little sleuthing. Neallanthra was never expected to wed, so she joined her sister as a lady-in-waiting. I'm using terms I doubt that the Orhanakai use, but it gives you an idea of the relationships."

"I get it," I said, nodding. "So, Neallanthra was foisted off on her sister since she couldn't—or wouldn't—find a husband?"

"Right. The best I can surmise is that Saílle heard about Herne proposing to you and had this plan set and ready to execute should you accept."

"When she saw my ring, she knew it was set and..."

"Right, and since she already had the plans in place, she made quick work of trying to lure you into her Court before Névé could."

I tried to follow the pieces. "But why Neallanthra? Why not someone from her own court?"

"My guess? She wanted me to have the appearance of nobility without sacrificing any of the women from her own court. Remember, you're..." He paused, frowning as he stared at the ground.

"I'm a tralaeth, even if I am to be a goddess. She had to find someone who wouldn't care, but would still give you some status as nobility. And Unkai's people—our people—they weren't really concerned about my half-blood heritage when we met them. Saílle must have her spies everywhere to know about this." I glanced around, wondering if she had somehow bugged the house. I wouldn't put it past her.

"She does. Trust me, those two? Saílle and Névé? Never underestimate what they're capable of. They have a network of informants that boggles the mind, which is why I didn't want to talk about this on the phone. Every inch of their cities has prying eyes and ears, watching and listening."

"All right. So she managed to find a princess willing to marry you, and that brings you into the court. She thought it would also force me to take her side, but that can't happen. Since she already said your marriage was happening, she can't go back on it now."

He nodded. "I suppose I could put up a fuss and get out of it, but the truth is, I don't want to be on her black-list. People who anger Saílle have a way of disappearing."

"Lovely," I said.

Angel stood. "Would anybody like more lemonade?"

Sharne smiled at her graciously. "I would, thank you."

As she headed into the kitchen, he leaned forward. "Be very careful, Ember. Saílle's going to be pissed about having to bend her knee to you, which will be the case once you become a goddess. She's *never* going to accept it. Once you go through deification, she can't touch you, but until then...accidents can happen."

I froze. I hadn't even thought of that. "You mean, she might try to kill me before then?"

"I told you, the Fae Queens are cunning and ruthless. They have little compassion, and massive egos. That's a bad combination if they feel they've been double-crossed or outwitted."

"I'll remember that," I said, my mood darkening. But I pushed it away for the moment, since there was nothing I could do about it at the present.

Instead, I fell into chatting with Sharne, asking him about his plans for after the marriage and how he would adjust to court life. As the evening wore away, I got a text from Herne, verifying that I was to head over to Annwn the next morning to bring back Neallanthra, and to meet him at his home at eight A.M. I texted back that I'd be there, but my mind was a million miles away, as I thought about all the potential ways things could go wrong before we were married, and how I wouldn't sleep easily until that day, now that I knew Saílle was gunning for me.

CHAPTER TWENTY

THE NEXT MORNING I WOKE TO THE SOUND OF RAIN outside my window. I dragged myself out of bed, groaning. Six o'clock was just too early. I glanced out the window to see pouring rain and opened the window, enjoying the breeze that gusted through the room to clear the air.

Then, moving as quick as I could, I showered and dressed, wearing jeans and a corset top.

Heading down to the kitchen, I found that Angel was up, yawning, and she had made me breakfast. Two sausage cheese muffins, a travel mug filled with twenty-four ounces of strong, iced latte, and a pastry that was oozing with glaze. She handed me the sack.

"I fed Mr. Rumblebutt, and I'll see you at work, later. Good luck." She beamed me a smile. "Oh, before I forget, Rafé asked if he could use our yard to work on his car? There's something wrong with it and he's trying to fix it himself, but his apartment building won't allow people to do that in the parking garage."

I waved at her as I took the paper bag filled with goodies. "Of course he can. Just so long as he doesn't leave a junk pile when he's done."

"Thanks! I'll let him know. Ember," Angel said, pausing.

"Yeah?"

"Be careful. Remember what Sharne said last night. Accidents can happen anywhere, especially if someone's out to arrange one. Saílle knows you're going over to Annwn today and she knows where you'll be. Don't let your guard down."

I bit my lip, realizing that Angel was absolutely right. "Hold on." I pulled out my phone and texted Herne. YOU ARE GOING WITH ME TODAY, RIGHT?

He answered quickly. YES, I WAS PLANNING ON IT.

THANKS, I texted back. "Okay, yes, Herne's going with me."

"Good, I feel better. And you be sure to tell him what Sharne said. Don't forget, okay?"

I nodded as I grabbed my purse and jacket and headed toward the door. "I won't forget."

THE PORTAL LED DIRECTLY to Cernunnos's palace. I was surprised. "I thought that we'd have to go into Y'Bain to pick up Neallanthra."

"No, I made arrangements for Unkai to bring her to my father's palace. I didn't want any chance encounters that could muck up things." He glanced down at me, his arm protectively around my waist. "What you told me—what Sharne thought—I have actually been thinking about since the parley. I know Saílle, remember? I know both of the Fae Queens better than they know themselves. And I don't trust them."

"Speaking of, how do you think they found out we were engaged...or rather, that you had proposed to me?" I tried to think about the people I'd told, but it hadn't been many.

Herne blushed. "I might have, in my anticipation, mentioned it. My parents knew I asked you, and so did Ferosyn, and Kipa, and Raven and...well, a few others. And while I trusted them to keep it quiet, there's no telling who might have overheard. I was just so excited, and so hopeful, that I had to tell someone about it."

I blushed, realizing just how much I meant to him. "I never thought I'd make such a difference in someone's life," I said, feeling askance. I had been so focused on how the engagement would affect *me* that I had almost forgotten his feelings.

Herne stopped. We were on the path to his father's palace. He turned to me, cupping my chin in his hands and tilting my head up. "Ember, never sell yourself short. I love you, more than you know. In one short year, you've become such a part of my world that I never want to let go. You're my lover, my companion, my friend. It doesn't matter that I'm a god and you're mortal. You are my world. I'll do my best to make you happy and that you never regret saying yes."

My heart fluttered and I threw my arms around his waist, pulling him close as I sought his lips. He kissed me, long and hard, and I hoped I would never let him down.

After a moment, he pulled back. "Come, love," he whispered. "We need to go meet Unkai." And with that, he wrapped his arm around my shoulders and we continued walking toward the massive tree palace.

CERNUNNOS'S PALACE still seemed steeped in summer, but even so I could see the tinge of autumn creeping one step behind. The leaves were just beginning to turn color, and eventually, the forest would be a riot of burgundies and rusts. The palace was always magnificent, but during the summer it was at its height, the massive oaks that made up its foundation clad in a thousand shades of green, like the world tree incarnate.

The guards who had greeted us at the portal led us to the throne room. Cernunnos's throne was in the center of the vast chamber, which was bigger than a football field. The room itself reminded me of a cavern, the walls formed of a swirling mass of roots and branches that wove together in a lignified fresco, a mural embedded into the walls and ceiling. Marble benches lined the walls, with matching tables nearby.

The ceiling glittered—literally—covered with dozens of stalactites. They flickered from within to form a web of light that spread through the room, illuminating every nook and cranny.

Cernunnos's throne was also woven out of a tangle of roots and branches, and it looked as though it had grown out of the ground that way. Crystals and gems peeked out from the knots and burls in the wood, and the seat of the throne was cushioned with a pad of green velvet.

But of course the most striking part of the throne room was Cernunnos himself.

A massive man-god, he sat with his chest bare, rippling with muscles that were finely hewed from his flesh. His hair flowed down his back, bound into multiple braids, as black as the night, and his eyes shimmered gold and green, very much like a cat's eyes. He was full-lipped and his smile was as beguiling as it was deadly.

I could see the resemblance between Herne and his father, and I wondered if in time, would my love grow to be as powerful and stately as the Lord of the Forest.

Cernunnos stood, his bearskin cape fastened around his shoulders with a gold chain and a knotwork brooch. He descended the steps from the seat of his throne and silently approached us as we stood in front of him. Without warning, he swept me up into a massive hug, his arms so strong they could have broken me into pieces. The scent of cinnamon and musk clouded my senses. He smelled like Herne.

I tried to catch my breath as Cernunnos's greeting thundered through the room.

"Welcome, my daughter-to-be. Congratulations are in order, I understand. You have enchanted my son. May you make a man out of him, and may he be worthy of your trust." As he let go of me, he kissed me on the forehead, then turned to Herne and held out his hand. Herne took it, and Cernunnos pulled him into an embrace.

"I'm so glad you're pleased." Herne admired his father, and though he had never said as much, I could read between the lines. He wanted to make Cernunnos proud.

"Pleased? I was ecstatic when your mother told me. But you didn't think to text your father when Ember said yes?" Cernunnos gave Herne a long look.

"I'm sorry, I just...things have been so..." Herne paused.

Cernunnos let out a hearty laugh. "Not to worry, my son. I'm just having some fun with you. I'm truly pleased. Morgana and I shall have to think of a good wedding present. Meanwhile, we have business today." His smile slid away as he motioned to the guard. "Clear the room."

The guard did so without a word, escorting everyone out of the throne room, leaving only Cernunnos, Herne, and me. Once the doors shut, the Lord of the Forest turned to us. "I have to tell you, I'm not on board with this sudden request from Saílle. The Orhanakai aren't happy about it, either. Unkai has spoken to me, and he asked me why I gave the Fae Queen leave to demand a bride from him." Cernunnos's eyes narrowed and he leaned forward. "What's going on? I want to know who planted the idea in her head that she could coerce one of Annwn's greatest chieftains into handing over an unwilling woman to be the prize in some game she's playing."

"What? We thought..." I paused, turning to Herne. "Did Saílle say how she came to find out about Unkai's sister-in-law? Or what exactly transpired when she made the arrangements for the woman to marry Sharne?"

"No," he said. "She didn't. I assumed that Unkai and the woman were both willing. I don't care what we've promised Saílle, if she doesn't want to be married, we're not handing her over to your uncle."

I groaned, rubbing my temples. "I have a headache," I said, leaning back in my seat. "I really don't want to deal with this at all. I know Sharne wasn't in on this. I talked to him and believe me, I've always got my bullshit meter running around him. He truly had no clue this was going to happen. He's resigned to it, and it may be good for him to wed at this point. But not if Neallanthra is unwilling. He wouldn't want that either. He's just trying to avoid Saílle's anger."

Cernunnos let out a blustery sigh. "All right, let's get to the bottom of this." He rang a bell and the servant who had been helping him returned to the room. "Bring Unkai and Neallanthra to me, please."

The guard bowed. "As you will, milord."

While we waited, I made small talk with Cernunnos. I found myself in the middle of a story about Mr. Rumblebutt when the chamber doors opened again and the guard returned with a man and woman behind him. The man I recognized.

I had first met Unkai when I had come to Annwn in search of Brighid's Flame, the sword I now claimed as mine.

Unkai looked like the typical Dark Fae—black hair, though it was seasoned with white, which meant he was very old indeed. His mustache was thin and well groomed. He was handsome, in a roguish way, and weathered from a life on the go.

The Autumn's Bane, or Autumn Stalkers as they were commonly called, were a warlike people. Nomadic, they had originally been both over on Earth and in Annwn, and they had swept through villages, enslaving the villagers, taking their lands, and moving on. Now, there were only remnants of them left on Earth. But in Annwn, they still thrived, though I had discovered they weren't as terrifying as they had first sounded. Unkai was actually a fair man, and just, and he treated his people well.

"Ember," Unkai said, stepping forward and holding out

his hand. I clasped it, and he gave me a quick hug, in the way of two warriors who were meeting after a long time apart. "It's truly good to see you." He was speaking in Turneth—the Dark Fae variant of Faespeak. But then, to my surprise, he switched to English. "It's been a time."

I smiled. "You're learning English?"

"I have studied, yes, since you left Annwn with Brighid's Flame." He frowned, picking over the words, but he spoke them flawlessly.

I glanced at the woman. She looked a lot like Unkai's woman.

"I present Neallanthra, my woman's sister." Unkai motioned for her to step forward and she did. "She hearkens from the Lekanhika clan."

"So I understand." I glanced at Herne, who was standing by silently, letting me take the reins. Still in English—I had my doubts Neallanthra spoke the language—I asked, "Tell me something, and please, in English if you can. When did Saílle arrange this exchange?"

Unkai glanced back at his sister-in-law, then motioned for me to walk to one side with him. When we were some ways from the others, he switched to Turneth. "I cannot speak that freely in your language yet, but I understand you don't want her to understand the question. The Dark Fae queen sent a contingent of her militia into our encampment and demanded a woman for marriage. They insisted the woman be nobility. I told them we don't have kings or queens among the clans, but they insisted on someone who would match a princess in power."

"As I figured. When did this happen?"

"One moon cycle ago. The only woman available was Neallanthra. The soldiers threatened to destroy the village we live in during the winter if we refused. They would have burned down every building so we had no shelter to return to come the snows, and they still would have taken Neallanthra. They also threatened to kidnap our children and take them back to Earth where we'd never see them again." His dark eyes burned. "Dark Fae do not go against Dark Fae over here, but apparently the rules are different on your side of the portal."

I let out a sigh. "Saílle's a queen all right, a queen bitch. Listen to me, she did this because of me. I had no knowledge of it, but here's what happened." I explained to him how she got wind of the fact that Herne had proposed, and that she decided to try to win me over to their side before Névé could. "She is using my uncle as a pawn, and your sister-in-law as an excuse. She thought it would give her favor once I go through the ritual of Gadawnoin."

Unkai's scowl grew darker. "The queens here may fight to the death, and many lives are lost, but they generally have more honor than *that*."

"I don't know if I believe that, but let's just say that her actions didn't surprise me, once I found out about them. So, is Neallanthra willing to go? I can tell you my uncle is a good-natured man and won't mistreat her. He's not thrilled about being pushed into an arranged marriage either."

"Then yes, she will go willingly. She honestly has always wanted to marry, but she doesn't fit in here. Maybe she'll adapt to your world better. She's too independent for some men, and far too domestic to manage with her own people. She was born for a life indoors, as we say in my clan. A house cat instead of a wildcat. The Autumn's Bane are *not* an indoor people." He sighed. "My woman will miss her sister, but at least Neallanthra will have a chance for happiness that is her own, and not lived vicariously through others."

We returned to the others and Cernunnos gave his blessing over our journeys—it was customary, I gathered, when someone relocated to the other side of the portals. Then, accompanied by a contingent of guards, we returned to the portal with Unkai and Neallanthra. Before we were even near noon, we transferred through, back to our world.

UNKAI BLINKED, looking around with wide eyes. Neallanthra looked shell-shocked. But we were in the woods near Herne's home, and they both relaxed as they saw the trees and foliage around us. I couldn't help but wonder what they'd think when they saw our cities, though. There were some similarities to the cities of Annwn—the bustle of people, the vendors and stores and shops—but where Annwn was steeped in magic and carts and horses, here we were steeped in cars and electricity.

I turned to Neallanthra and reached out for her hand. She looked at me curiously, but accepted the gesture and I held her hand as we walked ahead of the men, talking in Turneth.

"My uncle is a kind man, and he's pleasant. I think you'll like him." I wanted to put her at ease.

"What does he look like?" she asked. "What does he do?"

"He has my coloring. He's a tailor, actually. Though I don't know if he'll be allowed to keep his profession once you both move to the Court." I paused. "I need you to understand something and I don't know if it was made clear to you. I want you to know why you're here." I ran down what had happened. "Once she realized I'm going to become a goddess with power over her, Saílle laid this little plan into action."

"She must resent you a great deal. Unkai told me you were tralaeth, and to have you rise above her, to become a goddess?" Neallanthra shook her head. "I can't imagine that the Fae Queens would be happy. I am not saying they're *right* to feel this way, but..."

"But they *do* feel this way. You're correct in that. Farthing, my grandfather—Sharne's brother—plotted with my maternal grandmother to execute my parents. They would have killed me too, if I had been home. I was fifteen. Then, last year Farthing tried to destroy me."

She gasped. "I'm so sorry. What happened?"

I sighed. "I killed him. To avoid rumors, Saílle tried to buy me off. I took the money—hell, to refuse it would have set her up against me even more than she already was. But I will *never* forget what this incredibly stupid war between the Fae has wrought in my life. It murdered my parents, it tore my world apart, it almost killed me... There are days I'm ashamed to be Fae." I shrugged. "But I can't run away from who I am. I have to accept myself and make things better."

Neallanthra was a short, plump woman with gorgeous hazel eyes. She gazed up at me, smiling softly. "I have not been treated graciously by our people, either. Oh, Unkai and my sister treat me well, but I've never seemed to fit in. I have always felt like an outsider, looking into a world that I'm supposed to belong to, but never quite meshing with it."

"Welcome to Earth. Oh, there are cliques and groups and snobs and racists and xenophobes here, but you know what? The world is so diverse. There are many different kinds of people. You might fit in better here. Just don't be too surprised by the technology."

"Lord Cernunnos warned me about that. He didn't want me to be frightened. I'm actually looking forward to seeing some of your inventions. I like making things—I enjoy stretching my mind." Her eyes were glowing. Neallanthra's hair was caught back in a long braid. It was golden brown and her eyes were hazel, and she had that spark in them that indicated a quick mind and intelligence.

We came out of the park then, and Herne opened the gate that led to his yard, which buttressed up against Carkeek Park. Unkai and Neallanthra froze, looking around at the house and the car beyond. Unkai rubbed his temples.

"The noise—is it always this loud?"

I realized he was hearing the sounds of traffic, including the jets flying overhead. "Yes, most of the time it's this loud, at least in the city. When you get out in the country, it's not nearly as bad."

Herne motioned for us to follow him. "Come, let's break for a snack at my home, then we can drive you over to TirNaNog, where you can begin your new life."

And with that, we headed into his house to eat, and then to head over to meet Saílle.

CHAPTER TWENTY-ONE

We had barely stepped up to the gates of TirNaNog when Saílle's guards swept Unkai and Neallanthra out of sight with a terse thank-you. I had been hoping to see more of Unkai, but he needed to stay with Neallanthra, at least until she and my uncle were married.

Herne glanced at me as we headed back over the floating bridge. "Are you all right?"

"Yeah, though I wish Saílle could just keep her nose out of my business."

I was pissed. Saílle had disrupted Neallanthra's entire life, co-opting her as though she might grab a tool away from someone else. Except that Neallanthra was a woman, not a tool, and my uncle was a man, not a pawn.

"Well, get used to it. I have the feeling that until the wedding, Saílle will be doing everything she can to incur your favor or take you out. She's going on the premise that if you favor her, you'll align against Névé."

"A very black and white view of the universe." I sighed, resting my head against the headrest. "Listen, what—" I paused as my phone rang. "Viktor," I said, glancing at it. "Hello?"

"Ember, are you and Herne free yet? An emergency's come up."

"What's going on?" I put him on speaker so Herne could hear. "Viktor."

"What's up, man?" Herne said, keeping his eyes on the road as we navigated back to the office. Traffic was heavy. It was noon and everybody was out and about, looking to eat lunch and run errands.

"How soon can you get down to Whitemoor Nursing Home? It's in the Beacon Hill District, near the White Lodge Cemetery on Orcas Street." He sounded tense and I could hear shouting behind him.

"What's going on? We're probably fifteen minutes out, if we take the backroads," Herne said, veering off to the left onto a side street.

"Yutani and I are here. We've got more vrykos and they're trying to get into the nursing home. They've already killed two nurses and one cop. The cops are here and Yutani and I are trying to help them contain the creatures, but this is bad, Herne. The energy feels bad—like something big is on the way."

"We need our weapons—" Herne started to say, but Viktor cut him off.

"Already have them. I brought them in case you'd be back in time." Viktor shouted something and then said, "I have to go. Yutani's fighting one and it's getting the upper hand." He signed off abruptly as I cringed.

"Pull up the news. I know where we're going so I don't need you to navigate," Herne said, a grim look on his face.

I brought up a news station on my phone and turned up the volume of their live stream.

"We're down in the Beacon Hill District, where another group of vrykos are attacking a nursing home. It's believed they came out of the White Lodge Cemetery. Police are attempting to contain them, but the creatures have broken through a number of barriers already and some have vanished into the surrounding neighborhoods. Emergency calls are coming in from people who have been attacked. For now, there's no estimate on the number of victims. We do have verified reports of three deaths so far—two nurses and one police officer were confirmed dead. They were attempting to prevent the vrykos from entering the nursing home."

The reporter was blond and ditzy looking, but the alarm on her face had replaced the plastic everything-is-just-fine glow that a lot of newscasters wore nowadays, and she looked genuinely frightened. The footage cut to a clip from outside the nursing home.

"Those poor residents—they'll never be able to get away. Not if they're bed-bound." I watched in horror as one of the vrykos reappeared, dragging a screaming woman by her wrist. The woman was elderly, and she struggled but couldn't free herself. Right in front of the camera, the vrykos bent over and took a big bite out of her cheek, and the fucking camera operator kept filming. The woman barely made a sound, and I prayed she had either died of a heart attack, or had fainted so she wouldn't have to feel the pain.

"Oh my gods, Herne, step on it. This is bad," I said, looking over at him. "We need the militias—I know they aren't ready but—"

"There's nothing we can do regarding that right now. The time it would take to mobilize them would be too long. But…call Kipa and tell him to get his ass over here, and tell him to bring members of his SuVahta. They can fight."

I punched in Kipa's number and he answered on the first ring. I ran down what was happening. "Hurry. We need you."

"I'm already in the city. I'll be there with my guard in ten minutes." He hung up abruptly.

"He's on his way. He said ten minutes." I glanced around as Herne pulled into the parking lot of the nursing home. The cemetery was next door, and it occurred to me that it was a grim reminder to the residents of their stage in life.

We tumbled out of the car and I spotted Viktor over by what looked like a higher-ranking officer. "Viktor!" I shouted, and he looked up. Immediately upon spotting me, he spoke to the police officer, then jogged over to our car, where we were waiting.

"What the hell happened?"

"I don't know, but a call came in about twenty minutes ago. Yutani and I came down to check it out and found all this. Here are your weapons." He handed me Brighid's Flame, which I had left at the office, and he handed Herne a double-bladed axe. "They've managed to break into the nursing home. I don't think we'll find many survivors."

"I pray you're wrong. Let's go." Herne shouldered his axe and headed toward the building. Grateful I had thought to wear jeans and a sturdy top, I shrugged on my leather jacket and followed them into the building.

THE WHITEMOOR NURSING Home was a single-story building, sprawling three wings wide. Buttressed against the White Lodge Cemetery, the nursing home had that weathered feel that most homes for the elderly do. It was almost as though because their residents were fading, the walls and atmosphere around them shifted to match. Any beauty the home might have had was only a whisper—a memory long past.

The walls were painted two-toned, a pale rose on the top two-thirds of the walls, and the wainscoting was thyme green, but the colors hadn't been refreshed in a long time. There were cracks here and there, with water damage on the ceiling.

I brought my attention back to the screams that filled the halls. Even from where we were at the entrance, we could see one of the vrykos gnawing on an older gentleman, who was groaning and trying to pull away.

Herne took one look and went in swinging, bringing his axe around to neatly cleave the top half of the vrykos away from its lower half. The torso fell, and the creature tried to pull itself back toward its prey using its hands, teeth still gnashing. Once again, Herne brought the axe down, cleaving the torso in half, splitting it directly down the center from the top of the skull. The two halves of the vrykos fell apart and I averted my eyes from the resulting splattered gore.

I motioned for Herne to go past me while I knelt to examine the victim. He was still breathing, but he was pale and clammy and had obviously gone into shock.

Glancing around for someone who could carry him to

the medics, I saw a man running toward me. He was in a long brown leather duster, and his hair was the color of copper, swirling down his back. I didn't recognize him, but maybe he was one of Kipa's guards.

"Over here, we need to get this man out to the medics," I called to him.

He stared at me for a moment, then with a grim smile, headed my way. I stood to meet him and as he neared me, I saw Kipa running up behind him, his axe held high.

"Ember, get away! That's Gyell!" Kipa swung the axe as the man turned and right then I saw a blaze of light in the man's eyes that told me he was no ordinary man. He lashed out with one hand and a whip formed, an orange bolt of energy that coiled out from his palm. He caught hold of Kipa's axe with it, the tongue of fire coiling around the hilt, and yanked it out of the Wolf Lord's hand.

Kipa let out a loud curse. He raced forward, six massive wolves appearing to flank his sides. They tumbled out of a cloud of mist and snow, and were hot on his heels as they charged toward the shadow dragon.

Gyell's attention was on them, so I began to drag the old man out of the way, keeping my eyes on the dragon shifter at all times. At that moment, Viktor came running up.

"Herne said—"

"It's Gyell!" I pointed toward the dragon. "Be careful!"

Gyell jerked around at the sound of my voice. Once again, he raced toward me, eyes flickering with an unearthly light. I stumbled back, trying to get out of his way. I knew that even with Brighid's Flame, I couldn't take him on. I didn't have the strength. Kipa shouted something and lengthened his strides, but then the dragon was looming over me. He reached out to grab my wrist and I feinted right, then dropped to the left, trying to get out of the way.

Viktor broad-jumped over me, landing between me and the dragon, swinging his hammer as he landed. The hammer slammed into Gyell's side and the dragon let out a roar. He was taller than Viktor, at least seven feet tall, and he shot out another whip of energy, this time coiling around Viktor's arm. Viktor shouted as the energy constricted around his arm like a snake, and he dropped his hammer. Gyell yanked him close, grabbing hold of the half-ogre.

I had to help him. I brought Brighid's Flame up, snarling as I slashed at Gyell's back. But I missed, and I stumbled forward, unbalanced by the weight of my sword.

"Help him!" I turned to see Kipa closing in on the pair.

"I'm on it," Kipa said, leaping to close the distance between them. But at that moment, Gyell said something in a language I couldn't understand, and both he and Viktor vanished, disappearing as Kipa frantically grabbed for the dragon's coat.

I stared at the empty hallway. Where had they gone? What the hell had just happened? But Kipa gave me no time to think.

"We have to help the residents," he said, grabbing my hand.

"What about Viktor?" I glanced back over my shoulder as Kipa stopped to scoop up his axe from where Gyell had tossed it.

"There's nothing we can do for him right now. But we can save some of the patients if we get the fuck in there and stop these creatures." With that, he kicked open the nearest door and we headed in, leaving Viktor to whatever fate had befallen him.

THE VRYKOS WERE SWARMING, all right. I had never seen so many undead in one place, save for the vampires. Kipa's wolves shifted form into their human nature, or more-than-human nature. They were sturdy and muscled and armed to the teeth, and they began slashing their way through the mayhem.

Kipa pushed me toward the nearest room. "Check the patients. If they're safe, lock them in their rooms unless the windows look vulnerable."

"What about Viktor?"

He hesitated. "We'll find Viktor as soon as we can, but we have to take care of this mess first."

I nodded, realizing he was right, and turned toward the first door as he raced down the hall to join his men. From up ahead, around the corner, I could hear Herne shouting.

Opening the door, I peeked in. An older woman was in bed, and she looked scared spitless. She pulled her covers up to her chin, her eyes wide. A glance at the windows told me they were intact and they weren't low enough to easily crawl through.

"Stay here. We'll be back for you." I turned to the door but found no way to lock it. Hell, had the nursing home disabled all the locks? What the hell was I going to use to keep the door closed? I cast my gaze around the room, looking for anything that might help.

"What do you need?" the woman asked, slowly lowering the covers.

"I need you to lock yourself in here." I saw a hard-backed chair in the corner by a small desk. "Are you able to stand?"

She nodded. "What should I do?" She slowly got out of bed, and while she was older and looked frail, she seemed able to walk toward me.

I grabbed the chair and carried it over to the door. "The minute I leave, you prop this chair under the doorknob. Don't let *anybody* in. If you hear someone jiggling the knob, don't say a word unless they call out to you and identify themselves. Your life could depend on it." I held her gaze, hoping she would follow through.

"All right, dear. I'll do that." The woman waited by the door until I slipped outside. I listened and, sure enough, I heard her fitting the chair under the door.

"Tell me when you're ready and I'll test it," I called through the door.

I heard a faint "Ready," and gave the door a try. Sure enough, it wouldn't open. I wasn't sure if it would hold against the vrykos, but it was the best I could manage. I couldn't take her with me because she couldn't move fast enough, and I couldn't protect her and fight off the vrykos at the same time.

"All right. We'll be back for you. If anything tries to break through, hide in the closet or bathroom or under the bed and do your best to keep out of sight." I took off for the next room. The door was open there, and I peeked in, to see a very dead vrykos—apparently Kipa or one of his guards had gotten to it and chopped it into pieces—but also, a very dead patient.

I moved on to the next room. There, I found another patient, but he was nonresponsive and there was no way that he could help me the way the woman had. I grabbed a blanket and wedged it beneath the door as I left. It might give the vrykos some trouble in getting the door open, and if I could even frustrate them enough to move onto the next room, that was good enough.

Three more rooms, three patients either bedridden or nonresponsive, and three haphazard attempts to jam their doors shut later, I turned the bend at the end of the hall. I could hear a clash from up ahead, and I raced along the hallway, turning left into what appeared to be a cafeteria. There, the vrykos were fighting Kipa, Herne, Yutani, and Kipa's guards.

I looked around, spotting one of the creatures who was shuffling toward the door. I went in swinging, going full force on the offensive. I brought my blade around at neck length, aiming for the vrykos's throat, and Brighid's Flame sliced right through, decapitating it as the blade met flesh. The head fell to the side, but the body kept moving so I took another swing, this time from top to bottom, bringing the sword down on the headless neck. My blade cleaved through part of the torso before lodging right above the pelvis. I stepped back, pulling hard to free the sword. A moment later, it came loose and I fell backward, tripping and landing on my ass.

The vrykos was still trying to move, lurching around like some hideous monster out of a horror movie. I stared at it, panting, as the world seemed to slip into some surreal haze. My water magic wouldn't do any good, and there was nothing I could do except keep slicing and dicing my way through the tangle of undead.

I closed my eyes for a moment, feeling a rush of rage and futility. As the anger rose, it blotted out my thoughts, and the next moment, I found myself hacking away at the vrykos, frantically chopping it into bits. I was crying, furious that the only thing I could do to save people was to play the part of a woodchipper on legs.

Everything melded into that angry blur, the rage swelling into neon white, exploding as I took on another opponent and yet another. Everything stopped except the endless swinging of my blade, the crunch of bones, the smell of blood from the victims, and long-dead gasses from the vrykos being released. Everywhere the floor and walls were slick with brain matter and bodily juices and the odd thing that kept playing through my mind was there was no blood from these creatures, no sign that they had ever been human except their distorted shapes.

Some of the vrykos were newly dead, and they were the worst. When we cleaved into their flesh, the sounds that they made were hideous, a slurping, slithering noise. The older bodies were desiccated, a few almost mummified, paper-thin skin clinging to the bone.

But after a time, the room fell still and I lowered my blade so the tip was resting on the floor. We were standing in a house of horrors. The remains of the vrykos were scattered everywhere and we were all covered with bits and pieces of muscle and gristle.

My stomach lurched and I turned to the side, vomiting.

A putrid smell hung heavy in the air, and I suddenly couldn't breathe. I stumbled for the door leading into the hall and once there, leaned against the wall, barely able to hold myself up. I was exhausted, yes, but more than that, the fight had left me feeling like death warmed over. I looked down at Brighid's Flame. Her blade was covered in gray matter, and slowly, I sank to squat on my heels, still leaning against the wall, as I waited for the others to emerge.

Herne was the first to come out, followed by Kipa and then his men and Yutani. Herne looked around. "Where's Viktor?"

I shook my head and wiped my mouth on the sleeve of my jacket. "Gyell got him. I don't know where he took him."

"What?" Herne looked like he was ready to explode. "What the hell are you talking about?"

Kipa stepped in. "A shadow dragon landed and shifted form. He vanished around the corner and I hurried to follow. He was on the run, heading toward Ember, so I did what I could to throw him off."

"Viktor was trying to help me," I said. "He jumped in front of me. Gyell grabbed hold of him and before we could do anything, they vanished. But the vrykos...we couldn't stop to look for him." I pressed my forehead to my knees, not wanting to move or think or feel. "I'm sorry," I whispered. "We couldn't stop."

Herne leaned down and with gentle hands, lifted me to my feet. "No, you couldn't. And shadow dragons are terrifyingly powerful. But now we need to figure out what happened to Viktor." He motioned to Yutani. "Call Akron. Get him over here. Kipa, you and your men take one last look through the entire complex and make sure we got all of the vrykos. Then let the medics know they can safely go in for the residents." A raven shifter, Akron led a cleanup crew that took care of crime scenes.

I leaned against Herne's side, feeling drained. He helped me out of the facility and back toward the parking lot. The events of the day were so convoluted in my brain that all I wanted to do was shut out the world.

"We need to wait until Yutani and Kipa return," he said, "but you can sit in the car."

I shook my head. "I'll wait till they come back."

And so we stood there, waiting, until Kipa and his men and Yutani returned.

"Akron's on his way," Yutani said.

"Did you ride with Viktor or vice versa?"

"I drove." Yutani looked even more exhausted than I felt. He looked almost defeated. "I hate just leaving. What if he's somewhere on the grounds?"

Kipa spoke up. "My men and I will search the grounds and the cemetery. If Viktor's still around here, we'll find him. And that way, we can make certain there aren't any vrykos hiding in the bushes. We'll meet you back at the office."

Herne nodded his thanks, then helped me into the car. We headed out, with me silently staring out of the window, wondering where Viktor was, and if he was even still alive.

CHAPTER TWENTY-TWO

At the office, Herne and I took a shower together. We bathed silently, not talking about Viktor as though we might break a spell if we did so. But the half-ogre filled my thoughts as Herne soaped my back for me, rubbing my shoulders gently, offering comfort. As the water poured over us, he lathered me up with bath gel, then helped me wash my hair. We rinsed off and changed into the extra clothes that we both kept at the office.

I braided my hair back so that it would dry without my having to blow dry it, and headed for the break room. Angel was there, and she had ordered lunch. Steaming bowls of chowder were waiting for us, along with fried fish, biscuits, and coleslaw. Yutani went to take a shower while we sat down to eat. Angel was keeping his food warm in the oven.

"Yutani told me what happened to Viktor," she said, sitting down across from us. "Do you think he's still alive? What do we do now?"

"I don't know," Herne said, shaking his head. "If

anybody can survive being captured by a dragon, it's him. But we need a location spell. We need some direction as to where Gyell took him, because there's no way we can find him otherwise." His worry was evident in his eyes. "I've texted my parents. They're on their way."

Angel turned on the TV. The local stations were covering the incident at the nursing home. All told, eight out of the twenty-seven residents had been killed, along with three staff members and three officers. Fourteen dead from one little skirmish.

"The United Coalition has to tell the nation about the dragons soon." Herne shook his head. "I'll ask my parents to talk to the UC. While the Coalition is working with us, I think they can work faster if they do."

Yutani appeared in the doorway, looking clean and refreshed. "Lunch? Thanks." He sat down and Angel brought him his lunch.

At that moment, Talia hustled in from her office. "I've been doing research on Echidna this morning. I think Ember may be right with her hunch. I think Echidna might actually be in Death Valley. There have been several sightings of dragons around there over the past decade. I've called in the help of friends I have down there to do some sleuthing. Hawk shifters—they can see from a long distance overhead. Maybe she could help us with Viktor, if we found her."

"We really do need her, because things are just going to get worse from here on out. Why the hell Tartarus and Gaia had to go and create the dragon race, I don't know, but I could have done without them at this point," Herne said.

We had barely finished eating when there was a noise

in the hall. Herne started to rise, but before he could fully stand, his mother and father came striding into the room.

"We didn't want to bother you to open the door," Cernunnos said, motioning for us to stay seated. "You said something went wrong. Tell us what's going on."

That was one thing about Cernunnos—he didn't stand on ceremony. If there was work to do, he got it done. If there was something to find out, he went in search of it. And he didn't abide shirkers in his court.

Morgana gave me a weary smile. She actually looked tired and I wondered what could make a goddess tired. She accepted the chair that Cernunnos pulled out for her, sitting to my right. The Lord of the Forest then sat beside her, barely fitting in the average-sized chair.

"Viktor was abducted by Gyell, a shadow dragon who's been stirring up trouble with the vrykos," Herne said.

An idea suddenly struck me. "I know! We need to call Ashera. If anybody would have an idea of where Gyell took Viktor, it would be her." I jumped out of my seat. "I'm going to call her now."

"Good thought," Herne said, waving me on.

I moved to the sofa, putting in a call to Ashera.

She answered on the first ring. "Ember, what's up?" She had picked up on English faster than I ever thought anyone could, but then again, dragons were incredibly intelligent.

"Gyell captured Viktor. Do you know where he might have taken him? He grabbed hold of him and they disappeared." The words tumbled out of my mouth.

She gasped. "Oh no. Tell me what happened."

I ran down the attack at the nursing home and how Gyell had been there. "We couldn't do anything. They just vanished. We had to fight off the vrykos, and then, when we finished, there was still no sign of either one so we came back to the office and now we're trying to figure out how to locate him. Do you think Gyell killed him outright?" I added, dreading the answer.

She paused for a moment, then said, "No, I don't. Viktor's a good bargaining chip. My guess is that he'll try to use him to lure all of you in. You—the Wild Hunt—are a direct threat to Typhon, so it makes sense for Gyell to do his best to bring down the entire agency. He'll know enough to realize that he can't kill Herne, but he can destroy the rest of you. No matter whether he offers you a deal or not, you can't trust him. Shadow dragons are treacherous. All of the Luminous Warriors are. They beguile and charm and say whatever you want to hear in order to get what they want."

"Where do you think he took Viktor?"

"Into the Underworld," Ashera said. "That's where Gyell will be strongest."

My heart sank. "But…can Viktor survive there? He's alive. Can the living exist in the lands of the dead?"

Ashera cleared her throat. "Yes, for a while. Stay too long and you'll fade and become a wight. The Underworld is filled with wights and creatures that were once alive but haven't yet died. They live in the Between, the space between life and death. It's a shadowy world of fire and smoke, and endless twilight."

I closed my eyes, swaying. The Between… I had never heard of the realm before and now that I had, I wished I hadn't. It sounded like a horrible place.

"Limbo," I whispered.

"Yes, it's very much like limbo. But Ember…if Viktor

does fade into the Between, then you'll never be able to bring him back. You have to rescue him before then, or he'll be lost for good. Even ghosts can be freed from their state, but once you're caught in the Between, you'll never escape." Ashera paused, then added, "I'd offer to help you, but I cannot go there—the only dragons who can enter the Underworld are shadow dragons."

I thought for a moment. "What happens when you die? When dragons die, I mean. Where do they go, if not to the Underworld?"

"Our spirits travel to the Summerlands—some of us. Others actually end up in Valhalla, and still others, in darker realms. Like mortals, it varies depending on who we are and what we've done in our lives and the gods we may be connected to." She sighed. "I wish I could go with you, but I can't. However, you cannot enter the Underworld if you're still alive, not without a guide. And stay with that guide at all times. You might want to contact your friend Raven—she can guide you, given she's pledged to a god of death."

After asking me to let her know what we were going to do, Ashera signed off.

I returned to the table, feeling grim. "So, Gyell most likely will try to use Viktor as a bargaining chip in order to trap the rest of us. One goal the dragons have—Typhon's side, that is—is to destroy the agency since we're such a threat. And Ashera says that he's most likely taken Viktor into the Underworld."

Cernunnos let out a long sigh. "I feared that might be the case."

"Ashera suggested we take Raven as our guide." I sat

down again and Morgana reached out to pat me gently on the shoulder, a sad smile on her face.

"I concur," Cernunnos said. "But the trip will be dangerous and you'll have to make it short. It would help if we knew precisely where in the Underworld to look." He frowned, turning to Morgana. "My dear, do you have any oracles in your bag of magical tricks?"

She thought for a moment, then said, "Actually, I might. I can do an interdimensional location spell. That way we can find the coordinates for where to send you across. Think of it like...oh...latitude and longitude, only it applies between realms as well." She glanced around. "It would help if I could have something Viktor touched today. I can take his energy signature from that, and it will give the spell a much better chance of working."

Talia stood. "His jacket's in our office. He forgot it when he took off for the nursing home this morning. He wore it in, so the energy should be fairly fresh on it. Do you want me to get it?"

Morgana nodded. "Yes, but please don't touch it any more than necessary. Use a glove or something to carry it back to me, so your signature doesn't imprint over his."

Talia nodded and headed out of the room.

"You should call Raven," Morgana said to me. "If I find his signature, you'll want to head out as soon as possible, in case Gyell decides to move Viktor."

As I once again stepped aside, this time to call Raven, Talia returned, holding Viktor's jacket with a gloved hand. We kept plenty of disposable non-latex gloves around for examining evidence and anything else that might come up. Morgana took the jacket as Raven answered.

"Hey, Ember, what's shaking?"

"I have a big favor to ask, and it could be dangerous. Hell, it is dangerous, but we need you, Raven." I explained what had happened to Viktor and how we would probably need to travel into the Underworld to find him. "We could use a good bone witch with us."

I could feel her hesitation, but then she said, "I'm on my way. I'll be there as soon as I can. Kipa's here and he'll come with me. What should I bring?"

"Let me ask Morgana." I turned back to the table. "Raven wants to know what she should bring with her. And Kipa's coming too."

"Kipa cannot enter the Underworld," Herne said.

Morgana shushed him. "He's right, but that's no matter. Ask her to bring her heart-gift from Arawn." At my questioning look, she added, "Like the necklace I gave you representing your pledge to me. She'll have a heart-gift from Arawn. And also, the one from Cerridwen, for the Keeper of the Cauldron of Rebirth has free rein in the Underworld. They may offer some protection. I don't know."

I nodded and went back to my phone call. "Your heart-gifts from Arawn and Cerridwen, Morgana says."

"I'll see you as soon as we can get over the bridge." Raven signed off.

I turned back to the others, only to see that everybody had backed away from the table, giving Morgana room to cast her spell. I quietly took my place beside Herne, waiting.

The casting of spells varied depending on the spell-caster, but this was new for me. I had watched Raven cast her spells, and Marilee, and even Angel, as she was learning. I knew how I cast my own spells. But I had only seen

Morgana cast a spell once, and I was curious to see what she would do.

Morgana spread the jacket on the now-empty table and took the glass of water that Talia handed her. She trickled it out of the glass to encircle the coat, making certain there wasn't a single space left in the line of the circle. Next, she set a bowl from the cupboard on the center of his jacket and filled it with more water. Holding out her hand, she closed her eyes and whispered an incantation. A smooth, large pearl appeared in the center of her palm. It was as large as a marble, and more luminous than any pearl I had ever seen.

It suddenly occurred to me that as a goddess, I might be able to do things like this. I was learning to work with the magic of water, and Marilee had been teaching me, filling in the gaps of my magical knowledge. I had learned haphazardly, without my mother to train me. Oh, she had taught me some things when I was little, but she had died before I was ready to begin any formal training. Now, I was making up for lost time, but it was almost harder than starting from the beginning.

Morgana slowly circled the table, her hand stretched out above the jacket at all times. She held up her other hand, palm cupped upward holding the pearl. A trail of droplets drifted out from her fingers, hovering in the air behind her.

Through the mists, through the veils,
Carve a path, show the trail,
Sacred water, now I drink,
Waters creep through nook and chink,
Seek and find, deliver to me,

Viktor's location, for to see.

She paused, holding perfectly still and then suddenly, with one swift motion, plunged the pearl into the bowl of water and leaned over it, staring intently as the water foamed and churned. A moment later, the surface smoothed, still as ice, and from where I stood, I could see an image forming in it. I wasn't able to tell what it was, but Morgana watched intently.

Then the lights flickered and she stood, letting out a long breath. "I know where he's being held." She turned to Cernunnos. "I'll need your help to send Ember and Raven over there."

He nodded. "I can do that, my dearest." He paused, then turned to me as Talia helped Morgana clear the table. "This is neither the best time nor place, but while we're waiting for Raven, your mother and I discussed the matter, Herne, and we've decided you'll have the wedding in Annwn, at my palace."

There it was. Firm, no doubt, no wiggle room. I was glad Herne and I had already discussed the possibility of two ceremonies, one for show and one for just us.

"Thank you," I murmured, feeling suddenly shy. Cernunnos always made me feel spindly and awkward, though I knew he had no intention of doing so.

"Morgana's seamstresses will make your wedding dress, of course. Fit for a goddess." Cernunnos seemed more excited than I would have expected, and it struck me that it might be bringing back memories of his own wedding to Morgana. They might live in separate homes, but they still seemed happy together, and they meshed in an unexplainable way.

"All right, who will be going with you and Raven?" Morgana asked. "I can send three of you. No more."

"I guess..." I glanced at Herne. "You can't come, can you? Or Kipa?"

He shook his head. "I'm not a god over death. I cannot enter the Underworld."

I turned to Yutani. "I suppose that means you."

"I'm sorry, but Yutani can't go, either," Herne said.

Yutani jerked around to stare at him. "Why?"

"Your father is Coyote, and Coyote does not walk among the dead. You're a demigod, regardless of how recently you found out about it."

Yutani blinked. "I hadn't even thought of that."

"Then who do we take?" I couldn't imagine taking Talia. She wasn't weak, but she never went out on fights with us.

Herne turned toward Angel. "My instincts tell me to send you along."

Angel's eyes widened and she shuddered. "Are you sure? I can't fight my way out of a barrel. I'm learning but...my magic is still new. Wouldn't I just be in the way?"

I didn't want her to come with us, but something resonated inside, like a jigsaw piece fitting into place, and I slowly nodded.

"I think...yes. Angel, we need you." I wasn't sure why, but it felt clear as crystal now that she had to go along. However, that meant that I was the one who would do the brunt of the fighting, if there was fighting to be done.

"All right, if you're sure..." Angel looked like she was seasick, but she straightened her shoulders and asked, "What should I take?"

I turned toward Morgana. "Any suggestions?"

But it was Cernunnos who answered. "You're not going into a fight. You're to go in stealth, and you must rely on brains, magic, and cunning to win Viktor back. One thing I say to you," the Lord of the Forest said, leaning down to hold my gaze. "Remember why you are doing this. Should the occasion arise where you falter, remember the reason for your journey, and remember the friendship you share with the half-ogre."

Angel and I spent the next fifteen minutes getting ready. Regardless of whether we expected a fight, I still took my daggers. I wasn't going to risk losing Brighid's Flame—or even Serafina, my bow—over there, so I opted to take one of the agency short swords as well, buckling the sheath around my waist. Morgana told us to return before midnight.

"You must not stay longer than one day. If you pass midnight in the Underworld, you'll be trapped there. Viktor, too. He must return today."

"How do we get away?"

She pulled out a scroll, which I tucked inside the pocket of my jacket. "When you read it, you must all be touching—even by one fingertip. If any one of you isn't connected to the others, they'll be left behind. I would, of course, advise you to get the hell out of there before midnight if possible. You really don't want to become a wight. Watches won't work there, so be as quick as you can."

She stood back, taking a deep breath. "As soon as Raven arrives, we'll send you over. Now then, have you eaten?"

"That's another thing," Cernunnos said. "Neither eat nor drink while you are there. Remember the story of

Persephone? It's not a legend. It's real. If anything edible should pass your lips while you're in the Underworld, you'll be forced to stay. I cannot emphasize this point enough. Let neither food nor drink touch your lips. If it does, we won't be able to rescue you."

I caught my breath, thinking of Viktor. "I hope that Viktor hasn't eaten or drunk anything."

"I hope not, either." Cernunnos shook his head, the long braids draping down his back swinging almost like snakes. "Now prepare, and Morgana and I will open a vortex for you to cross through."

Angel and I ate a couple of candy bars for a little extra insurance, then we went to the bathroom, and by the time we were ready, Raven walked through the door. She, too, had dressed for the journey, wearing a thigh-length black tunic, a pair of black leggings, platform boots, and a leather jacket. As I figured, she had Venom with her, her dagger that had a poisonous bite to it.

"Do you have your heart-gifts?" Cernunnos asked.

She nodded, curtseying. "My skull necklace was from Arawn. The cauldron charm hanging from the chain was from Cerridwen. I'm ready."

We went back into the break room, where Cernunnos and Morgana had pushed the table to one side, leaving an open spot on the floor. They motioned for the three of us to step between them. My stomach fluttering, I took my place. I was afraid, but I had to be strong for Angel. This was her first big mission, and she'd need me to be steady. Raven joined me, her jaw set. Angel, with a nervous look at Talia, took her place.

"Tell Rafé..."

Talia shook her head. "You three will be back in no

time, along with Viktor. But…yes…I know what you're asking."

"Mr. Rumblebutt…" I said, looking at Herne.

"You'll come back to me and to him. I won't have it any other way. But don't worry about Mr. Rumblebutt." He started to say more, then stopped, and I knew that he was doing the hardest thing he could—he was letting me go, letting me do my job.

Raven simply gazed at Kipa, and slowly blew him a kiss. He touched his lips and silently tipped his hand to her.

"Hold hands," Cernunnos said. "Don't let go until you hear the sound of a bell."

Morgana and Cernunnos began circling us, their arms stretched wide. They moved slowly at first, Cernunnos humming a low note while Morgana began chanting in what sounded like an arcane language. I didn't know what it was, though I knew it wasn't a Fae dialect.

They moved faster and faster, and it was almost dizzying watching them as they spun around us, faster than any person could move. They became a blur of movement, waves of energy in their wake forming a circle. I couldn't see anything beyond them. And then, the world began to blur and all I knew was that I was holding hands with Raven and Angel, and that we were floating in a dark space while spinning lights—purple and green fire—arced in a wheel around us. The wheel spun faster as the floor vanished from beneath my feet. I tightened my grip on Angel and Raven's hands. My head was throbbing and I had to close my eyes.

Then, with a loud crack, we landed on something firm, our hands still connected. The blur of light began to recede and I squinted. All around me was a low rolling mist, and I realized we were standing in the middle of what looked like a field, though it was shrouded in shadows from the twilight around us.

Another moment and the wheel of light vanished.

"We're here," I whispered to Angel and Raven. "We're in the Underworld, the world of the dead." Now, we just had to find Viktor and bring him home.

CHAPTER TWENTY-THREE

AS WE SLOWLY UNCLASPED OUR HANDS, I WAS ALREADY looking around, trying to pinpoint our whereabouts. We were standing in what appeared to be a barren, dusty landscape. There was no grass on the ground, no trees that I could see, but there were foothills and rock formations everywhere, forming canyons around us. The soil beneath our feet was so hard that I doubted if I could have broken the surface with a shovel. I looked around. We were standing at a juncture of trails leading through the tall mesas. It looked as though some octopus of a river had carved its way through the area long ago, then dried up to leave the steep walled ravines of dirt and stone.

My stomach fluttered as I turned. There was a stillness to the air that was disturbing. It felt almost as though I couldn't breathe and I suddenly gulped, fearing I was suffocating, but the warm, dry air slid through my lungs and then out again as I exhaled.

"Cripes, this place is creepy," Angel said. Even though she whispered, her words shattered the silence, ricocheting off the canyon walls. She clasped her hand over her mouth, eyes wide, then mouthed, "I'm sorry."

I glanced around to see if we had attracted any attention. We were in a perfect echo chamber. Somehow, the canyons seemed set up to capture any sound and magnify it. But nothing stirred, nothing moved, and I slowly relaxed.

Viktor had to be close by. Morgana and Cernunnos had told us he would be within a quarter-mile's radius, which meant he could be behind one of the rock formations, or he could be holed up in a cave, or on top of a mesa. I motioned for Raven and Angel to fan out, but mouthed for them to keep in sight.

As I scanned the area, I noticed that about twenty feet up on a nearby cliff, a dark spot seemed to indicate a cave opening. I stared at it for a moment, then crossed over to Raven and Angel. I tapped Angel on the shoulder, then pointed up toward the cliff, mouthing, "Can you sense anything?"

Angel closed her eyes. A moment later she shuddered and stumbled back, a look of panic on her face. She pulled out a notepad from her pocket and a pen and began to scribble on it.

Viktor's there. The energy here is so magnified that I almost felt like I could read his thoughts. But there are...*things*...all around. And the ghosts. There are ghosts everywhere. I can sense them moving past us. Most of them seem clueless that we're here, but there are some angry, ancient energies in these canyons.

I stared at her note, then looked back at the cliff face. We would have to get up there somehow, and there didn't seem to be a path. Raven noticed what I was doing and took Angel's notepad, writing, "Maybe there's a path inside? There's a cave at the bottom, too."

I followed her direction and saw a dark splotch against the base of the cliff. Nodding, I motioned for them to follow me. As we moved forward, I unsheathed my short sword. Raven held out her hands, the energy crackling off of them. I wasn't sure what spell she was prepping, but whatever it was, I expected nothing less than fireworks from the sparks flying around her.

We came to the base of the cliff, skirting around various rockpiles as we moved forward, and sure enough, there was a narrow cave entrance. Only one could enter at a time, and I motioned for both Raven and Angel to stand behind me. I had brought a flashlight that was on a headband, and I slid it over my head and turned it on. It would give us away, but we had no choice. I wasn't about to walk into a dark cavern in the Underworld, not without knowing what we were getting into.

The tunnel extended about seven feet into the cliff, and the range of my light, while dim, illuminated at least ten feet ahead. I could see the archway and vaguely that it opened out into a larger chamber, though how large, I didn't know. I slowed. Hopefully, we were alone.

As I came to the opening, I motioned for Angel and Raven to stop. Then, easing my way through the arch, I quickly looked around the room, hoping that it would be small enough to see the other side. That way, if there were something in there, I'd catch it before we entered.

To my relief, we lucked out. The chamber was about seven feet in width, and about eight feet from where I was standing to the back. It was empty, with stalactites hanging from the ceiling. But against the back wall, opposite to me, was another opening. Even from where I was standing, I could see a rough set of steps leading up, into the cliff. With another sweep to make sure that there was nothing in the room, I stepped into the chamber and motioned for Raven and Angel to follow.

The only sounds were the sounds of our breathing. The air smelled just as still and lifeless as it had outside, and once again, I found myself focusing on my breath, forcing myself to acknowledge that yes, I *was* breathing. Yes, air *was* flowing into my lungs.

I glanced over at Angel. In the glow of my flashlight, her expression looked stark and worried. This was the first time she had been on a mission this dangerous, and I gave her a thumbs-up, trying to cheer her up. Raven, on the other hand, was glancing around at the walls and ceiling, scanning for something. She suddenly froze, then bolted, shoving me out of the way. As we went tumbling to the ground, a loud crash ricocheted around the room as a stalactite came hurtling down from the ceiling, landing directly where I had been standing.

"Oh crap!" I gasped as I realized I'd shouted aloud. There was a tremor in the air, and then another stalactite broke off and landed nearby. There were sounds now, all around the ceiling, the sound of rock cleaving from rock, and I scrambled to my feet, grabbing Raven's hand to pull her up. A third stalactite fell near the opening to the tunnel, and then a fourth, and I shoved Raven toward the steps. "Up!"

Angel scrambled, breaking into a sprint toward the steps and I followed. I had no more touched foot on the first step when a large stalactite plummeted to the floor, blocking the entrance to the staircase, barely missing my ass.

Angel and Raven were huddled a few steps up. I leaned my back against the wall, breathing heavily. Our way out was blocked. We had no choice but to follow the steps and hope they led to an opening higher up. Whatever the case, there was no doubt that if there was somebody else around, they knew we were here.

"Okay," I said, deciding to skip the whispers. The game was already up. "We head up the steps. Let me go first, Raven, you come second. Is your spell still ready?"

She nodded. "Those stalactites had a sentience to them, by the way."

"What?" I stared at her. "You mean they knew we were there?"

"Yep, I think they did. They're either some massively brilliant trap, or they're...alive."

"I don't really want to know which." I motioned for them to let me through. "Are there still spirits around us?"

"There are spirits everywhere," Angel said, her voice trembling. "I can feel them all over."

"She's right," Raven said. "The very land is riddled with spirit activity."

"Wonderful. All right, let's go." I stepped between them and, as they shakily stood, I began climbing the steps.

We had climbed over two hundred steps and taken ten turns by the time we arrived at the top. The top of the stairwell opened into a small chamber with an exit on the other side that looked like it led into a tunnel. The chamber was no bigger than a large coat closet, and I warily glanced at the ceiling, but there were no stalactites in sight. I paused, glancing at the walls, too, but saw nothing out of the ordinary.

But Raven tapped me on the shoulder. "Take a look at the archway. I have a weird feeling about this one."

I paused, then glanced up, shining the flashlight around the perimeter of the opening. Sure enough, on the ceiling, there were a series of small holes going all the way across the arch. They looked uniform in size and distance. I looked on the floor and there were the same holes, perfectly aligned with the ones on the ceiling. *Bingo.* I knew what this was. I knelt, cautious to keep myself from extending anything into the opening. Not even the tip of my nose.

I shone the light on the floor directly inside the small chamber and a glint of metal shining up told me what I needed to know. Then, I shone the light toward the exit on the other side, scanning the floor. Another glint. I turned around.

"There's a pressure plate the moment you step inside," I said, pointing. "And another on the other side. I'm not sure how big they are. Hmm… Let me try something first." I looked around and picked up a small rock, tossing it as far as I could so it wouldn't land on the pressure plate. It cleared the opening and landed on the floor about two feet into the chamber, about midpoint. Nothing happened. "Okay, so it's not just motion activated. So we go through. I'll go first. Step right by the rock, then another wide step to clear the other pressure plate. Understand?"

They both nodded. I steeled my courage, then stopped. If something went wrong, we only had one scroll to get the hell out of here. I turned to Angel. "I want you to hold the scroll. If things go wrong, get your ass out of here, and if you can, take Raven with you." I met Raven's eyes. She nodded. Angel started to protest, but closed her mouth as I shook my head. "We don't have time to argue."

After handing her the scroll, I took a wide step, clearing the first pressure plate, to the middle of the chamber. Then, steeling myself, I took another and managed to stretch my way into the tunnel beyond. Nothing happened.

Breathing easier, I cleared out of the way. Raven came next, and she too managed to avoid both plates. Angel was taller than either of us and for her, it was an easy pass. When we were all in the tunnel together, I motioned them to follow me and we headed down the corridor. My flashlight showed that it was a short jaunt, about seven feet, to the next opening.

As I neared the tunnel exit, I paused. The energy was growing thicker and once again, the feeling that I wasn't actually breathing swept over me. I gasped, leaning back against the wall to my right. As I fought to contain my fear, there was a sudden scuttling, and I jumped as something landed on my shoulder.

"Crap," I said, lurching forward.

Angel let out a muffled shout, pointing at my shoulder. "Ember!"

I looked down to see a large beetle on my shoulder,

about eight inches long and three inches wide. It hissed at me, and scuttled toward my chest. I knocked it off, sending it to the floor where it headed toward Angel.

"That's a death beetle!" Raven shouted, pulling out her dagger and swooping down to pierce it through its exoskeleton. The beetle went splat, and she shook it off her blade. "They can burrow into your chest and eat your heart."

I froze, hearing a hissing from all sides now. As I slowly swung my head around, looking at the upper walls of the tunnel, they seemed to seethe with movement, hundreds of the beetles climbing over one another.

"Run!" I shouted, pushing Angel toward the exit. She ran, leaping to clear the opening. Raven followed and I was right behind her. As I landed between them, I looked up to see Viktor, chained to the wall. He looked unconscious, draped forward, limp, as far as the chains would allow.

An opening on the opposite wall showed sky directly ahead. The floor was scattered with bleached bones, and several skeletons seemed humanoid in nature. Yeah, there had been others come through here, only they never made it out. And the next moment, I caught sight of the creature to which they had lost their last battle.

Standing between Viktor and us was a large creature that looked like the mother of all death beetles. Her shell scintillated with blues and greens, and she—I knew it was a she, though I didn't know how—began to move toward us. She had mandibles on her head, and they were opening and closing. She had to be eight feet long and three feet wide.

"Ember," Angel said, a wary tone in her voice. "Look behind us."

I glanced over my shoulder at the entrance to the tunnel. Hundreds of baby beetles—if you could call them "babies"—were swarming into the cavern. Before long, they'd be everywhere.

"Crap." I turned back to the massive beetle in front of us. "Let us have him and we'll leave you in peace."

To my surprise, a hissing noise echoed through the chamber, forming into words. "He's mine. I am to guard him. You cannot have him, and now you will feed my children."

"Looks like we're going to have to do this the hard way," I said, pulling out my sword. "Raven, whatever you've got, we need it. Angel, if we can give you an opening, get over to Viktor." It crossed my mind that Gyell might be nearby and we needed to get moving before he returned.

Raven circled to the right and I followed, drawing the beetle's attention away. Angel started edging slowly to the left, trying to keep away from the walls, which were rapidly filling with the death beetles.

"Can you use your lightning bolt?" I asked, my sword ready for action.

Raven was moving deliberately, one step at a time. "No, I think death beetles are immune to lightning. But I know they can burn." She paused, holding out her arms, palms up. Twin flames appeared in them, and she whispered something I couldn't catch. The next moment, twin streams of fire poured out, jetting toward the mother beetle. They hit her square on the face, and I felt a surge of joy.

The beetle let out a hissing screech. "For that, you will die," she said, her shell looking charred. She lurched toward Raven, and I jumped close enough to stab at her with my sword. I knew a slicing attack wouldn't work. The exoskeleton looked thick and hard to penetrate. But a piercing attack might do something.

I brought my sword down on her side as she listed toward Raven, and the tip of my blade met her shell with a loud *clang*. I pushed hard, leaning on the hilt, and there was a crunching sound as the shell splintered and my blade went through it, biting deep into the flesh below.

The beetle hissed again, swinging my way, and I lost my grip on the hilt of the sword, which was stuck deep into the beetle's flesh. I darted back, reaching for my daggers that were strapped to both legs. Raven cursed as she moved back to prep another spell.

By now, Angel was at Viktor's side, and she was frantically examining the locks on the shackles around his wrists. She reached up toward her hair for something and went to work on the locks.

I turned my attention toward the beetles on the walls and ceiling. They were still teeming out of the tunnel. One fell on me from overhead and I shrieked and shook it off.

Raven's eyes narrowed and she held out her hands again. "*Vedium, redente, mordenta caleth!*" As the words echoed from between her lips, a black smoke poured out of her fingertips to surround the mother beetle and the creature froze. I wasn't sure whether it was paralyzed or frightened or dead but when Raven said, "Get over to Viktor," I ran, passing behind her.

Raven followed me as beetles began dropping from the

ceiling. We dodged them, right and left and then right again, as the scuttling masses attempted to prevent us from reaching Viktor's side.

Angel shouted, "He's loose!" as Viktor slumped forward to the floor.

She shrieked as a couple beetles began to scamper atop him, swatting them away, sending them flying. Raven and I reached her side just as the mother beetle began to move again. Apparently she wasn't dead.

"Angel, get out the scroll!" I shouted, freezing as I glanced outside the cavern, only to see the shape of a large dragon winging our way. "Hurry! I think Gyell's coming."

Angel fumbled in her pocket, finally pulling out the scroll. Hands shaking, she tried to unroll it, but dropped it. I swept down, grabbing it up. As I unrolled it, the dragon shape was closing in on the opening.

"Quick, we need to be touching, grab hold me and one of you grab hold of Viktor!" I scanned the scroll. Thank the gods it was short and sweet. Well, at least short.

Raven grabbed hold of my right arm, Angel grabbed hold of my left with one hand, and she stretched down to grab Viktor's wrist with her other hand. I worried my lip as I mentally ran through the incantation. I didn't want to screw it up.

The dragon was shimmering, his head almost at the entrance to the cave. The next moment, a cloud of smoke appeared and a tall man that I recognized only too well appeared, landing on the floor. The swarm of death beetles immediately receded, as did the mother beetle.

"Crap!" I stared into Gyell's gorgeous eyes, trying to control the shaking in my voice.

He took in the scene and began to run toward us, eyes glinting with a malevolent light. I started to chant:

Powers of the vortex, heed my call,
Take us home, one and all!
By oak and thorn, by ocean's roar,
Transport us away from Death's door!

As my words echoed through the room, there was a massive groan, as though the Underworld was loath to give us up. Gyell reached out toward me and I thought he was going to grab hold of my arm, but his hand passed through me, and the last thing I saw, before the mists swept us away, was the anger in his eyes, and the blood-lust on his face.

CHAPTER TWENTY-FOUR

I wasn't sure where we were going to end up, but as the smoke and mist cleared, I realized we were standing the break room, in the exact position we had been in when we went into the Underworld. A sudden fear that Gyell had come through with us hit me and I whirled around, looking for the crazed dragon shifter, but he was nowhere to be seen.

There was a loud shout and the next moment, Herne raced into the room. Before he could grab me for a hug, I pointed toward Viktor.

"Get him down to urgent care!" And then, my knees weak, I collapsed into the nearest chair. Raven and Angel dropped to the floor, both looking as exhausted as I felt.

Talia and Yutani had followed Herne into the room. Talia immediately pulled out her phone and called the clinic, asking them to send up a medic.

Yutani knelt beside the three of us. "Are you all right? Are any of you hurt?"

I started to shake my head, but then Angel let out a

shout and slumped over. Turning, I saw she had fainted and there appeared to be something moving under her shirt.

"What the...oh great gods! It's one of the death beetles!" I ripped at her shirt, pulling it up and we saw one of the smaller beetles trying to burrow into her skin. It had managed to gnaw a hole in her side and was trying to eat into her thoracic cavity. I grabbed hold of the back end of the beetle and pulled. The scutellum of the beetle broke off from the head and thorax, leaving the guts of the beetle dangling. But it kept hold of the flesh in its mandibles.

"We need to cut that out immediately," Raven said. "The head can continue to live for a brief time—long enough to do more damage."

I pulled out my dagger and, biting my lip, cut the head away from the mandibles. The doctors could remove the rest of it from her when they got here. It hit me that I was staring into a small hole in my best friend's side. I turned to the side and leaned over, kneeling with my head on the floor as the room began to spin.

The next few moments were a blur. The medics arrived and they took both Angel and Viktor away, down the elevator to the clinic. Herne began stripping my clothes off, and ordered Raven to do the same.

"We can't take a chance that another one of those beetles is hiding in your clothing," he said. "You can tell me what happened while you're undressing."

Raven told him everything that had happened as we stripped. I was still feeling faint. By the time we had everything off, we had found no more death beetles, and I relaxed a little. But my thoughts were downstairs with Angel and Viktor, and I fretted the entire time.

Herne's phone rang as Raven and I got dressed again. He spoke in low tones, and then, he slipped his phone back in his pocket and turned back to us. There was a gleam in his eye that instantly made me relax.

"Angel will be all right, and so will Viktor. Angel is going to need a couple weeks' bed rest—she has an infection from the death beetle, but they caught it early and can knock it out with antibiotics. Viktor wasn't hurt, just drugged. He's awake now. So you pulled it off. The three of you saved Viktor's life. And I can't thank you enough. Sheila's on her way to take him home, but he wants to talk to you and Raven."

Wearily, we all trooped to the elevator and Talia locked it as we headed down to the first floor. Kipa helped prop Raven up, who was as exhausted as I was, and I leaned against Herne.

As we entered the urgent care clinic, the nurse led us back to the exam room where Angel was lying on the table and Viktor was sitting in a chair, looking groggy. I hurried over to Angel's side, taking her hand as she gazed up at me weakly.

"I hear you helped stop that thing from eating its way inside me." Her eyes were dilated, and she sounded slightly disoriented.

I glanced over at the nurse.

"Talk fast. We gave her something for the pain, so she'll be out of it for a while."

Turning back to Angel, I cupped her hand in mine, bringing it to my lips where I kissed it. "Oh, hon, I'd do anything to help you, even cut a freaking beetle off of you."

She smiled. "I guess it's my turn to take it easy for a while?"

"And you know I'm going to make sure you toe the line." I paused as Rafé entered the room. The expression on his face gave away his feelings. He crossed to my side and I slowly gave way, stepping back so he could take my place. Her face lit up when she saw him and he leaned over, kissing her gently.

As he murmured something to her, it hit me—Angel and I would always be best friends, but we were moving in different directions. I was engaged and she was in love. We'd always be important in each other's lives, but we were expanding, and other people had come into the picture. After I married Herne and moved in with him, Angel would be okay, because Rafé would be there for her. I could feel that, as clearly as I could see them there in front of me.

I turned away and Herne caught me to his side. "Are you all right?" he whispered. "You look teary eyed."

I shook my head. "Just tired," I said, gazing up at him. "I love you, you know. I love that you let us go after Viktor without trying to stop us. And I love that you're here, now, that you care about every single person that we work with."

"Oh love, if I didn't, I wouldn't be much of a boss, now would I? We're all family." He rested his forehead against mine, gazing into my eyes. "Come on, let's get the two of you home."

As he turned to the nurse to discuss moving Angel, Sheila bustled into the room, hurrying over to Viktor.

Yutani, Talia, and I stepped out into the waiting room to give everyone room to work. I dropped onto one of the sofas, leaning my head back. Images of the last few minutes of rescuing Viktor flashed through my head.

"Gyell is going to be on the offense now. He was so angry. He'll be back, and he'll probably bring reinforcements. We can't let down our guard," I said.

"We'll be ready for him," Talia said. "I have exciting news. While you were gone, I think I found out where Echidna is. Herne contacted Cernunnos, and Cernunnos is sending his right-hand military man down to talk to her."

I jerked my head up. "You found her? Is she in Death Valley?"

Talia nodded. "Yeah, we think so."

"I didn't know Cernunnos had a military force," I said, frowning.

"All the gods have warriors," Yutani said. "Well, most."

Before I could say anything else, Herne came out of the exam room.

"I'll go get my car. I'll drive Angel to your place. I'm taking you, too. Kipa will drive Raven home. Yutani can drive your car, then I'll bring him back to the office. Talia, can you drive Viktor home? Sheila will follow you in her own car, and then she'll drive you back to get your own."

Talia nodded, standing as Viktor slowly entered the waiting room, Sheila beside him. The half-ogre looked exhausted, but his eyes were clear and when he saw me, he gave me a huge smile that warmed my heart.

"Thank you, Ember. You, Angel, and Raven...without you, chances are I'd be dead."

"Gyell would have probably tried to use you as a

bargaining chip, but he would have probably made you stay in the Underworld. By the look on his face as we faded out of that cave, I think he would have killed every one of us." I pushed myself to my feet and gave the half-ogre a huge hug. "I'm so glad you're back, big guy. I love you, you know."

"Love you too, Ember," he whispered.

Sheila gave me a hug, too, before she led him out the door. Talia followed them.

The next few minutes were spent arranging Angel in Herne's SUV. Yutani drove my car, Kipa drove Raven home, and Herne ferried Angel and me back to our house. As he carried her up to her room, adjuring her to stay in bed, I asked Rafé if he could stay with us over the next week or so in order to take care of Angel while I was at work.

When everything was finally settled and everyone was home safe, I walked out to the side yard, staring up at the quickly approaching dusk. A crow landed on a nearby rose bush and let out a single caw.

I closed my eyes, sitting down as the wind ruffled my hair, and the next moment…

I found myself in a wide, scorched field. As I watched, a large dragon rose from beyond the horizon, but I wasn't afraid. She was silver and massive and she shone under the evening sky. She raised her head and let out a roar that shook the world. It was a challenge. I knew that to my very core. And then, from a great distance, another roar echoed in return, answering her call. It was beginning...the war was on the horizon and nothing would ever be the same...

One week later...

Angel sat at the kitchen table, frowning. "I'm feeling fine. The wound is healing, I want to go to work."

"No," I said. "Forget it. Rafé, you make sure she doesn't try to leave the house today."

"Will do," Rafé said. He set her breakfast in front of her. "Eat, and quit trying to convince me to let you go out and run errands. I'll take care of things."

"Just remember to set all the wards if you go out," I said, picking up Mr. Rumblebutt and giving him a big kiss. He purred in my ear and then squirmed out of my hands, jumping on the table. I stared at him. "What do you think you're doing? You know you're not supposed to walk on the table when there's food there."

Angel gave me a guilty smile. "Um, I might have..."

"You let him do it. Enabler," I said, picking him up and setting him onto the floor. "Okay, I'm off to work. Remember—"

"I'll set the wards, have no fear." Rafé followed me to the door, and as I swung my purse over my shoulder and headed out, I could hear him fiddling with the new security wards we had installed. After we rescued Viktor, we had added to our locks and wards and security systems. I knew Gyell wouldn't forget what we had done, and there was no doubt that he'd play dirty.

I paused at the car, bringing out the handheld gizmo that Yutani had given me. It scanned the car for any signs of tampering and I ran it across one side and then the other. Nothing out of the ordinary. I hated having to watch over my shoulder constantly, but it was what it was. Until we stopped Typhon—or at least Gyell—we'd have to be on alert.

Everyone was at the office already, except for Angel, Rafé, and Charlie, and I hurried into the break room for the morning meeting.

Herne motioned for me to sit down and, as I did so, Talia handed me a cup of coffee and a maple bar. By the look on Herne's face, I could tell that something big had happened.

"What's going on?"

"They found Echidna," he said. "Cernunnos is talking to her right now. He and my mother will be here soon to tell us what's going on."

Talia turned on the TV. "It can't come too soon. Klarkson? The city where the vrykos first attacked? Is empty. They couldn't stop the attacks there, and everybody either moved or ended up dead. There are more and more of the dead rising, so it's not just Gyell causing havoc here, it's other dragons in other cities."

"The United Coalition will be announcing the presence of the dragons this week," Herne said. "So expect wideset panic. And stupidity."

I let out a long sigh. "Well, I—" A sound from the front stopped me in midsentence. Herne quickly darted out the door, his sword in hand. We had taken to going around armed.

Viktor jumped to follow, but paused as Herne quickly returned, followed by his parents. Morgana and Cernunnos waved for us to stay seated as Herne brought his mother a chair, and Cernunnos swung one around for himself and straddled it.

"Well" Herne asked for all of us. "What happened?"

"Echidna knows how to put Typhon back into stasis. It's a tricky spell, and she's the only one who remembers it. She's talking to the Dagda, Danu, Zeus, and Hera right now. She's agreed to work with us, only this time, she wants to wound Typhon. If he's put into stasis wounded, the injury won't heal the entire time he's in there, so if he breaks out again, it will give us extra time to manage him." Cernunnos looked pleased—as relieved as I had ever seen him look.

"What do we do in the meantime?" Herne asked.

"Take care of outbreaks and work with Ashera, who is going to be the ambassador to the United Coalition for the dragons. There's no going back. The dragons are here to stay, but the Celestial Wanderers and the Mountain Dreamers have agreed to police the Luminous Warriors once Typhon is taken care of. However…" He paused and let out a long sigh.

"They want a seat on the United Coalition, right?" I asked.

Morgana nodded. "While I appreciate all the Spiral Web is doing for us, I was hoping they would agree to return to the Forgotten Kingdom. But the portal to their world is open, and there's no closing it up again."

A thought crossed my mind. "Does that mean *we* could go see their world?"

"Yes, but I don't recommend it," Morgana said. "It's far too dangerous there."

"So what comes next?" Talia asked.

"Echidna will call out Typhon. If he doesn't answer her challenge, he automatically forfeits, by the rules of the Dragonni. And then he would have to do as she orders. So he must either answer and fight, or let her drive him into stasis. It's going to be the most spectacular duel the world has ever seen. At least…since the last time." Morgana sat back. "Until then, just keep the Fae, shifter, and vampire militias ready to go, and suppress the attacks that the shadow dragons are bringing to bear." She paused, then motioned to Cernunnos. "Don't forget to give Herne and Ember the gift that Echidna gave to you."

"Oh, right!" Cernunnos reached down and picked up the bag he was holding. It was large and looked bulky. He rummaged around inside and then pulled out two quivers, each filled with shimmering purple arrows. One was a quiver of bolts, and it looked the size to fit my bow Serafina. The other looked sized for a compound bow. He handed the former to me, and the latter to Herne.

I took the quiver and it hummed in my hands. "What's this?"

"Allentar arrows and bolts. They're made of a very rare magical metal. They can pierce dragon scales. You could conceivably shoot down a dragon out of the sky with these. They won't work on Echidna or Typhon, but they can be used against all of their children, but each arrow can only be used once, so make them count." Cernunnos's voice was low, and I detected a note of respect and awe. "Echidna gave me enough to pass out to the other Hunt agencies. This will help control the damage done until she can rise and challenge Typhon, which will be several months."

"Allentar..." I had never heard of the metal but as I touched one of the bolts, it reverberated through my fingers and I felt a sense of—almost reverence.

Herne shook his head. "This is an incredible gift. I can't believe she entrusted us with them." He turned to me. "Always take Serafina with you, and at least one of these, when you go out. Gyell is still on the loose and we know he's focused on us."

I nodded, thinking that the tide was turning. The world would never be the same, but maybe we could make the changes a little more bearable. And thanks to Echidna, we had hope again. And hope held strong through the darkest of days.

Three days later...

Angel, Rafé, and Herne sat in the front row at the amphitheater at TirNaNog. The courtyard was filled with nobility and the sides of the halls were packed with onlookers from the city. I was backstage, standing beside my uncle. Sharne looked incredibly uncomfortable, though handsome, in his formal dress. He was wearing the colors of TirNaNog, deep indigo and dark plum and silver, with purple and blue trim. He fidgeted as I straightened his boutonniere, which was a white rose.

"Hold still. You're messing up all the work your valet did." I gave him a playful frown, still feeling out of place. The last thing I wanted to do was walk out there in front of hundreds of people who I knew would sneer at me, given the chance. But at least it wasn't me in the hot seat.

"You know, you're taking this very well," I said, giving him a long look. "You could still back out. You could leave TirNaNog and make a new home somewhere."

He shook his head. "No. Saílle would track me down and make me pay for embarrassing her. And her vengeance is usually deadly." He spoke in low tones, but we both knew that we were probably being overheard. "And she would punish Neallanthra for my acts."

"Well, I hope that you're happy. At least Neallanthra seems nice, and I really do like Unkai, so there's some consolation there." I grinned. "In fact, I've promised to show him the city, once the wedding is over and he's free to return to Annwn. He'll stay for an extra day or so. I promised when we first met that I would guide him around if he ever came over through the portals, and now I get to make good on that promise."

I finished straightening his jacket. "You look good," I said, patting his chest. It felt so odd. He looked so much like Farthing, but he truly was nothing like my grandfather in nature. Impulsively, I gave him a quick hug.

Sharne smiled fondly at me. "My great-niece, I hope you know how grateful I am you're in my life. I wish I could have known your father better, but...well...water under the bridge, I suppose." He looked around as the director—apparently important Fae weddings required their own theatrical attendants—motioned for us to get into place. "Are you ready?"

"As I'll ever be. Let's get this show on the road." I took my place in front of him. Instead of having a best man, Sharne had asked me to be his "best niece" and I had accepted, not wanting him to stand up there alone.

Taking a deep breath, I let it out slowly and began to walk forward as the director motioned for me to go. I was wearing a long gossamer ballroom gown with such a full skirt that I felt like a princess. It was black as night, with a thousand silver beads dappling the surface, and every step I took, the beads shimmered. I had allowed the queen's coiffeur to curl and coil my hair into a massive bouffant with curls draping down to my shoulders. I felt like an idiot—it wasn't really me at all—but hey, weddings were all about the bride and the other women were just there to make her look good.

As I stepped onto the stage, I caught my breath, staring at the massive crowd who were watching. They were silent as I crossed the stage, and I felt so conspicuous that I wanted to melt into the ground. But finally, I was at my mark, and I stood to one side as Sharne took his place beside me. I felt inside the secret pocket that had been sewn into the dress to make certain the rings were still there.

A solemn march that reminded me more of a dirge than a wedding song began to echo through the crowd, and then—from the other side of the stage—Neallanthra appeared.

I caught my breath. She was so beautiful that it was hard to look away. Dressed in a long flowing gown of pale lavender that shimmered with crystal beads and covered by a veil of the same color, she began to walk across the stage to Sharne.

Three women led the way, each in a black sheath, and each had been picked by Saílle herself. My uncle and Unkai's sister-in-law were pawns in a game far more deadly than anybody could imagine, and both of them knew it and accepted their parts.

As the ceremony wore on, I looked around and caught sight of Saílle. She was sitting in a box seat in the amphitheater, and she was staring at me. I gazed back at her, meeting her regard. We weren't done, not by any sense, and I realized that in the days leading up to my own wedding, I'd have to be crafty as hell, because the Fae

Queens were treacherous, and I had become a threat to the stability of their traditions.

Looking away, I focused on my uncle, hoping that he and Neallanthra would be happy. And who knew? Sometimes, arranged marriages worked.

"I'M SO glad that's over," I said, turning to Herne. I was still wearing the massive dress—it was mine, as a gift from Saílle—and we were in his SUV, heading home after the wedding. Rafé and Angel were driving together.

"You want to spend the night at my house?" Herne asked.

I nodded. "I'm hungry for you. And I want out of this fucking cupcake of a dress." I paused, then let out a long, slow breath. "It's all changing. Everything is moving so fast I feel like I'm on a roller coaster."

"I know, but love, life is like that sometimes. And then some years, it seems like time barely moves. It's all cyclical, you know. We'll take care of Typhon, hopefully with as little collateral damage as possible, and then...move on to the next phase." He pulled into his driveway. "I watched you up there tonight, and all I could think about was our wedding, and how I will be by your side."

He sounded so optimistic, I had to push away my negative thoughts.

As we headed inside his house, I paused, turning back to look at the park that buttressed against his home. It was beautiful, and it occurred to me that living here wouldn't be so bad—it would have its perks. I had given up the fantasy that Rafé and Angel and Herne and I could all share a house. I knew that Angel didn't want that, and when I really thought about it, it made sense. Angel and I were best friends, but even friends had to live their own lives.

I was just grateful she was healing up, and that Viktor was back, and that we were all alive. Typhon was out there, and Echidna was preparing to call him out in challenge. We had fought off more skeletal warriors, and more vrykos, and a few zombies had shown up, and I knew that Gyell was keeping his eyes open for any opportunity to strike at us. But all that was on hold for tonight. Tonight...was for Herne and me.

As I turned to go inside, a noise alerted me and I glanced at the park. There, sitting in the grass, was a little red fox. She watched me, unafraid, then turned and dashed back into the woods. I raised my hand as she left, feeling hope swell within me. Something about her had brought peace to my heart. Giving her a silent thank-you, I turned to go inside, to where my love was waiting for me.

If you enjoyed this book and haven't read the first twelve books of **The Wild Hunt Series**, check out **The Silver Stag, Oak & Thorns, Iron Bones, A Shadow of Crows, The Hallowed Hunt, The Silver Mist, Witching Hour, Witching Bones, A Sacred Magic, The Eternal Return, Sun Broken**, and **Witching Moon**. Book 14—**Witching Time**— is available for preorder now. There will be more to come after that.

I will be starting a new series this autumn (November

2020)—the **Blood Queen Series**. A darker Fae/Vampire series, this will be a six-book series to start. You can preorder the first three books: **Blood Roses, Blood Ashes,** and **Blood Dreams**.

Return with me to **Whisper Hollow,** where spirits walk among the living, and the lake never gives up her dead. I've re-released **Autumn Thorns** and **Shadow Silence,** as well as a new—the third—Whisper Hollow Book, **The Phantom Queen!** Come join the darkly seductive world of Kerris Fellwater, a spirit shaman in the small lakeside community of Whisper Hollow.

I invite you to visit Fury's world. Bound to Hecate, Fury is a minor goddess, taking care of the Abominations who come off the World Tree. Books 1-5 are available now in the **Fury Unbound Series: Fury Rising, Fury's Magic, Fury Awakened, Fury Calling,** and **Fury's Mantle.**

If you prefer a lighter-hearted paranormal romance, meet the wild and magical residents of Bedlam in my **Bewitching Bedlam Series.** Fun-loving witch Maddy Gallowglass, her smoking-hot vampire lover Aegis, and their crazed cjinn Bubba (part djinn, all cat) rock it out in Bedlam, a magical town on a mystical island. **Bewitching Bedlam, Maudlin's Mayhem, Siren's Song, Witches Wild, Casting Curses, Demon's Delight, Bedlam Calling, Blood Music, Blood Vengeance, Tiger Tails,** and Bubba's origin story—**The Wish Factor**—are available.

For a dark, gritty, steamy series, try my world of **The Indigo Court,** where the long winter has come, and the Vampiric Fae are on the rise. The series is complete with **Night Myst, Night Veil, Night Seeker, Night Vision, Night's End,** and **Night Shivers.**

If you like cozies with teeth, try my **Chintz 'n China paranormal mysteries.** The series is complete with: **Ghost of a Chance, Legend of the Jade Dragon, Murder Under a Mystic Moon, A Harvest of Bones, One Hex of a Wedding,** and a wrap-up novella: **Holiday Spirits.**

For all of my work, both published and upcoming releases, see the Biography at the end of this book, or check out my website at **Galenorn.com** and be sure and sign up for my **newsletter** to receive news about all my new releases.

QUALITY CONTROL: This work has been professionally edited and proofread. If you encounter any typos or formatting issues ONLY, please contact me through my Website so they may be corrected. Otherwise, know that this book is in my style and voice and editorial suggestions will not be entertained. Thank you.

CAST OF CHARACTERS

THE WILD HUNT & FAMILY:

- **Angel Jackson:** Ember's best friend, a human empath, Angel is the newest member of the Wild Hunt. A whiz in both the office and the kitchen, and loyal to the core, Angel is an integral part of Ember's life, and a vital member of the team.
- **Charlie Darren:** A vampire who was turned at 19. Math major, baker, and all-around gofer.
- **Ember Kearney:** Caught between the world of Light and Dark Fae, and pledged to Morgana, goddess of the Fae and the Sea, Ember Kearney was born with the mark of the Silver Stag. Rejected by both her bloodlines, she now works for the Wild Hunt as an investigator.
- **Herne the Hunter:** Herne is the son of the Lord of the Hunt, Cernunnos, and Morgana, goddess of the Fae and the Sea. A demigod—given his

mother's mortal beginnings—he's a lusty, protective god and one hell of a good boss. Owner of the Wild Hunt Agency, he helps keep the squabbles between the world of Light and Dark Fae from spilling over into the mortal realms.

- **Rafé Forrester:** Brother to Ulstair, Raven's late fiancé; Angel's boyfriend. Was an actor/fast-food worker, now works as a clerk for the Wild Hunt. Dark Fae.
- **Talia:** A harpy who long ago lost her powers, Talia is a top-notch researcher for the agency, and a longtime friend of Herne's.
- **Viktor:** Viktor is half-ogre, half-human. Rejected by his father's people (the ogres), he came to work for Herne some decades back.
- **Yutani:** A coyote shifter who is dogged by the Great Coyote, Yutani was driven out of his village over two hundred years before. He walks in the shadow of the trickster, and is the IT specialist for the company.

Ember's Friends, Family, & Enemies:

- **Aoife:** A priestess of Morgana who guards the Seattle portal to the goddess's realm.
- **Celia:** Yutani's aunt.
- **Danielle:** Herne's daughter, born to an Amazon named Myrna.
- **DJ Jackson:** Angel's little half-brother, DJ is half Wulfine—wolf shifter. He now lives with a foster family for his own protection.

- **Erica:** A Dark Fae police officer, friend of Viktor's.
- **Elatha:** Fomorian King; enemy of the Fae race.
- **George Shipman:** Puma shifter. Member of the White Peak Puma Pride.
- **Ginty McClintlock:** A dwarf. Owner of Ginty's Waystation Bar & Grill
- **Louhia:** Witch of Pohjola.
- **Marilee:** A priestess of Morgana, Ember's mentor. Possibly human—unknown.
- **Meadow O'Malley:** Member of the magic-born; member of LOCK. Twin sister of Trefoil.
- **Myrna:** An Amazon who had a fling with Herne many years back, which resulted in their daughter Danielle.
- **Sheila:** Viktor's girlfriend. A kitchen witch; one of the magic-born. Geology teacher who volunteers at the Chapel Hill Homeless Shelter.
- **Trefoil O'Malley:** Member of the magic-born; member of LOCK. Twin brother of Meadow.
- **Unkai:** Leader of the Orhanakai clan in the forest of Y'Bain. Dark Fae—Autumn's Bane.

Raven & the Ante-Fae:

The Ante-Fae are creatures predating the Fae. They are the wellspring from which all Fae descended, unique beings who rule their own realms. All Ante-Fae are dangerous, but some are more deadly than others.

- **Apollo:** The Golden Boy. Vixen's boytoy. Weaver of Wings. Dancer.

- **Arachana:** The Spider Queen. She has almost transformed into one of the Luo'henkah.
- **Blackthorn, the King of Thorns:** Ruler of the blackthorn trees and all thorn-bearing plants. Cunning and wily, he feeds on pain and desire.
- **Curikan, the Black Dog of Hanging Hills:** Raven's father, one of the infamous Black Dogs. The first time someone meets him, they find good fortune. If they should ever see him again, they meet tragedy.
- **Phasmoria:** Queen of the Bean Sidhe. Raven's mother.
- **Raven, the Daughter of Bones:** (also: Raven BoneTalker) A bone witch, Raven is young, as far as the Ante-Fae go, and she works with the dead. She's also a fortune-teller, and a necromancer.
- **Straff:** Blackthorn's son, who suffers from a wasting disease requiring him to feed off others' life energies and blood.
- **Trinity:** The Keeper of Keys. The Lord of Persuasion. One of the Ante-Fae, and part incubus. Mysterious and unknown agent of chaos. His mother was Deeantha, the Rainbow Runner, and his soul father was Maximus, a minor lord of the incubi.
- **Vixen:** The Mistress/Master of Mayhem. Gender-fluid Ante-Fae who owns the Burlesque A Go-Go nightclub.
- **The Vulture Sisters:** Triplet sisters, predatory.

Raven's Friends:

- **Elise, Gordon, and Templeton:** Raven's ferret-bound spirit friends she rescued years ago and now protects until she can find out the secret to breaking the curse on them.
- **Gunnar:** One of Kipa's SuVahta Elitvartijat—elite guards.
- **Jordan Roberts:** Tiger shifter. Llewellyn's husband. Owns *A Taste of Latte* coffee shop.
- **Llewellyn Roberts:** One of the magic-born, owns the *Sun & Moon Apothecary*.
- **Moira Ness:** Human. One of Raven's regular clients for readings.
- **Neil Johansson:** One of the magic-born. A priest of Thor.
- **Raj:** Gargoyle companion of Raven. Wing-clipped, he's been with Raven for a number of years.
- **Wager Chance:** Half-Dark Fae, half-human PI. Owns a PI firm found in the Catacombs. Has connections with the vampires.
- **Wendy Fierce-Womyn:** An Amazon who works at Ginty's Waystation Bar & Grill.

The Gods, the Luo'henkah, the Elemental Spirits, & Their Courts:

- **Arawn:** Lord of the Dead. Lord of the Underworld.
- **Brighid:** Goddess of Healing, Inspiration, and Smithery. The Lady of the Fiery Arrows, "Exalted One."

- **The Cailleach:** One of the Luo'henkah, the heart and spirit of winter.
- **Cerridwen:** Goddess of the Cauldron of Rebirth. Dark harvest mother goddess.
- **Cernunnos:** Lord of the Hunt, god of the Forest and King Stag of the Woods. Together with Morgana, Cernunnos originated the Wild Hunt and negotiated the covenant treaty with both the Light and the Dark Fae. Herne's father.
- **Corra:** Ancient Scottish serpent goddess. Oracle to the gods.
- **Coyote, also: Great Coyote:** Native American trickster spirit/god.
- **Danu:** Mother of the Pantheon. Leader of the Tuatha de Dannan.
- **Ferosyn:** Chief healer in Cernunnos's Court.
- **Herne:** (see The Wild Hunt)
- **Isella:** One of the Luo'henkah. The Daughter of Ice (daughter of the Cailleach).
- **Kuippana (also: Kipa):** Lord of the Wolves. Elemental forest spirit; Herne's distant cousin. Trickster. Leader of the SuVahta, a group of divine elemental wolf shifters.
- **Lugh the Long Handed:** Celtic Lord of the Sun.
- **Mielikki:** Lady of Tapiola. Finnish goddess of the Hunt and the Fae. Mother of the Bear, Mother of Bees, Queen of the Forest.
- **Morgana:** Goddess of the Fae and the Sea, she was originally human but Cernunnos lifted her to deityhood. She agreed to watch over the Fae who did not return across the Great Sea. Torn by her loyalty to her people and her loyalty to

Cernunnos, she at times finds herself conflicted about the Wild Hunt. Herne's mother.

- **The Morrígan:** Goddess of Death and Phantoms. Goddess of the battlefield.
- **Pandora:** Daughter of Zeus, Emissary of Typhon, the Father of Dragons.
- **Sejun:** A counselor in Cernunnos's employ. Raven's therapist. Elven.
- **Tapio:** Lord of Tapiola. Mielikki's Consort. Lord of the Woodlands. Master of Game.

The Fae Courts:

- **Navane:** The court of the Light Fae, both across the Great Sea and on the east side of Seattle, the latter ruled by **Névé**.
- **TirNaNog:** The court of the Dark Fae, both across the Great Sea and on the east side of Seattle, the latter ruled by **Saílle**.

The Force Majeure:

A group of legendary magicians, sorcerers, and witches. They are not human, but magic-born. There are twenty-one at any given time and the only way into the group is to be hand chosen, and the only exit from the group is death.

- **Merlin, The:** Morgana's father. Magician of ancient Celtic fame.
- **Taliesin:** The first Celtic bard. Son of Cerridwen, originally a servant who underwent

magical transformation and finally was reborn through Cerridwen as the first bard.

- **Ranna:** Powerful sorceress. Elatha's mistress.
- **Rasputin:** The Russian sorcerer and mystic.
- **Väinämöinen:** The most famous Finnish bard.

The Dragonni—the Dragon Shifters:

- The Celestial Wanders (Blue, Silver, and Gold Dragons)
- The Mountain Dreamers (Green and Black Dragons)
- The Luminous Warriors (White, Red, and Shadow Dragons)
- **Ashera:** A blue dragon.
- **Aso:** White dragon, bound to Pandora, twin of Variance
- **Echidna:** The Mother of Dragons (born of the Titans Gaia and Tartarus)
- **Gyell:** Shadow dragon, working with Aso and Variance to bring chaos to Seattle
- **Typhon:** The Father of Dragons (born of the Titans Gaia and Tartarus)
- **Variance:** White dragon, bound to Pandora, twin of Aso

TIMELINE OF SERIES

Year 1:

- May/Beltane: **The Silver Stag** (Ember)
- June/Litha: **Oak & Thorns** (Ember)
- August/Lughnasadh: **Iron Bones** (Ember)
- September/Mabon: **A Shadow of Crows** (Ember)
- Mid-October: **Witching Hour** (Raven)
- Late October/Samhain: **The Hallowed Hunt** (Ember)
- December/Yule: **The Silver Mist** (Ember)

Year 2:

- January: **Witching Bones** (Raven)
- Late January–February/Imbolc: **A Sacred Magic** (Ember)
- March/Ostara: **The Eternal Return** (Ember)

- May/Beltane: **Sun Broken** (Ember)
- June/Litha: **Witching Moon** (Raven)
- August/Lughnasadh: **Autumn's Bane** (Ember)
- September/Mabon: **Witching Time** (Raven) (upcoming)

PLAYLIST

I often write to music, and AUTUMN'S BANE was no exception. Here's the playlist I used for this book.

- **Air:** Moon Fever; Playground Love; Napalm Love
- **Airstream:** Electra (Religion Cut)
- **Alexandros:** Milk (Bleach Version); Mosquito Bite
- **Alice in Chains:** Sunshine; Man in the Box; Bleed the Freak
- **Android Lust:** Here & Now; Saint Over
- **Band of Skulls:** I Know What I Am
- **The Black Angels:** Currency; Hunt Me Down; Death March; Indigo Meadow; Don't Play With Guns; Always Maybe; Black Isn't Black
- **Black Mountain:** Queens Will Play
- **Blind Melon:** No Rain
- **Boom! Bap! Pow!:** Suit
- **Brandon & Derek Fiechter:** Night Fairies; Toll

Bridge; Will-O'-Wisps; Black Wolf's Inn; Naiad River; Mushroom Woods

- **The Bravery:** Believe
- **Broken Bells:** The Ghost Inside
- **Camouflage Nights:** (It Could Be) Love
- **Colin Foulke:** Emergence
- **Crazy Town:** Butterfly
- **Danny Cudd:** Double D; Remind; Once Again; Timelessly Free; To the Mirage
- **David Bowie:** Golden Years; Let's Dance; Sister Midnight; I'm Afraid of Americans; Jean Jeanie
- **Death Cab For Cutie:** I Will Possess Your Heart
- **Dizzi:** Dizzi Jig; Dance of the Unicorns
- **DJ Shah:** Mellomaniac
- **Don Henley:** Dirty Laundry; Sunset Grill; The Garden of Allah; Everybody Knows
- **Eastern Sun:** Beautiful Being
- **Eels:** Love of the Loveless; Souljacker Part 1
- **Elektrisk Gonnar:** Uknowhatiwant
- **FC Kahuna:** Hayling
- **The Feeling:** Sewn
- **Filter:** Hey Man Nice Shot
- **Finger Eleven:** Paralyzer
- **Flora Cash:** You're Somebody Else
- **Fluke:** Absurd
- **Foster The People:** Pumped Up Kicks
- **Garbage:** Queer; Only Happy When It Rains; #1Crush; Push It; I Think I'm Paranoid
- **Gary Numan:** Hybrid; Cars; Petals; Ghost Nation; My Name Is Ruin; Pray for the Pain You Serve; I Am Dust
- **Godsmack:** Voodoo

- **The Gospel Whisky Runners:** Muddy Waters
- **The Hang Drum Project:** Shaken Oak; St. Chartier
- **Hang Massive:** Omat Odat; Released Upon Inception; Thingless Things; Boat Ride; Transition to Dreams; End of Sky; Warmth of the Sun's Rays; Luminous Emptiness
- **The Hu:** The Gereg; Wolf Totem
- **Imagine Dragons:** Natural
- **In Strict Confidence:** Snow White; Tiefer; Silver Bullets; Forbidden Fruit
- **J Rokka:** Marine Migration
- **Jessica Bates:** The Hanging Tree
- **Korn:** Freak on a Leash; Make Me Bad
- **Lorde:** Yellow Flicker Beat; Royals
- **Low:** Witches; Nightingale; Plastic Cup; Monkey; Half-Light
- **M.I.A.:** Bad Girls
- **Many Rivers Ensemble:** Blood Moon; Oasis; Upwelling; Emergence
- **Marconi Union:** First Light; Alone Together; Flying (In Crimson Skies); Always Numb; Time Lapse; On Reflection; Broken Colours; We Travel; Weightless
- **Marilyn Manson:** Arma-Goddamn-Motherfucking-Geddon
- **Matt Corby:** Breathe
- **NIN:** Closer; Head Like a Hole; Terrible Lie; Sin (Long); Deep
- **Nirvana:** Lithium; About a Girl; Come As You Are; Lake of Fire; You Know You're Right
- **Orgy:** Social Enemies; Orgy

- **Pati Yang:** All That Is Thirst
- **Puddle of Mudd:** Famous; Psycho
- **Red Venom:** Let's Get It On
- **Rob Zombie:** American Witch; Living Dead Girl; Never Gonna Stop
- **Rue du Soleil:** We Can Fly; Le Francaise; Wake Up Brother; Blues Du Soleil
- **Screaming Trees:** Where the Twain Shall Meet; All I Know
- **Shriekback:** Underwater Boys; Over the Wire; This Big Hush; Agony Box; Bollo Rex; Putting All The Lights Out; The Fire Has Brought Us Together; Shovelheads; And the Rain; Wiggle & Drone; Now These Days Are Gone; The King in the Tree
- **Spiderbait:** Shazam!
- **Tamaryn:** While You're Sleeping, I'm Dreaming; Violet's in a Pool
- **Thomas Newman:** Dead Already
- **Tom Petty:** Mary Jane's Last Dance
- **Trills:** Speak Loud
- **The Verve:** Bitter Sweet Symphony
- **Vive la Void:** Devil
- **Wendy Rule:** Let the Wind Blow
- **Yoshi Flower:** Brown Paper Bag

BIOGRAPHY

New York Times, Publishers Weekly, and USA Today bestselling author Yasmine Galenorn writes urban fantasy and paranormal romance, and is the author of more than sixty-five books, including the Wild Hunt Series, the Fury Unbound Series, the Bewitching Bedlam Series, the Indigo Court Series, and the Otherworld Series, among others. She's also written nonfiction metaphysical books. She is the 2011 Career Achievement Award Winner in Urban Fantasy, given by RT Magazine.

Yasmine has been in the Craft since 1980, is a shamanic witch and High Priestess. She describes her life as a blend of teacups and tattoos. She lives in Kirkland, WA, with her husband Samwise and their cats. Yasmine can be reached via her website at Galenorn.com.

Indie Releases Currently Available:

The Wild Hunt Series:

The Silver Stag

Oak & Thorns
Iron Bones
A Shadow of Crows
The Hallowed Hunt
The Silver Mist
Witching Hour
Witching Bones
A Sacred Magic
The Eternal Return
Sun Broken
Witching Moon
Autumn's Bane
Witching Time

Blood Queen Series:
Blood Roses
Blood Ashes
Blood Dreams

Whisper Hollow Series:
Autumn Thorns
Shadow Silence
The Phantom Queen

Bewitching Bedlam Series:
Bewitching Bedlam
Maudlin's Mayhem
Siren's Song
Witches Wild
Casting Curses
Demon's Delight
Bedlam Calling: A Bewitching Bedlam Anthology

The Wish Factor (a prequel short story)
Blood Music (a prequel novella)
Blood Vengeance (a Bewitching Bedlam novella)
Tiger Tails (a Bewitching Bedlam novella)

Fury Unbound Series:
Fury Rising
Fury's Magic
Fury Awakened
Fury Calling
Fury's Mantle

Indigo Court Series:
Night Myst
Night Veil
Night Seeker
Night Vision
Night's End
Night Shivers
Indigo Court Books, 1-3: Night Myst, Night Veil, Night Seeker (Boxed Set)
Indigo Court Books, 4-6: Night Vision, Night's End, Night Shivers (Boxed Set)

Otherworld Series:
Moon Shimmers
Harvest Song
Blood Bonds
Otherworld Tales: Volume 1
Otherworld Tales: Volume 2
For the rest of the Otherworld Series, see website at **Galenorn.com.**

Chintz 'n China Series:

Ghost of a Chance

Legend of the Jade Dragon

Murder Under a Mystic Moon

A Harvest of Bones

One Hex of a Wedding

Holiday Spirits

Chintz 'n China Books, 1 – 3: Ghost of a Chance, Legend of the Jade Dragon, Murder Under A Mystic Moon

Chintz 'n China Books, 4-6: A Harvest of Bones, One Hex of a Wedding, Holiday Spirits

Bath and Body Series (originally under the name India Ink):

Scent to Her Grave

A Blush With Death

Glossed and Found

Misc. Short Stories/Anthologies:

Once Upon a Kiss (short story: Princess Charming)

Once Upon a Curse (short story: Bones)

Once Upon a Ghost (short story: Rapunzel Dreaming)

The Witching Hour (novel: Bewitching Bedlam)

After Midnight (novel: Fury Rising)

Magickal Nonfiction:

Embracing the Moon

Tarot Journeys

Made in the USA
Monee, IL
08 September 2020